MULTIPLE KARMA   By

MULTIPLE KA

By Rosemary Ravenblack
Copyright 2017 Rosemary Ravenblack
All Rights Reserved.

Copyright and other information

Multiple Karma is an 80,000-word-plus paranormal murder mystery novel, written for a mature adult audience.

Characters, events and some place names depicted in this novel are purely fictitious. Any similarity to actual persons, living or dead, or to actual events is purely coincidental.

No part of this book may be used or reproduced in any manner, including Internet usage, without written permission from the author, except in the case of brief quotations embodied within readers' reviews.

The author is British so the grammar and spelling in this novel are British style.

MULTIPLE KARMA   By   ROSEMARY RAVENBLACK

Table of Contents

CHAPTER ONE	- 6 -
CHAPTER TWO	- 9 -
CHAPTER THREE	- 18 -
CHAPTER FOUR	- 24 -
CHAPTER FIVE	- 40 -
CHAPTER SIX	- 47 -
CHAPTER SEVEN	- 50 -
CHAPTER EIGHT	- 63 -
CHAPTER NINE	- 71 -
CHAPTER TEN	- 76 -
CHAPTER ELEVEN	- 78 -
CHAPTER TWELVE	- 85 -
CHAPTER THIRTEEN	- 87 -
CHAPTER FOURTEEN	- 90 -
CHAPTER FIFTEEN	- 95 -
CHAPTER SIXTEEN	- 99 -
CHAPTER SEVENTEEN	- 103 -
CHAPTER EIGHTEEN	- 108 -
CHAPTER NINETEEN	- 111 -
CHAPTER TWENTY	- 115 -
CHAPTER TWENTY-ONE	- 131 -
CHAPTER TWENTY-TWO	- 137 -
CHAPTER TWENTY-THREE	- 145 -
CHAPTER TWENTY-FOUR	- 156 -
CHAPTER TWENTY-FIVE	- 161 -
CHAPTER TWENTY-SIX	- 174 -
CHAPTER TWENTY-SEVEN	- 183 -
CHAPTER TWENTY-EIGHT	- 186 -
CHAPTER TWENTY-NINE	- 188 -
CHAPTER THIRTY	- 196 -
CHAPTER THIRTY-ONE	- 200 -
CHAPTER THIRTY-TWO	- 202 -
CHAPTER THIRTY-THREE	- 211 -
CHAPTER THIRTY-FOUR	- 222 -
CHAPTER THIRTY-FIVE	- 228 -
CHAPTER THIRTY-SIX	- 230 -

CHAPTER THIRTY-SEVEN .... *- 235 -*
CHAPTER THIRTY-EIGHT .... *- 241 -*
CHAPTER THIRTY-NINE .... *- 247 -*
CHAPTER FORTY .... *- 251 -*
CHAPTER FORTY-ONE .... *- 256 -*
CHAPTER FORTY-TWO .... *- 264 -*
CHAPTER FORTY-THREE .... *- 267 -*
CHAPTER FORTY-FOUR .... *- 280 -*
About the Author .... *- 286 -*

CHAPTER ONE

Precious life poured from a frail old woman's lifeless body, like air rushing from compressed bellows as a murderer left her lying on a concrete doorstep at the back of her house. Her wide open eyes and mouth were evidence of how quickly death had claimed her. With pupils dilating, she saw nothing now but blackness, and then light.

Her arthritic bent fingers clawed at nothing. Her once immaculate clothing was now smeared with dirt and neglect. Decades of memories went with her as Rigor Mortis set in not long afterwards, rendering her as stiff as the hard surface she lay upon in the cold and wet night air. Droplets of water covered her, soaking her in seconds, merging with blood that spurted from the side of her neck.

The killer sprinted down her garden path, jumped over a low wall and vanished, concealed in between many trees that resembled silent sentinels; evil deeds observed by them yet remaining hidden, much like countless creatures swarming beneath murky undergrowth. This recent despicable act could never be forgotten, just like old Mrs. Robinson herself either. She'd been a busybody, a notorious gossip. Some residents in the street where she'd lived even viewed her as a troublemaker.

Despite having lived alone, neighbours – including her enemies – couldn't ever forget her; such was the strong impression she had made on all who'd ever come into contact with her over the decades.

An owl, its round and bright eyes scanning and surveying all around, had opened its beak and joined in with echoes of screams that had been snuffed out in a heartbeat. Eerie silence descended upon the area now, except for the consistent pitter patter of raindrops. But the quietness was soon about to change. Impending chaos was about to erupt into life.

Ben Thomas lived a few doors away from the victim. Smashing through two wooden doors with a sledgehammer, he further startled residents who were now swarming like bees outside and were huddling together under umbrellas by the old lady's house.

Police and an ambulance were on the scene within minutes; lights flashing furiously. Officers and medical staff raced up to the macabre display glaring at them as crimson and the beginning of decomposing flesh assaulted their senses.

The owl in the tree wasn't phased whatsoever as it digested a captured mouse. The wise and observant bird swayed on a branch surveying the night skies and undergrowth beneath it before flitting off in search of another warm meal. As it tore through mist near mountains, its tiny stomach convulsed, regurgitated tiny bones and fur. It dropped to the ground, scattering and joining others, all merging into a carpet of rodent bits and pieces. Beetles and other insects feasted, oblivious to nearby horrific events.

Mrs. Robinson's crafty killer watched and listened to everything going on in the street through a small slightly open bedroom window. They smiled a most sinister smile before changing their clothing and hiding the old in a hole in a bedroom wall. They then promptly joined the commotion outside, confident that nobody would suspect them of even going near the victim.

Several weeks passed and forensic officers and police had no other choice than to close the case. The killer smiled even more as they set about capturing the next victim on their list; a list quite long, and they had all the time in the world to work their way through it. Creeping around and picking them off one by one would be so easy, they thought. Getting caught was the last thing on their mind. It never occurred to them however, that someone would eventually balance the scales of justice and present them with a well-deserved dose of karma.

CHAPTER TWO

Mel Jones lived in Porthcawl; a charming Welsh seaside resort in Wales in the UK. Just a few hundred yards from the beach, she lived in a terraced street. Loving it there at first, the novelty had soon worn off when an unwanted presence had started choking all joy from her life.

She watched her annoying neighbour, Marlene Griffiths, from a kitchen window. Mel sighed. News of Mrs. Anita Robinson's sudden death had spread throughout the street like wildfire within minutes after screams were heard in the early hours on a Saturday morning.

Ben Thomas had informed police that she was lying on her doorstep, slumped in the rain. Her throat had been slit wide open, something he'd seen before in the past in town. Police hadn't solved that case either and with no evidence of who took Mrs. Robinson's life, all police and forensic officers could go on was a single strand of hair left at the scene of the crimes. But it was from a synthetic wig.

Her house was cordoned off with tape. It fluttered in the wind. Ben had been a suspect and had been taken away for questioning. Upon his arrival back home, much curtain twitching commenced as a taxi dropped him off outside his house. Living a mere few doors away from the victim, when neighbours saw him being carted off to the station, it turned their stomachs at the very though that it could be him responsible for such a horrific act. Trusted by residents for years, he was the last person they'd suspect of having it in him to commit such a terrible atrocity.

Several weeks passed before life began returning to some kind of normality again. Seeing everyone avoiding him and ignoring him had upset him. A lot. When he was cleared and word got about that he hadn't killed the old lady, people began apologising to him, but he wasn't interested. Their words fell on deaf ears. The damage had been done, he thought.

Today was Friday. Afternoon sunshine bathed the small village in golden light. Seagulls called to one another as they sped across rooftops and back toward the sea in search of a tasty fishy lunch.

Feeling her heart pound and her hands tremble, Mel turned around and walked away from her kitchen window. She leaned against a door frame and gripped her cup of steaming coffee; something she relied on a little too much to wake her properly from yet another troubled night's sleep. Despite wearing earplugs in bed, her vindictive neighbour's relentless banging on the wall and drilling when carrying out improvements on her property still woke Mel at precisely 6 am every single morning. The din always seemed to stop whenever Mel began to walk downstairs though; especially after stepping on a creaky floorboard on her landing.

An old house, every creak made her wince. She was already constantly walking on egg shells and afraid to speak her mind. She often wondered if the woman next door ever slept as she always seemed to be up and about long after midnight and well into the wee small hours. Whenever Mel tried to enjoy a film on TV, after writing all day, it was impossible to relax. She couldn't turn the volume up because it would wake the other neighbours, Alice, and her husband Ben. So she got used to putting subtitles on the TV screen instead.

Gazing into her cup through misty eyes, she sipped its refreshing liquid and felt as though she could take on the world as soon as the caffeine infused needed energy into her troubled mind. First thing in the morning, a nice cup of coffee was one of the few joys that she had. Nobody could take that away from her. She was already on edge so it wouldn't matter a jot she felt if it made her worse. So used to feeling like a prisoner in her own home, she rarely ventured outside. Only when absolutely necessary – anything for a quiet life. But it never was. Ever.

Once, after politely asking Marlene to keep the noise down late at night and to do repair work on her house after nine in the morning, and no earlier, her suggestion had been ignored. She was simply told, in a very abrupt manner, to go to sleep and to get up at exactly the same time that she did and then there wouldn't be a problem at all. How incredibly rude, Mel thought. Why do some people choose to be a pain in the arse, she wondered? She always treated people with respect so she felt bewildered why others retaliated with selfishness. She felt sorry for them and believed that they were lost in their own little world of self-centredness and bitter self loathing. Not even a psychiatrist could help Marlene, Mel believed. She really was the lowest of the low and not a very pleasant person at all.

With no choice at the moment other than to live next door to the unbearable person until she could sell her house and move somewhere better, Mel felt intimidated and controlled. It was a living Hell. Unable to bring herself to report the pain in the ass for creating excessive and unnecessary noise and anti-social behaviour along with it too, matters gradually progressed from bad to worse as months and years dragged by. So Mel simply learned to detach herself mentally from it all to the point that Marlene's behaviour was viewed much like an annoying gnat on the bottom of a horse and in Mel's mind, she flicked it off. Life was too good for her to let anyone or anything ruin her life. She had a lot going for her and treasured pleasant moments.

Entering her living room, she sat down at her computer and slipped on a pair of headphones. She also had a spare pair in a box - just in case. Sliding her long red hair over her ears with her fingers, she smiled. Feeling her heart calming and her hands still now, she thought how ridiculous things had become in recent years. It now felt so very surreal. Before then, her life had been completely different. Perfect in fact. But that had been well and truly destroyed since Marlene had moved into the terraced street.

She slid the headphones around to cover her ears fully and felt a sense of triumph and pride when her noisy neighbour began making a lot of noise again but Mel didn't have to listen to it. No longer bothered by the control freak, she laughed at the narcissistic bully's deliberate attempt to get to her. Opening her word-processing program on her laptop, Mel began writing several chapters of her new crime novel. Classical music soothed her soul through the headphones, some of the best things ever invented, she thought. She placed her stress on a back burner and would deal with it later.

She dreaded removing the headphones and sometimes envied deaf people before promptly feeling guilty for even thinking such a thing! She was a good person and was too polite and tolerant for her own good. She also noticed something unusual. Whenever she activated a voice recording device to make notes about books that she was writing, upon playing each sound file back, she not only heard her own voice but distant, other voices too. They seemed to be chatting with each other. She put it down to a radio being on in one of her neighbours' houses. She even began to convince herself that she was going nuts.

Outside, Marlene was talking about her. Again. Mel had an overwhelming feeling that she was being watched, let alone gossiped about. With hunger pangs clawing at her stomach, she took a break, prepared dinner and put it in the oven. Waiting for it to cook, she sat back down in her computer chair in the living room. Turning to face a large window, through net curtains she watched Marlene spewing verbal venom from her mouth to Alice, the other neighbour. No positive comments ever came out of her and Mel felt sad that Alice, who was a reasonably nice person, bothered to associate with the bitchy cow.

Mel turned around in her chair to face her computer monitor screen, blocking out the rising anxiety that filled her soul, day in and day out. Like a parasitic monster that always refused to let go, she just couldn't shake it away, no matter how much effort she put into it.

Feeling as if she were in some sort of macabre reality show and that all eyes were on her constantly, she decided that she had to do something soon to change the increasing feeling of having a constant and unwanted intrusion in her life. Regretting buying her house, she was hoping it would sell as soon as possible. Especially after reducing the price, twice.

Mastering the art of refusing to allow things to overwhelm her, by giving obscene gestures at the window with her middle finger and also with her index and middle finger, depending on what level of pissed off-ness she felt on any given day, whenever she caught even a tiny glimpse of her arch enemy, she distracted herself as much as possible in lots of different ways in order to cope with her very uncomfortable situation.

Heading for a nervous breakdown, a stomach ulcer or heart attack, Mel had learned how to clear her mind and to only let peaceful thoughts enter; through either music, writing, or creating art. But, deep down inside, way back in the darkness and depths of her troubled soul, she kept a boiling hot rage at bay, kept in a padlocked box, never, ever to be let out. It could never be allowed to escape. When her dinner was ready she sat in the kitchen and closed the door.

"Mel is such a strange one, don't you think, Alice?" Marlene, the neighbourhood Queen bitch and notorious gossip asked, taking her gardening gloves off and tossing them into a wicker basket by her feet. "I mean her entire attitude has changed over the past few years. She used to be so approachable and friendly with us when she first met us, but she's not anymore. What do you think about it all then?" She flicked through the morning newspaper that had just been delivered. Her shoulder length dark but greying hair was as immaculate as the ornaments in her garden. A slim woman, skin hung from underneath her upper arms like fleshy wings, so she always made sure she wore a long-sleeve blouse, even on a hot day. It was March though so nobody would see her awful arms through a big, thick coat. But all the operations to tidy things up could never improve her dark and cruel soul.

Alice, a shy but outspoken woman since getting to know Marlene, not only felt uncomfortable in her presence, it was like her confidence had crumbled away like stormy waves lashing away and eroding cliff faces. But she'd learned how to fake an air of self confidence and how to tolerate Marlene, rather than move home.

Listening to her neighbour slagging Mel off made her wither inside like a dry leaf curling up under burning heat of the Sun. But she knew that ignoring Marlene wasn't an option. Attempting to do that once, it just encouraged the bitch to stare at her whenever they were both gardening and Alice lived for gardening. Her garden was a stark contrast to Marlene's. It was filled with brightly-coloured objects, plants, and even the fence was painted in a cheerful and beautiful light blue. Marlene's was jet black and was as depressing as she was.

She and Ben had also purchased their house like Marlene had hers too and Alice had no plans on moving to anywhere else anytime soon due to Ben preferring the area because it was near his workplace.

A short-haired pretty brunette in her forties, Alice glanced at Mel's front door and then at her windows and finally back to Marlene's gossiping mouth again which always reminded her of one of those wind-up fake teeth novelty toys.

Net curtains ensured a degree of privacy in Mel's windows but as the windows were single glazed and not double, they deprived her of total privacy. Mel was younger than both women and as her dinner digested in her nervous stomach, she was back in her living room now and was cowering in a corner, unable to stop herself from listening to every word. Recording the conversation outside after placing the microphone near a small gap in the window frame, the file would come in handy if she ever needed to give it to police.

"Well, Marlene, you had to have that work done on your house. Maybe she's a bit aloof because you didn't let her know beforehand that there was going to be a lot of noise," Alice replied, her palms sweaty and her head feeling as if it were about to explode from a building headache.

The older woman stared at Alice, an icy look filling her arrogant green eyes. She brushed her hair through her fingers and simply shrugged. At the age of seventy, her wrinkled face portrayed decades of the result of an angry and bitter attitude and her eyes had a harsh and piercing stare. The only time she smiled was when anyone felt offended due to her blunt, unkind words and her abrupt and condescending manner.

"If she doesn't like it then she can move out. I can't let every neighbour around here know individually about any noise that me and builders are going to make. I always let you know of course, but I can't stand her, so I didn't bother. No, I think it's more than that, her avoiding me. Besides, you've had work done on your house too but she speaks to you in a civilised manner, you've always told me."

"Yes, but she lived here alongside us before you moved to the area, remember? Ben let her know beforehand that we were going to be renovating. Maybe she doesn't want to speak to you anymore because of that time you ran over her dog. Remember? I told you that she told me in confidence she felt you did it on purpose because you hate dogs. It could be that or maybe she is depressed and probably misses Mark. I don't know. She rarely speaks to me lately either. There's a personality clash. We can't all get along with everybody in this world. That's the way it is."

"Well, Alice," Marlene seethed, "remember when I first moved in ten years ago? She and Mark seemed so friendly towards me when they were first getting to know me. But she's altered. A lot. Especially after he ran off with your sister, Anna. I think Mel's depressed and chronically lonely too, but that's her bloody fault? You'd think she'd get another man to keep her company. It's not our fault that she chooses to be stuck indoors all the time. She's in there by herself every day because I never see her outside much, other than when she goes for a little walk and that's only for about an hour. It's not normal. Invite her over to yours for dinner one day and have a chat with her. See what you can find out for me. Don't make it too obvious though, just call me on the phone rather than come and knock my door. She's very observant, that one."

"She is, yes. She speaks a lot to Ben in the back garden but when I ask him what about he always says oh just about gardening, nothing more."

Both women gossiped some more and went their separate ways back indoors. Both of them, old enough to know better, they didn't stop for one moment treating an innocent person like Mel with such an utter lack of respect. They thrived on it, especially Marlene. Not even Alice's stabbing guilt prevented her from joining in, fuelling her nasty friend's fiery hatred and jealousy of the younger neighbour.

CHAPTER THREE

Five-forty-five approached and Mel had eaten and enjoyed her dinner for one. With headphones back on, she did some more typing. In the middle of writing her new crime thriller novel about a neighbour from hell who gets karmic consequences, she sipped another coffee. With the absolute joy of listening to classical music at the same time, it served two purposes: she ended up in her own quiet little world and it also helped her concentrate when drifting into another world along with her characters. She sat there blissfully for the next hour.

At the age of forty-four, regular exercise when dancing indoors and having a kind and calm nature ensured that she looked younger than her years. She smiled and laughed every day when she took a break every hour or so from writing due to watching online funny videos and comedy films on TV - anything to stop herself giving in to Marlene's negative personality traits.

Alice knocked on her back door. It was seven-fifty-five now and Mel was getting ready to enjoy a nice, hot and soothing shower. Alice knocked again but there was no answer. She went back to her own house, disgruntled and fearful that Marlene would be disappointed with her efforts.

"Ben, did you see her go out? I don't think she's in."

A handsome, forty-five-year-old dark-haired man scratched his bristly chin with dirt-covered hands and shrugged. He threw his t-shirt into a washing basket and kicked his boots under a table. Married when in their twenties and with Alice just two years younger than him, they'd been very happy for the first ten years but things had fizzled out over the next ten, like fleeing air deflating a balloon.

Going off sex due to an early menopause, Alice's dismissal of her husband's amorous advances slowly but surely drove him into the arms of other women. Never telling a soul, the secret ate away at him for every second of every day, resulting in digestion and dental issues that he put down to stress at work.

Owning a successful private detective company, his wage was more than enough to keep their expensive lifestyle going for years to come, and the wealth guaranteed to keep Alice distracted by buying nice things. But Alice just wasn't a happy person anymore and had drawn Marlene to her like a magnet. Birds of a feather and all that. Marlene much preferred hanging around unsuspecting happy people though. She enjoyed the process of sucking all the positivity out of them. She was an expert as an emotional vampire, and she thrived on it. Most people in Porthcawl however, steered clear of her.

"Mel doesn't go out often, so I expect she's typing."

"What do you mean? She can still hear us surely, and it doesn't take long to go to the door and to speak to us. How rude," Alice snapped.

"I've seen her through the window. She wears headphones when she's writing. I peeked through one day to see if she needed anything from the local garden centre. I knocked on her door but there was no answer so I went to the window. She types for hours on and off most days. I've tried seeing what she writes about by looking through binoculars but she always turns the laptop away from the window, so I don't know."

Alice stared at her husband, and frowned. "Do you think she writes about us?"

"No," Ben replied, shaking his head, "I've already asked her that and she said she doesn't write about real people. She told me she writes pure fiction, from her imagination. She was out on one of her walks the other day and I bumped into her. We had a long chat. That's how I know these things. In my line of work, I'm a pretty good judge of character don't you think?"

Alice chewed her fingernails, pondering over it all.

"Yes you are. You haven't made a mistake yet in your cases. You've helped police put a lot of criminals away, and as for cheating spouses, well, it serves them right I suppose. We reap what we sow and all that. So during your chat she never revealed anything then?"

"Nope. Not a thing worth us worrying over. No. Now can you leave it rest? What's the fascination with it, has the cow next door asked you to spy on the woman or what?"

"Of course not! I wouldn't do that. Hmm, then I guess we'll never know, unless I find one of her books online or in a book shop around here and read it myself to compare us to her characters."

Ben rolled his eyes and tutted 'Yeah, right. Believe that, believe anything, you lying bugger.' "I did see the cover of one book a few years ago though when I called in for a spare fuse she had for me, for a plug, but I can't remember the pen name she used," he replied, smacking the side of his head and scrunching up his face. "Nope, it's gone. I can't bloody remember now," he added, lying through his teeth and smirking. He knew all about Mel's books. She'd told him because she trusted him, and he trusted her; one of few people he felt comfortable around. He turned around, pulled out a chair by their kitchen table, and sat down.

"Marlene thinks it's a good idea if we invite Mel over for dinner. We can get some information out of her, find out what's going on in her life lately."

Ben gave her a knowing look.

"I can never hide anything from you, can I? You're like one of those bloody psychic know-it-all's. Well, the real reason is because Marlene wants to know what's going on in her life lately. You know what she's like. What do you think? Mel always gets on very well with you. She hardly bloody speaks to me nowadays so it'll be good to see if we can rekindle our friendship."

"Yeah, I don't mind having her over. When, and what time?"

"Tomorrow? About eight o'clock?"

"Yep, that's fine. Let's go shopping to get some food and booze in. It's Monday today isn't it?"

"It is, yes. Why? Did you think it was still the weekend?"

"It goes so fast. Back to work tomorrow for me. I'll take some painkillers," Ben replied, rubbing his aching jaw after dental treatment to have a back molar extracted in an emergency appointment two days ago. He splashed his favourite aftershave over his neck and chest before putting on a clean shirt. Combing his dark hair and checking he'd got everything, he and Alice both jumped into their car and sped off to the local supermarket a few miles away. And all throughout the journey, he couldn't get a word in as she wittered on about the neighbours. He wished he was at work. At least he could get some peace, there.

A sunset shimmered and glowed gold and red in the distance. Marlene finished off pruning her rose bushes in her front garden. They'd be in full bloom soon enough and she gave her plants and flowers far more respect than she gave to human beings. Occasionally glancing at Mel's garden, she had quite a disgusted look on her face.

Mel rarely went into her front garden, and it resembled a jungle. Once, a perfect-looking tidy one, it was now very unkempt-looking. She made an effort, but only when her cow of a neighbour was out; which wasn't often. When she was out though, it gave her just enough time to rip weeds out and to mow the lawn. She timed it like a military operation and always came back indoors as soon as she heard the familiar sound of Marlene's car engine, growling at the bottom of the street and approaching her house. On one occasion, she left the lawn half-mown and berated herself once back indoors at how silly it looked, but she convinced herself that that was so much nicer than being on the end of the cow's nasty tongue.

Mel rambled in her mind: Maybe Marlene thinks she's won. Maybe she knows exactly how unhappy I am.

And Marlene did indeed feel both things and absolutely loved it too. She even hoped that Mel's legs and hands were shaking. Often sticking pins in a voodoo doll she'd made that resembled her fed-up neighbour, she poked it mercilessly. She let slip one day to Alice about it, who naturally was horrified.

After Alice informed Ben about the doll, he went on to tell Mel who researched on the Internet how to shield herself in white light for protection from any psychic negative attack. An even better method, she found out, was to imagine oneself surrounded by lots of mirrors which would reflect any enemy's negative attacks. She didn't believe in the so-called power of voodoo dolls anyway so it didn't matter one way or the other, but Mel wanted to be safe, not sorry, so she did whatever it took to feel less anxious. But Marlene got off on it bigtime regardless, often with a disturbing and evil look in her eyes whenever she picked up the pins.

CHAPTER FOUR

The following day, the street was quieter than usual. Most of the residents were either in work or enjoying themselves at a local Spring festival. Mrs. Robinson's death was still very much playing on their minds so to stay away from the street as much as possible was a bonus, they thought.

Birds were still singing to their heart's content in the big trees that lined the street but there was an uneasy atmosphere as the morning of each new day swept into afternoon. No dogs barked so loudly for once and no sheep trotted down the country lanes in the distance. It was as if everyone and everything had vanished. It was unnaturally quiet, except for Mel's heart which beat against her tired chest like a drum. Trying to pluck up enough courage to venture out into her back garden, it was a small act that most people took very much for granted, but to her – it was worse than sitting in a dental surgery's chair.

She preferred to live a life of solitude lately. She had no other choice than to go into her garden today however, because she loved to feed birds at a bird table that she'd made a week earlier. Quite creative and an animal-loving and kind person by nature, to know that she was contributing to making her feathered friends' lives a little brighter warmed the cockles of her heart.

A million thoughts flew through her mind as she stood by her back door, like: What if cats get the birds? I'll have to come out to pick them up to put them somewhere else which means I'll have to go for a walk so Marlene will see me leaving? Why didn't I put a garden ornament there instead? She felt sick as she turned the key in the lock and grabbed the door handle. Don't be so bloody cowardly! You pay the mortgage on this house and this is your garden and you can go into it whenever you fucking like!

She opened the door. Keeping her eyes down, she stared at her shoes and hurried toward the bottom of her garden. The tension was unbearable. She felt like a pressure cooker about to blow its lid off. Perspiration dotted her forehead, and her armpits felt drenched within minutes.

Ben spotted her immediately. A glorious flash of her red hair swaying in the sunshine caught his eye. He sat sipping wine at a dark green and floral-patterned cast-iron garden table. A handsome and muscular man, he felt quite fragile today. His jaw was still aching but he decided that wine tasted far better than a painkiller.

"Hi Mel," he said, waving at her over their low fence.

"Oh hi, Ben."

She felt her tense muscles instantly relax a little, but her eyes still darted wildly all around in the direction of Marlene's immaculate garden. He walked over and rested both arms on his fence post and smiled at her. She returned his friendliness. She often felt like a high-tech robot, analysing every person in front of her. Friend, or foe? Ben was non-threatening. A good friend. She felt her body relax, despite her mind being in a state of constant turmoil.

"Thanks for letting me read one of your books the other day. It's very good. I hope you're enjoying working on your new one that you told me about. I've had a big tooth taken out so I'm killing the pain by forgetting all about it," he said, waving a half-empty bottle of red wine in one hand and his full glass in the other. Some splattered against his side of the fence and landed on several Begonias that Alice had recently planted to infuse borders with colour instead of dull brown earth, and dead leaves. "Oh bugger," he said, trying to brush the wine off petals with his shoe.

"Anytime. Yes, I'm loving this one that I'm working on. It's another crime thriller." "I can hear your radio sometimes too. The walls are very thin aren't they?"

"Radio? I doubt it. I can't hear anything coming from your house and I've got excellent hearing. It must be coming from Marlene's house. Maybe her walls are thinner than ours."

"Yeah, could be. I just wondered, that's all, just how much can be heard exactly. These houses are very old after all."

"A bit like me, yes," Ben replied, rubbing his jaw and wincing; a sudden twinge of pain stabbing his face as his tongue inspected a tender tooth socket and inflamed gum. "Hey, maybe you're hearing voices, you know? In your head. Maybe your house is haunted!" He made a scary face at her. She shuddered and slapped his arm playfully. He slapped her back and grinned. He was very much like an annoying older brother: loveable but a pain at times as well.

"Ouch! Behave yourself!" "I hope you feel better soon. I hate going there and only go when I absolutely have to," she replied.

Marlene had nipped out to get some groceries and was on her way back to her house. Mel recognised the familiar din of her car engine as her old vehicle chugged up the road.

"Listen, I have to go back in. Speak to you next time. I hope the pain goes away very soon. And if you run out of wine," Mel shouted, looking back over her shoulder at him, "let me know. I've got tons of the stuff!" "Christ, I need alcohol to put up with certain people in this bloody street. Let's get drunk one night, just for a laugh."

"Mel, listen. Fuck her! Life's too short. Don't let her get to you. She's not worth it. I don't like the cow either as you know, so no worries there. She hates me. I think she hates all men to be honest. I don't know what you're doing tonight but me and Alice were wondering if you'd like to join us for dinner later about eight. It'll be a welcome distraction from the bitch, don't you think? C'mon, let's catch up as it's been a while," Ben pleaded, his puppy dog eyes irresistible to her. Hey, and don't forget what I suggested! Write about Alice and Marlene. Get them bumped off by your protagonist. You know you can trust me. Do me a signed copy, I'll hide it in the attic. Alice never looks up there. You should see the stack of porn mags I've got," he continued, tittering to himself and holding onto the fence to stop himself from falling onto his lawn.

Mel carried on with briskly walking back up her garden path. "Coming to yours sounds great. Okay, I'll see you later. Thank you. Please make sure that she's not there though. You know how I feel," she said, rolling her eyes and pointing in the direction of her arch enemy who was carrying groceries from her car to her house.

"Trust me, she won't be. You have my word. I'll go and tell Alice now then," he replied, gulping back another mouthful of wine as he watched her shapely body in her figure-hugging pretty summer dress. It billowed and blew up in a breeze, giving him a glimpse of her sexy legs. Alice seethed as she watched from an upstairs open bathroom window.

"Mm, beautiful," he whispered. He wondered if he'd ended up with the wrong woman. Mel disappeared back indoors.

She was far more interesting than Alice was, he thought. Mel had a good heart and she and Ben shared a very strong bond of friendship. He wondered if the grass really would be greener if he was with her, or if he was just so bored of being with Alice that he was simply indulging in a silly middle-age fantasy. He had a secret girlfriend on the side too, a stunner named Jan. As a frustrated and red-blooded man, he just couldn't get enough.

Seven-forty-five arrived. A nervous Mel brushed her hair and applied make-up to her naturally pretty face. She wore a knee-length dark blue dress and minimal jewellery. At the age of forty-four, she looked years younger. She picked up her favourite bottle of perfume. A misty spray of floral infusions caressed her neck. She was now ready to go out. She felt excited and grateful to get away for once from the confines of her brick and mortar prison.

Stepping outside, she felt familiar butterflies fluttering away in the pit of her stomach: some for fear of seeing Marlene and others out of pure happiness at the thought of spending the evening with Ben. Although she didn't turn around, she keenly felt Marlene's bitchy eyes burning into the back of her head like a red-hot fire poker. Trying her best not to stumble over anything, even her own feet on her garden path, she calmly opened an iron gate and gripped her handbag. It helped to stop her hands from trembling.

With pride and restrained anger assaulting her senses all at once, she closed the gate behind her with with a firm nudge of her bottom.

MULTIPLE KARMA   By   ROSEMARY RAVENBLACK

Walking to Ben and Alice's front door and unwilling to glance at Marlene's house, she focused instead on beautiful flowers lining their garden path. Holding her head up high, she felt her confidence rising. Marlene noticed, scowled, and moved away from her window. Also living alone, she believed an entertaining evening was soon to start for herself too as she grabbed a plastic beaker from her kitchen cupboard.

Going back into her living-room, she held it against a wall with one hand, a second, large glass of wine swaying in her other. "This should be interesting," she said, smirking and pressing her ear against the beaker. Muffled sounds came through. Still, it was better than nothing, she thought.

Mel knocked on Ben and Alice's door.

"Hi! Come in. So glad you could make it. You look great, Mel. Wow," Alice said. She too was dressed up to the nines and wore a white, short lace dress. It had a collar going right up to her neck, just below her chin. The collar was buttoned so tightly, it threatened to cut off her oxygen supply. She held two glasses of white wine, one in each hand. Ben welcomed their neighbour with a hug and ushered her inside.

"What would you like to drink?"

"Hi Ben. I don't mind. Whatever you've got, thanks. And thank you for inviting me too. It's been a while hasn't it?"

"It has. We should have chatted more over the years, like we used to," Alice replied, regret in her eyes.

"Work's been busy, sorry," Mel replied, maintaining a respectful manner as Alice handed her a drink while Ben closed the front door. He walked behind the younger beauty and admired her curvaceous figure. He inhaled her perfume and felt his body responding to her womanly charms. She glanced over her shoulder and their eyes met with mutual warmth.

"It'll be okay. If Marlene knocks on the door I'll ask her to leave and I'll say that we've got company," he whispered.

"Thanks," she replied.

Turning to look at Alice, she tried to think of things to talk about. Every time she set eyes on her, Alice was a painful reminder that her sister, Jan, was with Mel's ex-husband, Mark.

"I love what you and Ben have both done with the place! You've repainted in here. It was pale yellow last time, if I remember correctly."

"It was, yes. You've got a good memory. I thought lilac would be better for this room. It's such a soothing and beautiful colour isn't it? Ben did most of the painting. I helped a little but upstairs is where I spent most of the time redecorating and it looks amazing now. Remember that leaky cistern we had? We bought a new one, knocked a wall down and made the bathroom much bigger. I'll show you later."

"That would be great. Thanks, Alice."

Mel sipped her wine and wondered what Marlene was doing just a few inches away in her own house. And Marlene was wondering exactly the same thing about Mel too. It was as if both women had an invisible psychic and telepathic radio station that they both tuned in to and oblivious to anyone else but them. Rubbing her ear, she moved away from the beaker and wall and sat down to watch TV. But she never heard a word of the film that was on.

An hour into dinner, there was a knock on Alice and Ben's front door. Mel almost choked on her morsel of food. Her heart skipped a beat. Ben looked at her immediately. He rose to his feet and sprinted across the room.

"I'll get it!"

He saw the familiar shape of Marlene through frosted glass. He sighed. Opening the door, a little, he peeked through a gap. His foot was also right behind the bottom of the door too.

"Hi, Marlene," he said, resentment evident in the tone of his voice. "we've got company. We'll see you tomorrow, sorry." He moved his foot and began closing the door.

She wasn't taking no for an answer though and barged past him, only to find that he'd put the chain on the side of the door.

"Charming," she snapped. "I've got a cake that I've baked for you and Alice. She asked me to drop it in as soon as I finished it," she replied, her stern face momentarily softening. Although almost seventy years of age, years dropped off her whenever she could be arsed to smile.

Ben had a moment to decide. He slowly moved the chain across and then opened the door again. Deliberately standing in the way as she tried to get past him, he rested one hand on her shoulder and grabbed the cake with his other hand. Much taller, younger and larger, he had the advantage. In the other room, Mel's anxiety level was sky-high now as she'd heard her horrible neighbour's shrill voice.

"Ben, let me in for one moment. I need to speak to Alice about something! Women's matters, you know?"

"Marlene, like I said, we'll see you tomorrow. We have a guest," he insisted, not budging one inch. Although a man, she soon caused him to feel as if he were wilting like a scorched flower destroyed by the heat of a thousand suns. But he hid his anxiety very well. An expert in body language skills, he didn't let her see it for one second as he held her stare, not blinking even once.

"For God's sake! Men are so awkward!" She scowled and flounced off in a huff. "Fine! Please let Alice know that I'll see her tomorrow. You could have let me in for a few minutes. How bloody rude!"

Ben simply smirked and made a one-finger gesture behind his back.

She slammed the gate shut and stormed off to her own house. He watched her go, understanding fully why she was single.

"Stupid fucking bitch," he whispered, before going back inside and locking the door this time. Spitting on her cake, he carried it into the kitchen. Composing himself, he rolled his eyes at Mel and didn't even look at Alice who didn't look happy at all and was wittering on like a parrot on drugs.

"Ben, you could have let her in for just a bit."

He didn't reply.

Mel looked up from her half-eaten meal and Alice saw fear in her eyes. Her hands were shaking. She moved them under the table. Her eyes darted all around and she didn't know what to do with herself. Although sitting in a chair, she thought that she may as well have been wandering through a dark and scary tunnel, desperately trying to get out.

"Why do you get yourself into such a state, if you don't mind me asking? You never used to be like this. What's causing it? Is it because Mark's not with you anymore so you blame me because he ran off with my sister? Or is it because Marlene has had all that building work done and never told you first about the amount of noise that was going to be made? Or, is it because of work?"

Mel tried to relax her shoulders and tasted bile in her throat. Having Marlene almost in the room was bad enough, but to also have Alice verbally attacking her and putting her on the spot like this, it felt just as bad. But she had to answer her. If she got up to leave right now, there was a good chance they'd never speak ever again. Or worse...Marlene would still be outside and the thought of a confrontation in the street after alcohol was too much to contemplate.

"Look, Alice. I just avoid her, okay? I don't like her, I haven't for years and that's that. I don't mind you and Ben. You are good neighbours and I understand that work has to be done on houses. It's not Mark. I'm over him, it's finished, and I have never avoided you because he ran off with your sister. That's not your fault. I'm just on edge and am working very hard. I also have trouble sleeping. Maybe that's it. I'm very tired. So tired of it all to be honest." Confident that that was the end of the conversation, it had felt good to vent.

Alice persisted. "But why though? I don't understand. She's never done anything to me. So why do you feel the need to avoid her? She's a good person. She even gives to charity. And she goes to church every Sunday!"

Goes to church? What a fucking hypocrite, Mel thought, seething. Grinding her teeth and feeling lightheaded, she felt rage begin to boil and bubble in her mind, and nausea, lurking like a thief in the night. Taking Ben's advice that he'd given her several years prior to this, she went into self-help therapy mode. Visualising lying on her favourite beach, it was so wonderful to hear the wonderful sounds of gulls and waves lapping against rocks. It was an effective mental technique and it soothed her worries away within moments. Visibly calmer now and easing herself back into the room and the here and now, she picked her knife and fork back up and continued eating her meal and drinking her glass of wine.

"It's a very long story, Alice. Can we change the subject please? Let's have a nice evening."

Alice shrugged, whispered "Stubborn woman," under her breath and the matter was put to rest.

Ben walked back into the room. He was managing to balance two plates on one forearm and another two on his other.

Marlene was back by the wall and listening through a beaker. She'd had enough and had a plan.

"Cake? Yum!" Alice shrieked, visibly delighted.

"Marlene made it. Said you were expecting her to drop it in. You should have said."

"I forgot. Sorry."

Mel saw her face flush and also guilt peeking out from behind a fake expression as the woman, sensing she'd been caught out, refused to make eye contact. Mel felt disappointed that Alice had dared to stoop so low, but was very thankful that Ben hadn't let Marlene in.

When Alice was digging into her slice of Victoria sponge cake with a fork – missing it at one point and clanking metal on ceramic - he mouthed reassurance to Mel: 'It's okay. Relax.' She flashed him a brief smile and mouthed back: 'Thanks.'

"Aren't you having any then?", Alice asked both of them, cake crumbs spitting from her mouth, onto her plate and narrowly missing her husband and neighbour. "Oops, how unladylike of me!" She wiped her mouth with a serviette.

"My gum hurts. I've had a tooth out, remember?" Ben replied, holding his jaw and pretending that it hurt far more than it actually did.

"I'm full. Thanks anyway," Mel said, moving her hand back and forth in front of her and feeling sick at the thought of consuming anything made by a bully's hands. She'd much prefer to starve to death than ever lower herself to do that.

Two hours later and after several bottles of wine had been demolished and enjoyed, along with most of the delicious cake, saliva and all, Ben and Alice showed Mel around their house for her to see all the work they'd done on it since she was there last, a very long time ago. Their old, very small bathroom had since been transformed into a much larger and brighter one, complete with a brand-new roll-top bath, featuring lovely gold-coloured taps, and in the far left corner of the room a beautiful row of palm plants and seahorse ornaments gave the bathroom a fantastic tropical feel. Lots of multi-coloured decorated ceramic fish lined one wall, and dolphins, starfish and coral reef the opposite one. Two walls were painted in pale blue and the other two in lemon yellow. Mel felt as though she were in an entirely different house altogether to the dreary and drab one she'd seen ages ago.

In the other corner of the room, an amazing water feature caught her attention. Relaxing sounds of trickling water and classical music were playing on low volume. The bathroom used to look so boring before they improved it and Mel felt very calm now just being in such a nice atmosphere. It was also a welcome distraction from Alice interrogating her. Mel stared at the rocky water feature and imagined drowning both women in it. She was very tempted to include such a scene in her new novel too.

"I don't know what to say. It's incredible! You've done a great job here, Alice. And you too, Ben. I wish my bathroom looked as good as yours."

"Thanks. I did most of it but Ben helped me with the water feature and he and builder friends knocked a wall down and rewired the electrics. The floor tiles and roll top silver bath cost a fortune but the others that we had are years old. I thought because he's earning a lot of money at work lately, why not spend a bit more of it on the house?"

A bit? Mel thought, admiring the vastly different room. More like twenty thousand quid!

Ben looked at Alice and then back at Mel. "If Alice doesn't mind, I can ask my mates to alter your bathroom too if you want. Let me know. I can get a massive discount for you, seeing as I know you well."

"I'm sure that Mel has her own contacts, Ben," Alice chimed in. "We need your friends to finish off our spare room. And then there's the garden to finish off too." Wide-eyed and with jealousy tearing at her soul, she instantly created an uncomfortable atmosphere.

"It's fine," Mel replied, as Ben ground his teeth and glared at his wife. "Yes, I do have my own contacts. My father's friends are in the building trade as well so if I need anything done to my house I can ask them, but thanks all the same, Ben, very kind of you to think of me," Mel replied, startled at the obvious, icy look that Alice was giving him. Feeling that she'd outstayed her welcome, Mel decided to go back to her own place.

"Thank you both for a lovely evening. It was very kind of you to ask me over and the meal was delicious."

Ben and Alice nodded in unison. "Anytime, more than welcome," Alice replied, a false smile on her now very pissed off face.

Mel felt as though she could cut the atmosphere with a blunt knife, let alone a sharp one.

"I've got something for you both," she said, pulling two pieces of paper out of her handbag and handing them to the couple.

"Gift vouchers! Brilliant! We'll save them for Christmas. Thank you, Mel. That's very thoughtful of you," Ben replied, very grateful for the kind gesture lightening the mood. He took his wallet out of his trouser pocket and slipped the vouchers into a small compartment. There were no photographs of he and Alice in there. And certainly no photographs of he and his secret lover either. Shudder the thought!

"Yes, thanks, Mel. Much appreciated," Alice added, still looking as if she were sucking on a lemon, or an angry wasp. "There's no need to go just yet. Stay a while longer. We can show you the back garden and what we've done to it. The solar-powered pretty lights and ornaments are in those boxes over there. They can be set up in about an hour and you can help us if you like."

Mel felt her stomach lurch and she shook her head. "I have to get back, sorry. It's late. Got an early start tomorrow on this new novel I'm working on. Maybe some other time. I'm sure your garden will look even more amazing that it already does. I'll take a look when it's all done."

"Okay. Shame you won't stay longer but maybe next time, yes," Alice replied, feeling frustrated that she'd failed to find out more about the woman's life so that Marlene would know. "We hope you've had a nice time tonight. Lovely to see you again. Please keep in touch more. I thought you'd moved out as I hardly see you lately."

"Well I am looking for a new place as it happens. Hopefully I'll be somewhere else by Christmas. We'll see."

Ben felt sad as he watched her walk to the front door with Alice by her side. Mel deliberately stood to the right of her so that she could look over the woman's shoulder and through a window opposite. There was no sign of Marlene. The coast was clear! Or so she thought anyway...

Opening the front door and stepping outside, Mel thanked Alice again for inviting her round in the first place. Ben ran towards the door to try to alert her about Marlene, but it was too late. Mel came face to face with her bitch of a neighbour on the garden path. Her heart leapt and she feared that it would stop beating. Adrenalin coursed throughout her veins and she didn't know whether to flee or fight; her initial reaction. But, like rabbits in blinding headlights, she froze on the spot.

"Oh hi, Mel. I didn't know you were here. I hope you enjoyed some of my cake. Did you?"

"I was full after dinner, sorry. Couldn't fit another morsel in," she replied, frantically trying to get past the woman to get back into her own house where it was all nice and stress-free but Marlene was having none of it as she put her hand on her victim's shoulder. Mel immediately tensed up and felt her bowels move, dizziness threatening to capture her mind and body.

"I have to go. I've got to telephone someone and it can't wait. Bye, Ben. Bye, Alice. Thanks for the invite, I had a great time."

Rushing past Marlene and flinging the garden gate open until it rebounded off a wall, she waved and hurried through her own gate and up her own garden path. Without looking at anyone she pulled her key from out of her bag and prayed that it went into the door's lock straight away. The thought of hands trembling with the three of them watching would feel so demoralising. The key slid straight into the lock. She felt herself slide mentally into her own little safe bubble again. Opening her door, she stepped inside. The very second she closed her door and locked it, most of her anxiety left her. Slumping to the floor, she began sobbing uncontrollably into her hands, her heart feeling as heavy as stone and a huge headache beginning to squeeze her temples in a vice-like merciless grip.

A solitary owl was making a din outside while Marlene was getting on Ben's nerves next door.

"Alice, I asked him why he didn't invite me in and he said that you were entertaining a guest. Not one to barge in, I thought as she's a neighbour that you wouldn't mind my company. I must say, I feel quite put out that I was excluded."

Ben looked at her in disgust. He walked into the back garden to get away from her, and before he said something that he wouldn't regret getting off his chest, but Alice would tell him off for being so blunt – despite the fact that her friend always got away with being like that. He thought how suited both women were and that they should be married to each other. He loved women but the mental image of the both of them getting it on sexually as he watched, made his last meal almost exit from his stomach.

"Marlene, I'm sorry. All I could find out was that she said she doesn't like you and that maybe she's tired due to overworking. I did try."

"I know. I heard. I was listening through the walls," the bitch replied, giving her friend a sly wink. Ben noticed though and had the urge to throw her through a window.

"You cheeky...," Alice replied, pushing Marlene's shoulder playfully. Grinning like maniacs and gossiping like two old witches, they both sat down and enjoyed a coffee each. It was approaching midnight but as both women didn't sleep much, the night was still young as far as they were concerned.

Ben stood in his garden and glanced at Mel's back door. He felt a longing to go in to see how she was but with Alice getting drunk with Marlene, all hell would break loose. He hoped that she was ok and wasn't too upset. He kicked a plant pot over and kicked it even harder the second time, shattering it into tiny pieces as fragments of terracotta hurtled through the air and landed on a low brick wall.

CHAPTER FIVE

Time whizzed by. Marlene went out early in the morning. She planned on staying out all day but often returned at different times; something Mel hated. At least if she returned at exact, specific times, Mel could go outside and not have to endure the very uncomfortable situation of being in her obnoxious presence.

Expecting Mel to be pottering around in her back garden, Ben felt disappointed to see that she wasn't there. He also sometimes timed meetings, knowing all to well that if he was to ever engage in conversation with her, he had to imitate her movements. Once, when he went into Mel's house to speak with her, Alice came knocking at the door. Suspicious as always, she had eyes like a hawk and ears like a bat.

Alice came out and was carrying a box in both hands. She appeared to be struggling to hold it up. Ben used to rush to her side to help but couldn't be bothered anymore. It was full to the brim with solar-powered lights and lots of varying-sized garden and patio ornaments. Indoors, a delicious Sunday roast dinner was next on the agenda as pots and pans held cut and sliced vegetables and a meat tray covered in foil held a plump and expensive piece of lamb.

"I think we were far too drunk last night to set these up."

"Well I wasn't. You certainly were!"

"I was not drunk. I was merely...merry!" Alice replied, squinting in the sunlight and feeling worse for wear.

"You look rough today. Hangover? Serves you right. You still look gorgeous though."

"Gee, thanks. I think. Are you being sarcastic?"

"No, I'm being nice. Why do you always assume that I'm being awkward or sarcastic?"

"Because you're an expert at it, that's why. I never know when you're being genuinely nice to me or are having a little go at my expense."

"Well I'm not. You do still look gorgeous. I can't win can I? Whatever I say or do or don't say or don't do I'm always in the wrong. I'm going to the supermarket to pick up some batteries for the smoke alarm. Do you need anything else?"

"Yes. More wine. We drank the place dry last night."

"You mean you did. Mel hardly touched a drop. And you could have let her know that Marlene was going to call in with the cake. Maybe Mel would have also drunk the place dry and would have told that cow off for once. Somebody needs to!"

Alice glared at him. "You mean you'd like to, but you haven't got the balls to, have you?"

"I will, one day. She's intrusive, a gossip and a troublemaker and one day she'll turn on you too. If she can talk about others behind their back, she's probably doing it about you as well."

"She's my friend. I trust her. She'd never do that."

"How do you know though? Mel was your friend too once, remember? But even I can see how cool things are between you two nowadays, despite having her round last night. You could have cut the tension in the air with a piece of that cake, let alone with the knife!"

"Oh shut up."

"Don't tell me to shut up. Look, I'm going out. See you later."

"Bye!" "And don't forget the wine!" Alice shouted, and wished that she hadn't. Her head hurt but not as much as Mel's heart did next door. She had been listening to every word and a part of her felt sorry that their marriage was as crumbly as the cake had been.

As Ben got to his car, and as he was just about to turn the key in its ignition, he noticed that Mel was watching him through her net curtains. The way the light dimmed in the sky as the sun hid behind dark clouds for a few seconds gave him enough time to see a little glimpse of her, before she disappeared into a blaze of golden rays and then whiteness of the material of her bright white net curtains as they changed from see-through to opaque. She moved them and waved and smiled at him. He smiled and did the same back and then gestured to her if she wanted to join him. Normally she wouldn't dare leave the house in case she bumped into the bitch next door but she suddenly thought 'fuck it', grabbed her bag and coat and closed the front door behind her as she sped away to the shops with him. Alice was cursing in her back garden and picking up broken plant pot fragments. Still, it was better the pot than his foot against her, she thought.

"How's your gum now?" Mel asked him, as they drove down the street and turned a corner.

"It's hardly hurting now. Well not as much as it was yesterday. It comes and goes. That's the unpredictable nature about pain. A bit like cow face next door. Seeing Marlene in front of you and your reaction hurt me more. I saw her at the last minute when I looked out of the window. I did try to get to the door before Alice did. I'm so sorry."

"It's fine. You might think I'm silly but I didn't have to make a telephone call. I lied. I sat by my front door and cried my eyes out. I wouldn't have come around to your house at all if you hadn't been there. I can deal with the bitch as long as I'm not alone with her."

"Actually, I think when the time is right and you've had enough, you'll stand up to her. I've known you a long time and we've spoken a lot over the years and I believe you're much stronger than you realise."

"Maybe. We'll see. I'd rather avoid her if I can though."

"Come on, let's push the boat out and have something nice for dinner. Alice doesn't have to know. Not around here though."

"Thank you, Ben. You're a good friend."

Her words, although lovely-sounding, weren't what he had hoped for. He wanted to be with her all the time and couldn't bring himself to confess that to her. For now, he was content to just spend a few hours in her company and away from Alice. He loved his wife but his love for Mel was growing not only stronger as time went by, it was a love that he'd always dreamed of, always deserved and always had searched for; never fully finding it with Alice, or with Jan either. They were content in each other's company and he loved his wife, but if he had a choice, he'd leave.

He rested his left hand on Mel's. It felt welcome there. Natural. She didn't want him to move it and he only moved it when changing gear, promptly returning it when not. They drove five miles. She felt happy for the first time in a long time. Truly happy. And safe. And very, very calm. She always thought that he was in the wrong job and becoming a counsellor suited him much better than a private investigator.

Marlene's car was parked in the same car park that Ben's would soon be in and when both he and Mel reached the same area and parked about fifty yards away they both got out and slowly strolled across tarmac until they reached the huge entrance of a large and popular supermarket. And Mel was about to have quite a shock.

They wandered up several aisles and she felt relaxed and at ease in his company. To anyone else in the supermarket they appeared to be a happily-married couple, browsing through products. Ben prayed deep down inside that his secret girlfriend, Jan, wouldn't be there, even though she lived miles away and was always discreet. He'd told her where he and Alice shopped so she stayed away to avoid an awkward and embarrassing situation. He didn't know that much about Jan; just where she lived and how great she was in bed. Their affair had been going on for nine years and he had a lot of affection for her but didn't love her. Not in the same way that he loved his wife anyway. She loved him but knew that he'd never leave Alice. Age thirty, and very attractive, she could have any man she wanted but had chosen him instead.

Marlene spotted Ben and Mel from the corner of her eye when browsing in the wine aisle. She looked around for Alice but she was nowhere to be seen. With an air of arrogance and judgement in her swagger, she walked straight over to them. Tapping Mel on her shoulder, venom laced her tongue.

"Ben, what is it?", Mel asked.

"Well, hello you two! Alice not here then, Ben?", she sneered, one eyebrow raised.

He put his hand on Mel's tense shoulder and steered her away. Mel had turned an alarming shade of white and had accidentally dropped a tin of soup, denting it on the floor. It rolled a few yards away in a wonky fashion before disappearing underneath a stack of shelves and price displays.

"No, she's at home. We thought we'd nip out to pick up a few things. We're going back soon."

"I bet you are. I'm going to the checkout now, I'll call in to see Alice and tell her you're on your way then."

Put on the spot and searching desperately for a suitable response, Marlene walked away from them before he could speak. Marlene turned around and glared at Mel.

"I hope you two are not having an affair. Alice is my best friend and I'd hate to see her hurt."

"How dare you! We're out shopping. I told you!"

"Bye! See you later!" Marlene shouted, as she made her way to the checkout, pushing her shopping trolley and narrowly missing a pensioner in front of her.

"I should have spoken up. I should have said something," Mel said.

"You weren't to know that she'd be here. You're in shock, it's fine. Look, let's get back before she does."

Mel looked at him and suddenly felt an icy calmness wash over her. She stood upright and smiled, feeling her anxiety dissipating like condensation upon a window pane in a sunrise's heat.

"No. We'll carry on as we are and finish our shopping. We're out in public for God's sake! It's not as if we're having an affair and sneaking around behind everyone's back."

Ben felt a pang of guilt stabbing at his gut and heart. Before he could confess to her about his secret affair with Jan, he noticed that Marlene had turned around and was now coming towards them again. Mel put her hands on her hips and did her best to hide her fear. Ben had taught her how to use body language to mask inner turmoil and now was the perfect time to use it.

"I forgot to say, Mel, I know you don't like me. Alice told me. The sooner you move out of our street the better, do you hear me? You're nothing but trouble!"

Mel forced herself to look Marlene in the eye and as sick to her stomach as she felt in her presence, she knew that she had to speak up, or endure another day, another week, another month and another year of the horrible woman. But telling herself off for choosing not to be assertive and to protect her self-respect from completely crumbling and dying was far worse and she'd had more than enough of that.

"I'm going nowhere. I think you should move," Mel replied, trying to control her masked panic. It sounded, to her, like a totally different person speaking and not she herself. And she liked how it sounded and felt. If she'd known how great it could make her feel, she wished she'd done it a lot sooner than now.

Marlene was so taken aback by her neighbour's blatant and unexpected confidence, she swiftly turned around and marched off, seething and muttering obscenities under her breath as shocked shoppers whispered to each other and tried not to make it too obvious that they were staring at her.

Ben patted his shaking friend's shoulder. "Bloody well done! Now that wasn't so hard was it?"

"It was actually. You have no idea!"

She jumped at his touch and then felt enormous relief sweeping over her, followed by elation. Although her heart was still thumping and her stomach churning, a voice inside her head congratulated her on mustering up the guts to finally speak out. They finished their shopping and for the first time in a long time, Mel actually looked forward to returning home. The gloves were well and truly off now!

CHAPTER SIX

Upon arriving back home, they got out of the car and she surveyed the street. It was empty. Usually averting her gaze away from Marlene's property, for the first time in a long time she stared right at it. There was no sign of her aggressive neighbour. She doubted very much that the bitch was hiding and afraid but as long as she couldn't see her, everything was alright.

Shrugging her shoulders, she turned to Ben who was grabbing bags out of the boot of the car. He smiled at her and whispered: "You're going to be fine. The worst is over now. You stood up to her, good on you. I'm proud of you."

"It was difficult and very uncomfortable back there but I feel great. Thank you for the support, I really appreciate it."

"I'll see you in a few days' time. Got a lot to do in the house, DIY and all that and a barrage of questions to answer. You know what Alice is like. Best to get on with it but we can catch up soon I hope. It was the best laugh I've had in years."

"No problem. It's been good to get out. We must do it again. See you soon then. Call in anytime, you can tell me over a coffee what needs to be done in my house as you know more than I do about renovation."

"I'll try. Alice may suspect something's going on between us though if I'm found in your house, so best I speak to you in the garden instead."

"Okay. Whatever's good for you. I don't want any trouble."

They went their separate ways. Mel walked toward her kitchen to make a coffee. As she stepped across the floor she noticed a stickiness underneath her shoes. A horrendous smell accompanied it too. Lifting one foot off the floor she was greeted with the disgusting sight of a warm and wet lump of dog shit. Looking around and then at the smeared brown trail behind her, she seethed. Her mouth fell open as the realisation that someone had deliberately shoved it through her letterbox flashed through her mind. After cleaning up the mess, her shoes, and spraying a whole can of strong air freshener around her house, she tried to calm her rage. Sitting down, she had to get up again and paced the floor. Her entire body shook like a leaf caught in an angry and powerful storm, and she felt pains in her gut.

"Stop it!", she said, glaring at herself, willing her body to keep still. Despite using the air freshener, it only seemed to mask the awful stench of excrement for a few minutes, not get rid of it completely. She closed her eyes and forced bile back down her gullet.

Opening the front and back doors wide, fresh air improved things somewhat, but in her mind, memories of stenches were much harder to eradicate. She wrapped the shit in newspaper and a plastic bag and braced herself to walk to the bottom of the back garden to put it into a bin. Carrying it at arm's length and screwing up her face, she lifted the bin lid and threw it in. Flies began hovering and they soon swarmed around the lid of the smelly bin.

As she turned around to walk back up the path, movement of net curtains on a bedroom window next door caught her eye. Marlene was pissing herself laughing. With not much breeze around today, the movement of the curtains had been done by a person. Mel glared at the window and didn't take her eyes off it for a second as she reached her back door and stepped inside her kitchen. Marlene sat on her bed, holding her sides.

"Oh there's plenty more where that came from. Stupid bitch. That'll teach you to humiliate me in public," she growled, under her breath.

Little did Marlene know however, that Mel was in the process of totally and completely snapping, now. And it wasn't going to be pretty at all.

CHAPTER SEVEN

Ben's secret girlfriend decided that she needed to see more of him. Despite being told under no circumstances not to approach his house, ever, she sat outside in her car, huddled under a blanket. Peeking through her car window from beneath the rim of her hat, she couldn't look more suspicious if she'd tried.

A Monday evening, bats flitted around a nearby street light; circling, and catching moths and other bugs. Tunes played from Jan's CD. Drumming polished fingernails on her dashboard, she chewed gum and anticipated being in his arms once more.

The street itself was silent but drum beats from her heart sounded as though they were about to deafen her ears. Normally a person with inner calmness and poise, she was a nervous wreck. Checking her phone for the tenth time, she began sending Ben a text message.

Marlene spotted her through her bedroom window. Colour drained from her face. Having not seen her sister for years, she raced downstairs, shrieking like a mad woman. Yanking her front door open, she ran in her fluffy black mule slippers up to the car. Joanne panicked. She detested her sibling. Living in the same house when kids, Marlene had made her life a living hell, picking on her at every opportunity and always having the first pickings of everything; from new shoes to clothes, even to the advances of potential boyfriends whenever Jan brought them home. So she simply stopped bringing them home and went to their place or to hotels instead. Before she could turn the engine back on, a loud rap on the window made her jump.

"What are you doing here so late? Why didn't you let me know you were coming? Come on in!"

"Hi, Marlene. Good to see you again," Jan replied, forcing herself to sound sincere.

She climbed out of her car and returned her sister's welcoming embrace.

"Come in! Long time no see. Let me see that beautiful face of yours," Marlene said, lifting the hat off Jan's head, just at the exact moment Ben wheeled his bins out to the front of his house to be emptied the following morning by council bin men. He felt faint and steadied himself in the shadows by a wall. Both women don't see him. Jan locked her car and headed into her older sister's house. He bites his nails and mutters to himself: "What the hell?"

Marlene hurried to her kitchen to put the kettle on. Jan was already sitting down and fidgets with a zip on her coat. Checking the living room out, she nods approvingly.

"Gorgeous house you've got here, sis. Much nicer than mine. You're doing well for yourself I see!"

"Well, it's taken me years but I'm getting there. Why didn't you telephone me or at least send me a text to let me know you were coming to see me?"

"A surprise visit. You know me, spontaneous."

"Yes, you've always been like that. Never mind, it's good to see you again. I've got loads to tell you! Tea or coffee?"

"Coffee please. One sugar and lots of milk. Thanks. You always did love a good old gossip didn't you. You haven't changed one bit."

"And what's wrong with that? You usually listen to whatever I've told you. I don't see you storming out or putting your hands over your ears."

Jan placed her hands over her ears, mockingly. She then removed them to pick up a steaming mug of hot coffee and sipped it slowly, enjoying its delicious taste. It was so cold outside and the heating in her car had packed up. Marlene sat beside her and stared. They hadn't seen each other for ten years due to the fact that they wouldn't stop bickering, but neither could remember what the conversations had been about now.

"Look, I just fancied calling in to see how you are that's all," she lied, wondering if Ben had seen her loitering in the street. She had the same car they'd made love in but hotel rooms were much better nowadays.

"Well, I'm glad you have. I'll sort the spare room out after a chat. How long are you staying?"

Caught off guard, Jan stumbled over her words. "I do-, I don't think I can. I'm not sure."

"Stay a week! I don't see you enough. Please stay a week. We've plenty of food here and I've got enough booze to sink a ship. You're the same size as me and you can wear my clothes. It's fine," Marlene suggested, resting her hand gently on Jan's head. Jan felt as if she'd been knighted and given permission to do whatever she wanted to – a stark contrast to when they were growing up, when her older sister always got her way.

"Sis, you're two dress sizes bigger than me. What are you on about?" "Do you have a radio I can listen to in the spare room? You know how much I love my music."

"I don't, no," Marlene replied, visibly offended by her true but blunt comment about her weight. I can nip out and get one though if you want me to."

"No. It's fine. I'll probably drop off to sleep straight away, so no point."

Marlene patted her stomach and looked around the room. Changing the subject, she swallowed a mouthful of coffee and coughed as the hot liquid scorched the lining of her mouth. "See? This is what surprises do for me. Plus, I've got some juicy gossip for you, young lady. God, you're going to spit yours out when I tell you what's been going on here lately."

Jan wondered if Ben was listening through the walls. Her pulse had returned to normal now but butterflies still fluttered around inside her. Marlene continued to witter on about Mel.

"You look miles away. Haven't you heard a word I've said?"

"Course I have! I'm just tired that's all. What were you saying about Mel?"

"Keep this to yourself but I put dog shit through her letterbox and I've really got her rattled now. Oh and the old lady down the road has been killed. You must have heard it on the news, surely?"

"I don't really watch it but I heard something about it on the radio. I'm kind of busy you know?" "Sorry to hear that. She seemed a nice woman but from what I remember about her she was a bigger gossiper than you, and that's saying something," she replied, laughing.

Marlene cocked her head to one side. "I'm not that big a gossip, but yes, she was far worse, you're right."

"Did they find out who killed her?"

"Not yet, no. Police have been swarming the area for a while but have cooled off lately. I wonder if they'll ever catch who did it to be honest. I mean they would have caught them by now. Apparently there wasn't enough DNA evidence to get the murderer, so how they'll get them is anyone's guess."

"But they got some, you say. What evidence was that then?"

"Footprints in the garden and scuffed shoe marks on a wall. Undergrowth was disturbed too. That's about it."

"Oh? Male or female shoes?"

"They're not a hundred percent sure because the garden's been soggy from all the rain we've had, so a lot of detail has been washed away and distorted, I heard. And the shoes, anyone within a fifty-mile radius probably wears the same kind of footwear so it's very difficult to pinpoint or track down anything of significance really."

"How do you know all this? Good God, you should be a policewoman, not a retired Headmistress."

"Jeremy, my friend, he lives a few doors down and he told me that he overheard police discussing the matter the night it happened. You should have seen the body, there was so much blood. So much of it!"

"I see. Good coffee. Thanks," Jan replied. They both sat in silence for several minutes and the hairs on the back of their necks stood on end.

Ben cupped his palm to a wall and strained to listen to them. Nothing. Frustrated, he paced up and down his living room. Alice couldn't help noticing whenever she occasionally walked past, carrying wet laundry in a large, oval-shaped red plastic basket to a utility room.

"What are you doing? What's wrong? You're up and down like a blue-arsed fly!"

"Nothing. I've just got a lot of energy tonight that's all. Do you need a hand with that?"

"You don't normally offer. Are you sure you're alright tonight?"

"I do offer! But here's the bloody thing though you see, whenever you're doing housework you always tell me off, that I'm usually in your way and you ask me to move or to watch the telly so that you can get on with things. No wonder I get confused."

"You're just acting strange. Not quite yourself, Ben."

She handed him the basket. He carried it into the utility room. Fortunately for him it had thin walls and was adjacent to Marlene's living room. As he draped each garment over a clothes horse to dry, he heard muffled speech. He could make out the odd word here and there but not enough to work out what the conversation was about.

Pressing his ear up to the wall he narrowly missed his cheek becoming embedded on a large nail that was poking out from between breeze blocks blocks. A big, dark brown spider spun its web and seemed oblivious to Ben's peculiar behaviour. Ben marvelled at how clever the insect was and watched in fascination at how creative it was too. It's amazing what you notice when you're not moving much, he thought. He heard the words "Ben was in the garden," and, "He found her on her doorstep. Blood was gushing from her neck. It was awful for him to see her like that."

Alice walked into the room and stood with her hands on her hips like a stern mother about to tell a disobedient kid off. She could frown for Wales and deep ridges had formed over the years above the bridge of her nose. He often wondered what her face would look like if a surgeon ever stretched the surface of her face taut.

"You're worse than those curtain twitchers you are. You're turning into the old lady. She was exactly like this; always sticking her nose into other people's lives, always involving..."

"Sssh! Shut up for one second, woman, will you?", he interrupted. "I'm trying to hear!"

"Hey, don't speak to me like that. Why are you listening through the wall anyway? What's so interesting about Marlene that you need to know?"

"Nothing. I'm just seeing what's on TV. I'm curious as to what she watches."

"You little liar!"

"I'm not a lair. Don't speak to me like that!"

"I'm going upstairs for a bubble bath. See you later when you're back to your usual normal self. Well, as normal as you'll ever be anyway," she teased, walking up to him and placing a pair of wet knickers on the top of his head. Laughing, she ran away and headed upstairs.

He threw them across the room and cursed under his breath. Although it was a pleasant change to hear her laughing and not her normally sullen menopausal self, now was not the time for frivolities, he thought.

Pressing his ear against the wall again, making sure he missed the nail and the spider too, he sighed. Marlene had now put music on, making it even harder to work out what she and Jan were talking about. Giving up altogether, he finished hanging wet laundry up to dry. He then carried the empty basket to the far side of the room. Putting it down in a corner, he slumped in an armchair and switched TV channels to watch the news. He ran his fingers through his hair, and sighed. He couldn't wait to get back to work.

Next door, Jan chatted with her sister in the kitchen. She'd gone outside into the back garden to have a cigarette. Despite disliking Marlene, she decided to put up with her. Staying in her house for a while was the only way she could be anywhere close to Ben. Becoming possessive over time, she was now well and truly stalking him. He'd warned her several years ago to stay quiet when she'd suggested that he tell Alice about the two of them. She hadn't liked the expression in his eyes, it had chilled her to the bone at the time, stopping her in her tracks, making her change the subject. Wining and dining her and fucking her senseless always melted away any concerns she ever had for her own safety, but deep at the back of her mind it always festered.

"He found her. He was the first person to find her sprawled out on her doorstep. Her mouth was open and her eyes were looking terrified, like she'd seen a ghost or something. The blood was everywhere and running down the step like a stream in the rain. The poor woman. I know she upset a lot of folk over the years but she didn't deserve to be murdered. Bad timing."

"Marlene, aren't you worried that whoever did that to her might do it to another person? Do you want to come and stay at my place for a while?"

"No, it's OK. We can't live our lives terrified all the time. Police have arranged for two officers to patrol the area every night, every few hours or so, so I feel safe knowing that. I've got too much to do here with the house but thanks for the offer anyway. You always were thoughtful. Despite our differences over the years, I do love you."

"I know. And I love you too. But the offer's still there if you change your mind. I know it's a long drive to my place but the break from doing all of this renovating might do you the world of good. Give it some thought."

"I will. I'm fine, honestly. Hard work never harmed anyone and even though I'm older than you, I've still got my mojo you know. You should see some of the lazy buggers in the street. Some of them refuse to work. They disgust me. When I was their age I was working two jobs. Mam and dad always taught us that; to be conscientious and never slobs. I'd rather be doing something. The doctor says I've got a low boredom threshold and bipolar disorder but I don't believe him of course. He's also suggested that I'm suffering from menopausal mood swings, especially paranoia. What rubbish!"

Jan smirked and rolled her eyes in sarcasm. "No, you're perfectly normal, sis. Just like me."

Marlene looked at her and blinked, hard. She then smiled. "So good to see you again. Let me run a bath for you and while you're having one I can get on with sorting out the spare room for your stay. And I won't take no for an answer!"

"You can't kidnap me. I'm too old. You did that when we were kids, but you can't now."

"I can if I want to. Don't think age matters! You're my younger sister and you do as you're told, young lady!" Marlene teased.

"Got to bloody catch me first!" Jan replied. She ran away, feeling nine-years-old again. "By the way, what's that smell?"

"Ah memories. Those were the days," Marlene whispered. "What smell?"

"In your back garden. I had a smoke out by the shed. I walked down to the back, by the wall."

"I can't smell anything whenever I'm down there."

"That's strange," Jan replied. "I'm a smoker and I can smell it but yet you can't? I thought you were burning sage or something but there was no fire, just the smell of it. I'll go and have that bath then. See you soon."

"Aye, take your time," Marlene replied, watching her sister wander upstairs.

Ben had had enough and braved it to go outside. He stood by his garden gate and glanced up at the house next door. Jan drew curtains and then a light went on in the front bedroom. He watched her shadow move around the room. The bathroom light went on next. He looked up and down the street. Bats were still chasing moths and other bugs and an air of trepidation rumbled in the skies. He opened the gate and went for a short walk down the pavement. Shivering, he placed both hands in his trouser pockets and felt reassured when he noticed two officers were strolling towards him.

"Evening, officers. Heard anything else yet about the murder?"

"Hi, Ben. Not yet, no. We're still going over things in and forensics are examining whatever they can. I'm sure we'll catch the bastard who bumped her off though. Fancy doing that to a little old lady. I'd string them up if they did that to my grandmother. Sooner or later they'll trip themselves up. They always do. Few get away with things for too long."

"Great to hear. I'm sure the case will be solved in time. How long are you here for?"

"Just another hour or so. We've been keeping an eye on the houses for three hours before other officers take over for the night shift. My feet are bloody killing me."

"New shoes, Joe?"

"No, I've had these a while. I run in my spare time and I hurt my leg on a wall recently. Check out this bruise!" He pulled his trouser leg up and revealed a large dark purple bruise near his shin bone.

"Ouch. That must have hurt like hell."

"Ben, it hurt like a motherfucker, I can tell you."

"You hurt it on a wall you say?"

"Yeah," officer Joe replied, pulling his trouser leg down and facing the man's curious eyes. "I ran into a wall. Came around a corner up the lanes up there and a van didn't signal it was around the corner. I went one way and the van swerved the other. Both lucky to be alive. I booked the driver for reckless driving and was tempted to bloody send him a bill for medical treatment I've had, but as I know his father, I let it go."

"I see," Ben replied, his mind trying to fathom the man's whereabouts and the timing of matters.

"No rest for the wicked, eh Ben? See you next time. Better get indoors, looks like rain any minute now. I hate the bloody rain. Typical Welsh weather, eh!"

"Aye, Joe. It's always bloody raining around here. I'm sick of it. I'm tempted to move up North but I've heard it's not much better; depending on which part you live in of course."

"Move abroad. My mate did. He lives in sunny California now and wished he'd done it sooner. You should see the tan on him when I video call him. He's unrecognisable now. He used to be pasty white all his life. I've never seen him so happy either. Especially with the women flocking to him. With your looks, Ben, get your arse abroad. Sunny California, Ben. And bloody take me with you, mate. I could do with a holiday. I could do with women flocking around me too, come to think of it!"

"I've got one on the side, here, I don't need to go there."

"Does the wife know?"

"No. But she might well find out tonight."

"Shitting a brick then are you? Going to tell her are you? You're brave."

"No, I'm not going to tell her. Look, it's a long boring story. I'll see you around okay? Send me a postcard if you do leg it to sunnier climes and describe in graphic detail what any women do to you."

"Oh I'll do that alright. You never know, I might just do it one day. Got a murderer to catch here first though!"

"I won't keep you then. I hope you get them. I've never seen residents stay indoors as much as this, it's not normal to see the street so deserted. It's always been so full of life."

"One less now though, Ben."

"Hmm, yes. Not good. Not good at all."

They stared at black clouds hovering above them. Ben waved to him and headed back up the street.

Jan was soaking in a sumptuous bubble bath while Marlene opened an expensive bottle of Merlot while singing to herself in her usual out of tune way. Ben came in out of the cold. He shivered and rubbed his hands by the log-burning fire. He then sat on a large settee. Alice cuddled up to him and they both found a good film on the telly to enjoy. He didn't take in a word of it as his mind was a million miles away with thoughts of Jan just yards away; so near and yet so far. He felt Alice's head against his shoulder and he closed his eyes, imagining Jan's there instead. His fingertips lightly brushed up and down Alice's skin. She moved her head to rest it on his muscular chest and watched the film as his mind travelled even farther.

Jan had her eyes closed too. She inhaled a beautiful and relaxing scent of Ylang Ylang and Lily as she gathered countless fragrant bubbles over her naked body, imagining that they were Ben's hungry lips on her instead. Pleasurable waves soared through her. Her lustful cravings for him were at boiling point as her fingers explored beneath the steaming water. She thought of his handsome face, his ragged breathing and final release. A single tear slid down her cheek, mingling with the bath water. Ben thought of her sleeping alone and he felt his heart sinking in his chest, like a boulder from a mountain hurtling into a deep, deep sea. He never felt so alone. Useless. Unwanted.

CHAPTER EIGHT

The following morning, Jan snuck out and left the area before Ben stirred from his slumbers. Marlene had begged her to keep in touch more and was met with a half-hearted response.

Mel yawned next door and dreaded another day, despite feeling a renewed energy source and sense of not wanting to be a doormat anymore. Marlene was slowly losing her ability to control her and the biggest realisation that Mel herself had seen was that she had allowed her to. But no more. She had choices in her life and this was now one of them, a good one for once. She made herself breakfast and cheered up. She had more positive matters to focus on today. Her novel was almost finished.

A sinister atmosphere clung in the air like a sodden filthy blanket over a rail; poisoning everything around it. The old lady's killer sat and pondered on who to bump off next. Unbeknownst to them, another murderer was plotting their demise, and soon too. Cats meowed and dogs barked in the street and bin men emptied bins. Just another ordinary day. Clouds gathered over the street and droplets of rain soon covered everything in sight.

A postman hurried along, clutching letters, parcels and whatever else he managed to carry for residents. Seagulls hovered over crashing waves lining Porthcawl beach, occasionally swooping down to feed on fresh, tasty fish. Fishermen cast their nets and hurled their rods, bristling against fierce and stormy winds that battered their cold faces without let-up.

The lighthouse's door creaked and banged against stone, little bits of wood flying in all directions as howling gusts swirled inwards and upwards, climbing the spiral staircase to the huge light's area. A few boats bobbed around on the waters outside and the scent of wet seaweed strewn all along the sandy dunes and grass filled many nostrils of cold and impatient shopkeepers who were busily setting up for the day to sell their many wares. Cars lined the coastal street outside hotels and bed and breakfast establishments and the hustle and bustle of life continued as it had for decades before and will for decades to come in the future too. Strong coffee aroma invited crowds of people to be enticed into little cafes and the delicious smell of bacon, eggs and all the trimmings were irresistible.

Three workmen had arrived to start digging up a section of the road to lay new broadband Internet cables, but were on a break and were sat at a table awaiting their breakfast – much-needed fuel to last the long, long day. Salty air had stung their faces in the street overlooking the beach. Weather beaten and fed up, they cursed under their breath. They were paid well so couldn't really moan about anything, but still, they did.

Dressed in weatherproof waterproof clothing and smeared in grime they wiped their dirty hands on their trousers and listened to each other's stomach's rumbling like thunder, angrily seeking something to silence it.

The nearby fairground was quiet today, devoid of the usual happy faces and excited hearts anticipating a ride or arcade delight, with the potential to win many a prize, if lucky enough. It was opening later than usual due to maintenance work being carried out on nuts, bolts and electrical wiring. Usually opening much later in the year, it was unusual to see it up and running in March.

Recent tempestuous weather ensured much jolting of machinery which had to be made as safe as possible. Milder and calmer weather was due in the first week of April soon. Caravans were parked in the area next to it and children impatiently ran around and caused a din to many visibly annoyed parents.

Sugared ring doughnuts were being cooked in batches, along with other tasty offerings for hungry crowds later that day. The gorgeous aroma of seafood also filled the air. Fresh cockles filled polystyrene cups full to the brim. Colourful balloons of all shapes and sizes swayed in the wind as they clung to metal bars.

Back home, not too far away, Mel rubbed her tired eyes and got into her shower, soon fully awake and alert when she forgot to wait a few seconds first. Shrieking as cold water hit her skin, she giggled and shivered. Once under the waterfall of liquid warmth, she sang to herself instead of switching on her shower radio.

Ben read his newspaper and thought of Jan. Having had a disturbed night's sleep, he felt grumpy and wasn't looking forward to his day at all; especially as Alice was wittering on and on about how much more they both had to do to the house. He just wasn't in the mood for drilling, hammering nails and painting and racked his brains for a way out.

"I'm going into town today to pick up some more DIY supplies. Do you need anything from the other shops while I'm there? A new set of curlers perhaps? Or a facelift?" he whispered, smirking.

"What was that?"

"I said I'm going into town. Do you need anything?"

"Yes, please. Can you get me four pints of milk and some eggs? I might make a cake today and we're running low on those. Thanks. Try not to be too long because that wall in the bathroom needs another coat of paint. I can see the old colour coming through on it. It looks awful. What will Marlene think if she goes in there?"

"Oh for God's sake. Why do you care so much about what she thinks, Hun? It's our bathroom, not hers. Let her worry about her house and we'll worry about ours. We've got all the time in the world to finish this place, there's no rush is there? We don't have the Queen coming here do we?"

"Oh you're in a bad mood today. Got out of bed the wrong side did you?" Alice snapped, hands on hips and glaring at him.

"I didn't sleep well that's all," he replied, hoisting his newspaper higher so that she couldn't see his irritable expression aimed directly at her like a sharp dart heading towards the bullseye.

"Can you get a few more things too? Look, I'll write a list now."

She walked into the kitchen while he sighed and then rubbed his face with a sweaty hand. At least it'd get him out of the house and away from her insufferable and lecturing attitude, he thought. He wondered if Jan would be there, but doubted it. She rarely visited the town and usually stayed closer to home; not so much to avoid Alice seeing them together in a romantic embrace, it was more that she couldn't stand Alice. Ben went out and was glad to be away from the house for some peace and quiet.

Reaching town, he stopped his car as he approached a swarm of police cars and several ambulances. Jan lay on a pavement. She was covered in bruises and splattered with blood. A hammer and kitchen knife lay at her twisted feet. Rain began pelting the roof of his car accompanying tears trickling down his face as he watched her lifeless body being zipped up in a body bag and then carried into the waiting ambulance. The doors closed. He began hyperventilating and then fainted, banging the side of his face against his car door.

Coming to later, fists banging against the window of his car door startled him, making him jump. He wound the window down.

"Are you alright, Sir?"

"Oh yes, officer. Just shaken that's all. I hate the sight of blood. What's going on then?"

"Well I can't say too much but a young woman was found by a member of the public not too long ago and we're trying to find out if anybody saw her being attacked. Who are you and where are you going?" a dark-haired policeman asked him, scrutinising his anxious face for the smallest sign of guilt.

"I'm Ben. I live not too far from here and I'm just going into town to pick up a few things. Like I said, the sight of blood makes me queasy. I've only just arrived. I haven't seen anything, no, sorry. From the police station out of town are you?"

"No, this local one. I'm new. I just wondered why you had the expression on your face that you did, that's all. Did you know the young lady, Sir?"

Ben sighed and slumped in his chair. "I didn't know her, no," he lied. "I recognised her as I've seen her out and about in the shops now and again. Such a tragedy. I hope you catch whoever's done this."

"So do we. OK, thanks for your time. We've cordoned off the area here so you'll have to go around the other way. This is a murder scene now, Sir. Forensics are on their way and we'll do what we can to clear the street as soon as possible. Sorry for any inconvenience caused."

"Thank you, officer. I'll reverse and then go that way then."

"Good day to you."

"And to you too, officer," Ben replied, feeling nauseous. He reversed into a lane and switched the engine off. Burying his face in his hands he sobbed his heart out. "Oh Jan. Why did it have to be you?"

Ben composed himself and thought about heading back home. He could explain to Alice that the street was closed due to a murder, but she might wonder why he hadn't gone to a different street. Feeling trapped, he quickly drove to an adjacent street and picked up a few household bits and pieces, including a bottle of strong vodka.

Driving back home, despite keeping his eyes on the road, all he seemed to be seeing was his dead girlfriend's gore-covered body; a beautiful woman's body that he'd planted many kisses upon on many occasions. A body he'd worshipped often and loved and that housed a good soul, a decent and lovely person who was not only his lover but had been a good friend too. But she also had a big mouth and had upset many people over the years. But bad enough to lead to her death?

He felt as though his entire world had been crushed in an instant, just like her legs, feet and other parts of her body had with the bloodstained hammer and her throat had been slit open with the knife. He and Alice had the same kind of knife in their kitchen.

Alice certainly didn't know about her, and although he didn't know Jan's friends and family, he believed that she had some.

Pulling up outside his house, he paused and ran his sweaty palms across his forehead. His face felt clammy and he felt lightheaded again. He groaned at the thought of going into his own house where there would be endless questions and a barrage of talking. He just wanted to curl up alone, and sleep.

Marlene was chatting with Alice in the back garden; gossiping more like, as usual. He could hear Marlene's cackling laughter and shuddered. Maybe if he sneaked in the wouldn't notice him. He closed his car door as quietly as he could and gently opened his garden gate, praying it wouldn't squeak. He felt a hand rest on his right shoulder and jumped. Turning around, he came face to face with a worried Mel.

"I heard on the news. A young woman was killed. I hope you didn't see anything. Are you ok?"

"I saw the body. I passed out at the wheel of the car. I wasn't driving, thankfully. It's awful. Police asked me a few questions but other than that it's a mystery. I hope they catch the bastard who did it though. Such a waste of a young life."

Mel noticed a look in his eyes of faraway distances and longing. Of deep sadness and unrequited future affection.

"You knew her didn't you. Women know these things. Intuition and all that, like a sixth sense. It's OK, you know you can tell me anything."

"Yes. Her name was Jan. I'm trusting you not to say a word to anyone about this, especially to Alice. I do love Alice but Jan was very special to me. Very special," he replied, feeling tears welling up in his eyes the moment Mel's hand touched his. Imperceptible to anyone but him, there were a thousand sympathies and understanding in that touch; far more than anything his own wife could ever give to him. Mel moved her hand away and felt her eyes tearing up too.

"Listen, I can hear those two in the garden so I'm going to go upstairs to have a hot shower. She's very observant, that one. She'll know something's up. Thanks for the concern, you're a good friend, Mel. I'll speak to you when I can, next."

"You know I'm here anytime, day or night. I'm only a doorstep away, Ben. When you're feeling up to it, tell me whatever you want to. I prefer getting my feelings out through talking, but some men bottle things up don't they, and it's not good for the mind or the body. But I'll respect you the same way even if you don't want to talk about anything, OK?"

He nodded. His lower lip was quivering. He rubbed her arm and he forced a smile through a haze of tears. He turned around, closed the gate before walking up his garden path and rummaged in his pocket for the house key. Letting himself in, he hurried upstairs and cried until his chest ached.

CHAPTER NINE

Alice had since come indoors and had heard on the news about the young woman's murder. Telephoning Marlene immediately, screams echoed down the telephone line and then uncontrollable sobbing.

Alice went to see her friend in person to console the heartbroken woman. Ben listened to relaxing music through headphones and sipped several large vodkas. His hands were shaking like a leaf and he could just about hold himself together. Alice told Marlene she'd call in later to see her after Marlene had finished speaking to police officers who were due to call to interview her. Chief inspector Don Hallows also wanted a word. A rugged man, weather beaten and cynical by nature, he didn't have time for small talk and was rather abrupt in his manner. Often glowering at people and appearing miserable all of the time, he frequently reduced many people to gibbering wrecks.

Alice walked back into her own house and stood behind her husband who was oblivious to her presence. She watched him for a few moments before pulling his headphones off his head. He wiped his eyes, trying to conceal his upset.

"Terrible news isn't it?"

She waved a hand in front of his face but he ignored her and closed his eyes. Prodding him in the arm, she persisted. He ground his teeth and finally looked up at her; a sea of unanswered questions flooded her curious eyes.

"What?" he blurted.

"Didn't mean to disturb you. I said, terrible news isn't it? About the young woman in town. Marlene's sister too. The poor woman's distraught. Police are calling in on her soon to ask her a load of questions as she's not in a fit state to go to the station. What happened when you got there in town? Did you see anything? Did you find out anything about it because if you did you really should go next door and tell them when they arrive?"

"A police officer asked me a few questions and then instructed me to drive up the other street. I saw a woman's dead body, it was covered in bruises and blood. That's all I know. There was a hammer and knife by her feet. Why don't you ask Marlene, she probably knew the ins and outs of a cat's arse before I even got back home! I didn't tell you straight away because I didn't want to upset you. I'm upset too you know. It's not every day you see a dead body in town is it, for Christ's sake?"

"No, she didn't! Don't be so callous!" "She was her sister. Have a heart."

Alice stared at him, her mouth open and eyes narrowing. She began shouting at him and telling him off for being so cruel, but he didn't care and didn't hear a word as he slipped the headphones back over his ears and closed his eyes again. She prodded him again but he moved his body away from her, an angry expression on his face. She eventually left him alone.

He sat there for what seemed like an eternity as soothing Rachmaninov calmed his soul and healed his heart, even if only for a short time. He always found solace and comfort in classical music and retreated into it so deeply whenever speaking about things was impossible, and far too painful. Alice ran a hot bath and spent more time than usual upstairs. He didn't hear her crying. And she didn't know the depths of his grief. And never would either.

Marlene paced up and down her back garden, muttering away to herself and rubbing her sore and red eyelids. She'd spotted Mel staring at her through her bedroom window that overlooked the gardens and she was almost sure that she'd displayed two insulting fingers up at her. What Mel had actually done was to replace hooks in her curtains combined with a two-finger gesture at the same time. Smiling to herself like a Cheshire cat, Mel had loved how annoyed it had made her hated neighbour feel. If she'd known it was that easy to get to her, she would have done it a lot sooner, she thought.

Not long after, Mel played her sound files back to get an idea of what to write in upcoming chapters of her new novel. For a fleeting moment she was sure she'd heard a woman say:

"I know who did it."

Mel transferred the file to her computer, slipped on her headphones and strained her ears to listen to it again. Among her own words, twenty seconds into the recording the voice was definitely there:

"I know who did it."

She gasped and blinked hard before scanning the room for the slightest sign of ghostly presences. All she could see were ornaments, furniture and nothing ghostly at all.

"I'm going crazy. Knew I'd been overdoing things. I'm losing my bloody mind now!"

She rewound the sound file and turned the volume up and listened to it again. The voice was there alright. She wasn't going crazy at all. Not only that, there were other words and both male and female voices too and they seemed to be speaking over her words and between pauses as well. They were louder when she was speaking and fainter when not; like her own voice amplified theirs. White noise. The female's voice was much easier to understand. She turned the volume up a little more, closed her eyes, and concentrated.

"They ran down the garden path after killing me!"

Mel's eyes opened wide and she put one hand over her mouth in shock. She rewound the previous bit of recording and the exact same sentences were still there. Panicking now, she took the headphones off and paced back and forth across the room, visibly agitated; like she had the biggest secret in the world and didn't know who the hell to tell it to.

"I am. I'm going crazy! I'm hearing things. It wasn't a radio coming from next door at all. It's coming from this house. Oh my God. Oh my..."

A Gothic dagger, next to a row of four other Gothic daggers fell off their little platform and landed on their side in a glass cabinet nearby. Metal clanked against glass but the glass didn't break. She collected them and in all the years she had them not one had ever done that before. Turning a small silver key, she opened the cabinet's door and placed the daggers back into small one inch slits and pushed the blades downwards. Shrugging her shoulders, she closed the door and locked it.

Turning around, she heard the same sound as before. Metal landed but this time but it didn't just clank against glass, it tapped against the glass on and off, every few seconds or so. She stood there for what felt like an eternity before burning curiosity got the better of her. Slowly moving her head to the side, she tried to see from her peripheral vision at first.

The silence in the room became deafening. Her nerves were on edge. Feeling dizzy, she held her stomach with one hand. Waves of rising bile threatened to spurt out. She fought back the revolting sensation as best she could. Unable to stand it any longer, she turned around fully, absolutely dreading what she'd see. Not only was one dagger now on its side the other four were too and were stacked upon each other at a vertical, upright angle. She gasped and ran out of the room, slamming the door behind her as her sound file began playing over and over again, all by itself:

"I know who did it. They ran down the garden path after killing me!"

CHAPTER TEN

The killer sat and wiped another bloody knife clean. In a sink full of warm water, globules of blood mingled and spread like watercolour paint on a wet canvas. The murderer crouched and lifted up a corner of a carpet and pulled at least a third of it across the floor until a trap door was exposed. An old and rusty chain lay by the side of a large iron ring. They gripped the chain with one hand and the door rose with an eerie and slow creak.

Moving a piece of wood, they held the door open and then, feet first, they lowered themselves into blackness until they touched a stone step. Holding onto the sides of the edges of the ceiling, they carefully turned around and held onto metal railings. Stepping downwards, they sang a song.

Upon reaching the last step, they flicked on a light switch and a large room was bathed in bright light. The room stretched out across the entire length of the large house and was littered with an assortment of knives, hammers, chainsaws and other gruesome-looking tools. It was an immaculate and spotless area and not an object was out of place.

The murderer strolled across a wooden floor, the knife still in one hand. They prised open an oblong-shaped box on a wall and carefully placed the knife back in its leather sheath before closing the box lid. Smiling, and still singing a tune, they walked over to a computer and booted it up. A pair of ghostly eyes watched them from a corner where the temperature was icy cold.

Once fully booted up, a bookmarked page appeared in front of the killer and they refreshed it by pressing Ctrl and F5 on their laptop computer. The page refreshed within a second. On it were recent reports of deaths and crimes in the area:

Here is the Porthcawl news for today, March 23rd: A man in his twenties, fair skinned, having strawberry blonde hair, blue eyes and being six-foot-two was discovered dead in the early hours of this morning in Sand Street. He'd been poisoned. Police are interviewing residents in the town and no other details are available until further notice. The young man left a wife and three children and there are no indications that he'd had any enemies. Police are baffled. If anyone reading this knows anything about the incident or if they saw any unusual or suspicious activities or persons, they are strongly advised to contact the local station immediately.

It is of utmost importance that any witnesses to this horrific crime come forward as soon as possible. Forensic officers are at the scene and Sand Street is closed off. Motorists are advised to follow the detour signs and are forbidden to enter the street itself. Chief inspector Don Hallows assures the public that he, other officers and forensic examiners are doing everything they can to secure an arrest. Further details will be given in due course. Residents are advised to stay indoors but if they must venture out, to never be alone when doing so. Safety in numbers will keep the public safe until the murderer, or murderers - are in custody.

The killer sat back in a leather swivel chair, placed their hands in their lap and they chuckled after reading the warning. Having contempt and no respect for the law or its upholders, they cursed and mocked the announcement's empty promises. Ghostly eyes continued watching them from the corner of the room, anger consuming them as they got up and approached the person. With breath visible now, the killer shivered and switched off their computer, got up from their chair, walked straight through the ghost and headed back upstairs. The spectral being followed them.

CHAPTER ELEVEN

Mel downed a large glass of wine. She gingerly opened a door and peered around a small gap, expecting the worst. Shuddering, she searched every inch for any signs of weird activity. Everything seemed perfectly normal. The Gothic daggers were back in their normal positions and she stood there shaking her head and gulped another mouthful of wine down, the glass and liquid held in a very trembling hand.

"I am. I'm losing it. I've been way overdoing things lately and with that cow next door, no wonder I'm hallucinating," she whispered to herself. Stepping into the room, she left the door open. Just in case... Slurping the rest of her strong drink, she wiped a red droplet from the corner of her mouth with the back of her other hand. Shrugging her shoulders, she turned around and walked back out, closing the door behind her and made her way towards her kitchen.

Ten minutes later, there was a knock on her front door. She noticed a tall figure through frosted glass and thought it odd that anyone would call today as the postman wasn't normally due until later. It was ten in the morning and he was at least two to three hours away yet. Assuming it was a religious caller, she sighed and thought of what to say to them to get them to leave.

Opening her door, a safety chain allowing nothing wider than a small gap, she stared through it into the eyes of a male police officer.

"Good morning. I'm speaking to residents in this area and you're next on our list if you don't mind us coming in for a moment to speak with you," a middle age man asked as he glanced over his shoulder at his colleague who was closing the garden gate behind him.

"No, of course, officer. Come on in."

Mel slid the chain across and opened her door wide, gesturing for the two men to enter. They replied to other officers on their walkie talkies and strolled around the house as Mel closed the door and turned to face them. She wondered if Marlene had sent them and was causing her yet more trouble.

"Sit down, please. What's this about, officer...?" she asked, looking into his rugged weather-beaten features as she searched his soulful brown eyes for answers. His colleague, a younger and shorter man was looking around the living room and seemed a million miles away.

"Well, Miss..."

"Mel, please call me Mel."

"Officer Jones. And this is officer Davies," he replied, pointing to the other man who was now looking at the two of them. "Have you heard the latest news this morning at all?"

"No, not yet. I haven't. What's this about, please?" she said, anxiety building inside her yet relief soothing her soul that they weren't there to tell her off about something Marlene had done to provoke her. She felt guilty for feeling this way but wasn't going to let them know that. "Please, make yourselves comfortable. Would you like a cup of tea or coffee? It's quite cold out there today."

"Tea would be great, thanks. Officer Davies here drinks coffee. Two sugars, please. Milk in both too. Thank you." They both sat on a large settee and watched the attractive woman walk to the kitchen where she switched a kettle on and walked back into the living room, questions still bombarding the two men as she felt slightly annoyed that they seemed to be taking their own sweet time with matters and she had a ton of work to do.

"While we're here, Mel, your neighbour, Marlene, has informed us that you've been causing her a bit of grief. Is that true? We never take sides and are impartial so let's hear your side of matters. If we find that you are provoking her however, we have to warn you that you must stop. We've enough on our hands lately as it is without residents wasting police time," the older and taller officer said, removing his jacket as the heat from a log-burning fire began thawing out his chapped, cold hands.

Mel's face dropped and she felt rage growing deep inside her. She imagined Marlene pressing her ear against the wall and trying to listen in on the conversation. She stood there with her hands on her hips and glared at the man.

"No, actually, it's the other way around. I've had to tolerate that woman for years and I've had enough. I'd like to move away from this town to be honest but it's not that easy. I'd appreciate it if you had a word with her, not with me, officer Jones."

"Look, we have a lot of neighbour disputes and bickering most days to deal with but the main reason we're here is because a young man was found in Sand Street, dead. We're still waiting on forensics, a pathologist and coroner's findings. To cut a long story short, have you noticed any suspicious activity going on around here lately? Any prowlers? Anybody acting out of the ordinary, you know? Anything at all like that?"

"Well I'm sure you already know about poor old Mrs. Robinson's death already, and my neighbour's sister, Jan, but other than that, no, I haven't noticed anything else of a similar nature. But please pass on my condolences to the young man's family. That's awful. When did that happen exactly?"

"A few hours' ago to be precise. We can't divulge any more information but as I said just now, we're interviewing everybody around here and it's bloody freezing out there so the sooner we can get this investigation over with the better. I'm forty tomorrow and I'm going away for my birthday. We're still not sure if Jan' death is related to the other deaths. We're looking into it and are trying to see if there's some sort of connection, if the killer knew these two women, and this man too."

"Forty-one," officer Davies piped up, smirking."

"Oi, I'll have you know that I'm forty. Don't add an extra year onto me or I'll have you demoted on the force, is that clear?" he joked, rubbing his hands together as he sat forward and gazed into the flames in front of him. "We've got one of those, they're lovely on a cold day like this aren't they?"

"Oh the log burner. Yes, yes they are. I don't know what I'd do without it. That reminds me, I'm having a delivery of fresh wood later, not for about another hour yet though. The postman is calling soon. I've ordered a spare electrical fire, you know, for emergencies."

"Good idea. Listen, we'll wrap this up here then. If you don't know anything else, then best we be off and we'll speak to your neighbour. I'll tell her to stop wasting our time. We're a good judge of character, Mel, and you don't strike us as the sort of woman who goes around causing trouble. She however, is well, a different kettle of fish by the looks of it isn't she?"

"Do you still want that tea?" Mel asked, grateful for their company.

"Nah, you're alright. We've already had two cups this morning as it is and two officers bursting for a pee isn't a professional-looking sight now is it when we're walking down a street. Cross-legged policemen would be a laughing stock."

"OK. I appreciate you calling. It's good to know that you're patrolling the area. I feel safer knowing that. Thank you."

"Our pleasure, Miss. That's what we do. Thank you for helping to thaw us out," he replied, pointing to the fire and smiling.

"Call in anytime. I'm writing a novel but I can always have a coffee break and chat."

"Ah, you're a writer! Me too," the younger officer replied, eyes wide with excitement like he and she were the only two people in the room as the other looked on.

"I write thrillers. What do you write? If you don't mind me asking that is?"

"Sci-fi, and thrillers too. Have you sold many of yours?"

"Enough to pay the bills, that's about it. What about you?"

"Same. Fingers crossed we write a best seller one of these days, Mel," officer Davies replied, beaming.

"Right, you two authors, I do hope you sell a truckload of books, you can give me millions and I can retire!" "Come on, we've got a lot of people to interview," officer Jones said, poking his smitten colleague in the shoulder with a finger.

"I have to go I'm afraid. Nice meeting you, Mel."

"Likewise, officer. Hope to see you again. Call in anytime, we can maybe give each other writing tips. It's good to speak to another author. I think I'm the only one in this town."

"Call me Simon. I'll be in touch!"

"See you, Mel. Thanks for your time."

"No problem, officer Jones. I hope your hands have thawed out enough now. Shame you have to go back out there."

"I should have listened to my wife, Mel, she's always buying me gloves for my birthday and for Christmas. I've left them at home. Must have a drawer full of them by now!"

Mel watched the men open the front door and Simon looked over his shoulder at her, a huge smile on his handsome face. He waved before closing the door behind him. She smiled and headed back into the kitchen to make herself a cup of hot chocolate. Normally she drank mostly coffee but fancied something different for a change. The wine had gone to her head. She also felt a little lightheaded due to the unexpected admirer paying her so much attention. It had been a long while since she'd encountered such a good-looking man, and an officer of the law too!

She poured hot water into a mug. Feeling anger rising again deep inside her at the thought of Marlene deliberately trying to piss her off, she hoped that both officers would indeed tell her off for wasting their time. The thought of her little nasty plan backfiring on her pleased Mel enormously and her anger was soon replaced by smug satisfaction. She sipped her hot chocolate and thought about the strange voices she'd heard on the sound file. She wanted to hear more, or to double check at least that she hadn't been imagining it.

Next door, she could hear the sound of Marlene's shrill voice getting louder and louder. Mel spat her drink back into the mug as she coughed and laughed at the same time. She couldn't be bothered to listen against the wall so she sat down at her computer desk and slipped on her headphones. Pressing 'play' on the file, she closed her eyes and focused again, trying her best to hear even more than she had the last time.

Aware of a very cold draught clinging suddenly to her left arm, she shivered. Removing the headphones and placing them back on her desk, she got up and walked toward her front door and was very surprised to see that it was firmly shut.

"That's strange."

Confusion swept across her face. She sat back down and continued with what she was doing. In between her own voice and words, the other, female voice said the exact same words she'd heard earlier. Male voices were chatting away too but they were far too faint to make out. Mel sipped her drink and stared at the monitor screen.

Over her left shoulder something, or rather someone, appeared. An elderly face gazed at hers. Mel dropped her mug, shattering it on the wooden floor. Hot chocolate spilled and splashed against her legs. Turning around, she found nobody there. She sat there for several minutes, dabbing her legs with an old rag. She felt her entire body tensing up. The air crackled with anticipation. The cold spot gradually vanished as warmth enveloped her arms and shoulders again. She made herself another hot chocolate and considered making an appointment to speak to a psychiatrist. Or maybe a demonologist or priest.

CHAPTER TWELVE

"She's nice, yes. Good job I'm single!"

"Simon, she is, but do try to keep your mind on the job. We've a possible murder case on our hands and we've got to keep our wits about us. We have to make sure that we notice any giveaway body language of these residents. From what I've seen of some of them, they come across as a shifty-looking lot. We could be speaking to someone today who could do it again. We must be on the lookout for suspicious behaviour; even a slightest glimpse of guilt is enough grounds to get them to the station for further questioning. Come on, we can't hang around here for too long. Let's finish this street and then move on to the next one," officer Jones insisted, as Marlene continued ranting in her house so loudly that she was heard outside too.

They both walked down the street and skipped old Mrs. Robinson's empty house. Weeds were growing out of control and all was still and quiet; unnaturally quiet. There were no dogs barking and no people going about their day. It resembled a ghost town. Frost clung to their clothing and goose bumps sprung up over their skin as they shuddered in the cold.

"I'll listen to Janice next time and will wear the bloody gloves. Women are normally right you know, Simon. Just don't ever let them know that we know that."

"Right. Good tip."

"Well, you may be courting soon, so listen to some advice from a married man. You never know, you could be married this time next year," he replied, grinning at his younger friend.

"I doubt that. She's lovely and all but let's not rush into things. I'm not as old as you yet, Sir."

"Hey! You're not that much younger than me. Watch your tongue!"

They both chatted and laughed as they approached the next house to call on.

Mel had wiped her floor and changed her trousers and slippers after putting the soaked ones in the washing machine. She was now back at her computer and typing the next chapter of her new thriller novel.

Marlene was moaning to Alice on the telephone about that morning's occurrences and both women were yakking non stop about Mel too. As usual.

Ben was in his shed out of the way, in the back garden, deep in thought about Jan. He sipped a steaming cup of strong coffee and winced as heat reminded him of recent dental work. He gazed out of a small, cobweb-framed window at a very old Oak tree opposite. He also thought of Mel and wondered how she was. Maybe they could meet up and get drunk, he thought, remembering what she'd said. Alcohol would numb his pain and help him to forget. He looked at an old ornamental wishing well nearby and wondered if wishes and hopes really did come true.

CHAPTER THIRTEEN

The following day, Ben knocked on Mel's door after Alice went out into town to do some shopping. She was going to have her hair done in a salon too so he gauged the time and estimated that she'd be gone a good few hours at least, giving him ample time to spend with Mel. Getting away from his wife made him feel a mixture of guilt and also relief; just to speak to another person who would understand him the way Mel did meant everything to him and it wasn't as if he had many male friends in the street. They were either in work a lot or drinking in the local pub. He used to accompany them and enjoyed things, until Alice had nagged him to stay home more to spend time with her. Relenting and wanting peace, he'd given in and resigned himself to the fact that spending time and money on decorating and refurbishing their home was more important – to her anyway.

Mel didn't hear him knocking on her door at first. She came up out of the bubble bath she was relaxing in and wiped bubbles out of her eyes as she spluttered. Hearing knocking now, she slumped in the bath tub and cursed. It was Sod's Law that whenever she couldn't answer the door straight away, due to either being in the shower or bath tub or sitting on the toilet having a damn good crap, that seemed to always be the precise time when a visitor called.

She got out of the tub and wrapped a large, white fluffy towel around her. Running downstairs, she got to the door just as Ben was leaving. She knocked on her own door, alerting him that she was there. He turned around and walked back up to it. Opening it, she smiled upon realising that it was him.

Letting him in, she tightly held the towel around her, praying that it wouldn't fall to the ground. He didn't care and hoped that it would.

"Sorry. I didn't know you were taking a bath. You didn't have to come down, I could have called another day. I just need someone to talk to that's all and well, we are friends after all. You're the only person I want to talk to about this, Mel, to be honest."

"No, it's fine. Give me five minutes and I'll join you. Go and make yourself a drink. I won't be long now," she replied, sprinting upstairs, her towel rising and falling, giving him a good eyeful of her shapely legs. He sighed and watched her disappear around a corner before stepping into the kitchen to see if she had anything stronger than a cup of tea or coffee.

Opening a cupboard door, he found nothing but tins of beans, tomatoes and other essentials. Opening a different one he found other foodstuffs. In the last cupboard at the end of the wall he grinned as he saw several bottles of different types of wine, all lined up in a row. Mel didn't just have panic attacks, she also had chronic OCD.

He remembered that he'd left his reading glasses in the glove box in his car. Unlocking the front door, he opened it a little before returning to the kitchen for a few moments.

"Red today I think! Why the fuck not. I deserve it," he muttered to himself, grabbing a bottle of Merlot and searching for a corkscrew. Feeling in a more upbeat mood than before, he whistled a song and made himself at home.

Mel was completely naked and laying on her bed, thinking about his strong hands and how good it would feel if he came up and touched her. She revelled in a cool breeze coming through a small window. Fine hairs prickled across the skin.

Ben went upstairs to speak to her. He found her and no words were spoken. They kissed passionately for several delicious moments before Alice found herself standing there after walking into the house through an unlocked door and getting no response to her 'Hello Mel, are you there?'

A loud audible gasp destroyed any hopes of simmering passions becoming a reality as both Ben and Mel turned to look into the eyes of a betrayed and very angry woman. Before either could even attempt to make amends, she left the house and rushed straight to Marlene's side to cry on her shoulder.

"No point in going after her then is there? I should have left her years ago, Mel. Just stay put."

"She's ruined what could have been a wonderful experience between me and you. No thanks. She doesn't half know how to kill a nice mood doesn't she? I'm sure I locked that door!"

"You did. I was going to get my reading glasses from my car. Sorry."

"I'll get dressed and will lock it again. Leave the glasses for now. I don't want her just walking into my house. I wouldn't want anyone to do that. It's my private space," Mel replied, getting off the bed as Ben cursed under his breath and punched the mattress.

CHAPTER FOURTEEN

The following morning, after a night of listening to Alice screaming through the walls and hammering them with her fists, along with Marlene's unwanted interference, taking great delight in joining in the barrage of verbal abuse aimed at Ben and Mel too, Mel decided that she'd had enough. Storming around to next door, she banged on their front door. Her face was purple almost as she cursed under her breath.

Alice opened the door. Before she had a chance to speak, Mel barged past her and confronted Marlene. It was now or never. Mel didn't even give herself time to think about it, she was too pissed off. The woman stood, hands on hips, ready and well prepared to hear whatever it was her arch enemy had in store for her.

"You! You've caused me nothing but upset," Mel shouted, pointing at her. "What's wrong with you, for fuck's sake? Why can't you be normal? Why are you so inconsiderate of other peoples' feelings?"

Unlike Mel, who had totally lost it now and was screaming like a banshee, forever the Ice Queen, Marlene simply stood there, a mocking expression on her wrinkled face.

"Have you any idea what it's like living next door to a cow like you? I've tried to move, what more do you want, you sour-faced old bitch?"

This one really got Marlene. She took great offense at being referred to as 'old'; the rest she could brush aside, having been called far worse to her face, but 'old'? No, she wasn't standing for that. She prided herself on trying to retain as much youth as possible and wasn't having a much younger woman demeaning her, and in front of her friend too.

"Never mind me. What about you then? Running away with another woman's husband. Now that's bad. Really, really bad."

Mel turned to look at Alice, and rather than apologise she offered her the same look of contempt she'd given to Marlene too.

"And before you open your mouth, he's told me all about you; how much of a pain in the arse you are to live with. No wonder the poor man's had affairs over the years. Can you blame him? You used to be a nice person once, Alice, but since you've started associating with this old trout you're becoming like her. What a pity!"

Marlene's face was priceless. Alice just gasped in shock. As Mel turned to leave, Marlene lunged at her and grabbed her by the hair. Swinging around in a heartbeat, Mel smacked the woman in her face, her punch landing right in the centre of her wrinkled nose. It began bleeding within seconds. Marlene slumped onto the settee and Alice rushed to get a cloth from the kitchen and a First Aid kit.

"Don't bother calling the police, it's my word against yours. I'll be long gone by the time they get here. Me and Ben are pissing off from this bloody town, for a break. God knows we need it. I hope none of you are murdered while we're gone because I haven't finished telling you exactly what I think of you yet!"

She slammed the door shut and raced up the garden path. Her heart pounded loudly in her ears and she couldn't stop shaking. Ben's eyes were on stalks and his mouth was open.

"For God's sake. What on Earth has happened now? The whole street could hear you! It's not even nine in the morning yet and this is how you behave?"

"Hey, you know how she's treated me so I hit her in self defence. She went for me first. If you even think for one minute that I'd throw the first punch you're wrong and you don't know me as well as you thought you did."

Fuming, she almost fell over a plant pot that had fallen off her wall. Kicking it out of the way, she kicked her gate open too and went to pick up a few things for her trip away. Ben suddenly understood how she felt, as he too recalled kicking one in the garden recently; how frustrated he felt at the time and how white hot anger builds into fury in a matter of seconds after provocation.

"I'm sorry," was all he could blurt out. He watched her go into her house, and followed.

"I don't know if you heard me just now, I said I was sorry. Look, I know what you've gone through, you've told me enough times, but I apologise for not realising just how bad it's been for you. I hate the woman as you know, but it must be much worse for you. It's you she's targeted the most, not me."

Mel felt his arms slide around her waist from behind. He clasped his fingers in front of her, just above the navel and he rested his head on her left shoulder. She felt tears trickling down her face as her shaking subsided a little at a time.

"Let's go. Let's just get out of here and have a break away from this place. They've got each other, they'll simmer down and you never know, they might be okay with things by the time we get back, and with us too. Hitting her and her seeing that you're more than capable of standing up for yourself may have shocked her to the point that she'll start respecting you more and maybe even..."

"Don't even go there!" Mel interrupted, "If you think for one minute me and those two can ever be friends you're sadly very mistaken. We'll never be friends. I tried that in the beginning. I tried more than most people would. I hate the pair of them even more now. To put me through this, as well as years of provocation and humiliation, all the gossip and other stuff too? No, we'll never be friends. I don't want to speak to them, look at them or have anything to do with them. Let's bloody go!"

Ben shut his mouth and just nodded, as meek as a lamb. They got a few bits and pieces of clothing and essentials and made sure they'd turned the water off and whatever else needed doing. A week or two away would do them the world of good, they decided. A weekend wouldn't be enough. They took a last look around Mel's house and used the toilet just before leaving.

"You calmer now? Not going to hit me too are you?"

"No. I'm not," Mel replied, scowling and rubbing her sore knuckles.

"Of course you're not. I'm too cute for you to hit aren't I? You couldn't possibly damage a handsome face like this."

She looked up at him and his gorgeous face melted her anger like sunshine on snow.

"They're not worth it. Imagine a few hours from now really enjoying yourself; some music you know? Some nice drinks. Me in your arms too. Hell, what else do we need to be happy?"

"You're so sure of yourself aren't you!" Mel replied, nudging his stomach with her elbow as he tried to catch her as she ran past him. She playfully slapped one of his ass cheeks too.

"I am, yes. If I don't love myself who else is going to?"

"Stop fishing for compliments. You know I love you. Come on, let's go. Let's enjoy that music, drinks and you in my arms."

"Oh goodie! Now we're talking. Have you decided what hotel or B&B we're going to check into yet, and where?"

Mel gazed into his eyes and for the first time in a while, smiled a lovely and soft smile.

"Anywhere would be nice, as long as it's with you."

Ben leaned in and kissed her gently on the lips. He sighed and cradled her in his muscular arms. She felt so tiny and so vulnerable, even with all of the strength and feisty spirit that she had. When angry, she scared him, but to see her calmer now, much calmer and being all affectionate with him, it was this side of her he felt was the real her and he loved that side of her the most.

They locked the front door and inhaled the morning's fresh air. Not even looking over their shoulders at his house, they both felt Alice's and Marlene's nasty eyes boring into the back of their skulls.

"Don't look back. Never look back."

Mel looked at him and squeezed his hand in hers. "Oh I'm never going to. Onwards and upwards from now on. I've been through a lot, now it's time for some fun and a new life."

"That's my girl. I've been through a lot too so yes, let's have as much as we can."

They got out of the street for a weekend or week of peace and quiet. Rushed packing of suitcases with whatever came to hand, they simply didn't care anymore. It was out now, the secret, and years of pent-up frustration on his part in living with a woman who was never truly interested in him from the start. He felt relieved to get away.

CHAPTER FIFTEEN

Back in the house, a ghostly hand rested on Alice's shoulder as she continued ranting about the crumbling of her marriage. Stopping in mid sentence, she stared at Marlene whose eyes brimmed with endless questions. Believing that it was the hand of Ben, he coming to apologise and to make things right, or Mel, who she felt definitely needed to apologise, she wiped her tears with a handkerchief. Marlene was wiping her crusty, bloody nose with a different handkerchief.

Alice spun around, hopeful of heartfelt words and regrets. But nobody was there. She fainted where she stood and lay in a crumpled heap on the carpet. Marlene, frozen to the spot did see something though: a large, black, ghostly dog. Its teeth were bared and a snarl from the depths of Hell itself began to frighten her to death.

A trickle of yellow liquid ran down her legs and collected in a small puddle by her feet. She could do nothing but stay rigid as her fingers shattered her wine glass. Even blood oozing from a cut didn't make her leave the spot.

As the apparition floated toward her, palpitations of terror gripped the woman's heart. She felt her world darken into nothingness as an icy breath consumed her life force as spectral jaws tightened around her neck; a neck that would no longer spew torrents of nasty gossip, not on this side of life anyway. Mel's spirit guardians planned on ensuring that on the other side of life she wouldn't be able to get to within a hair's breadth of Mel's auric field, or sensitive psychic ears.

Alice opened her eyes and stared at a ceiling. Rubbing a bump on her head, she flinched. Bursting into tears, it was all too much for her to cope with. To see her friend lying there, a mere few feet away from her and with her eyes all glassy and lifeless, Alice suddenly felt all alone in the world.

She managed to get up off the floor and steadied herself against a wall. Telephoning the police, they arrived on the scene within ten minutes. After she'd filled them in on why her husband wasn't around, he and Mel instantly became prime suspects.

"I don't expect any of you to believe me, but we saw a ghost. As for my waster of a husband, and her next door, I don't know where they've gone. I don't care either. I'm getting the locks changed and I'm also filing for divorce."

"Alice, that's understandable after what you've told me but our priority right now is to make sure that you're not alone in this house. Can you stay at a relative's or a friend's until you've come to terms with things do you think?"

"She was my best friend and I don't know what I'm going to do without her," she replied, sobbing uncontrollably as the friendly officer looked on, sympathy etched on his face. He took her to the police station as other officers scoured her entire house for DNA of anyone other than Ben, Mel and Marlene.

Ghosts listened to every word. The house was riddled with them. Some floated through walls, others lurked in a corner in the room. One or two sat in the back of Ben's car, getting there faster than the speed of light. Mel instantly felt that she and Ben were no longer alone. Developing her psychic and mediumship abilities over the years and especially recently through conducting EVP experiments and also going through a traumatic time, she tried to tune in to see who was there in the back seat. A shield met her psychic vision and the spirits refused to let her see their identities. They did touch her hair though, gently stroking it. She didn't feel afraid.

Ben, oblivious to any of this, rambled on, telling her all about the times that Alice had either belittled him in public, mocked him in private, neglected him sexually and many other countless situations. Although hearing every word he was saying, Mel was also scanning her auric field for evidence of additional spectral company. There was most definitely something, or someone there. She sensed male and also female companions. One was new. They weren't young, a new spirit, they had roamed the Earth for many lifetimes, when not at Home back in the spirit realms and dimensions.

"You seem a million miles away. Have you heard anything I've said?"

She turned to look at Ben. "Yes, yes I have. Of course. I'm just looking out of the window that's all, it's a nice day."

"Well it is now. And with you by my side, my gorgeous, of course it's a nice day," he replied, gazing at her for a moment and kissing the back of her hand, his warm eyes melting into hers.

"Look, just put it down to experience. Remember the good times you've both shared over the years and try to focus on your future, without her. Unless you can mend things. Do you feel that you can?"

"Not a fucking chance in hell. No," he protested, shaking his head before going off on another verbal rant about how Alice hadn't been the kind of wife he'd wanted.

Mel rolled her eyes and reached into her jacket pocket for some chewing gum. It was going to be a long, long journey. The cold spot hanging around her had vanished and warmth from the car heater circulated, stopping her shivering.

CHAPTER SIXTEEN

A week later, after returning back to Mel's house, he saw an envelope on the floor and noticed it was addressed to him. Opening it with some trepidation, he read a police notice. He was to contact them immediately upon receipt of the letter. Mel stood by his side and dropped bags to the floor as she felt his anxiety rising.

"We've got to contact them. They won't say why but it's crucial that we do. There's tape around my house so something's bloody happened. No point in me trying to get in through my front door so I'll ring them now."

"I'm involved with you so if you need me to come with you I will."

"You probably need to anyway."

Ben rang the station and was informed that both he and Mel were to get there as soon as possible. They both left and drove off.

Familiar faces greeted them across a large wooden counter top as they both stood and waited for further instructions. Officer Davies escorted them into a side room where they sat down after getting a fizzy drink from a nearby vending machine. It was going to be a difficult day. What else is new? they both thought.

"Right, Ben, good to see you again but I have some bad news I'm afraid, mate, I'm sorry to say," the officer said, looking at him and then at his notes.

"It's Alice isn't it? What's happened? I saw the tape around the house."

"According to your wife, she thought you were standing behind her and had come to apologise for your, how can I put this? Your romantic moment with your neighbour Mel here," he said, glancing at her. She was blushing profusely, picking her fingernails, and most of all she was desperately trying to find anywhere in the room to look other than in either of the men's eyes. "When your wife turned around, she said there was nobody there. She fainted, and when she came to on the floor she saw Marlene lying there, dead. So I've had to call you two in because you were two of the last people we know of who saw both your wife and the deceased when she was last alive."

Mel's face turned white and she gasped out loud.

"What are you charging me with? I wasn't there."

"Nothing yet, Ben. That's it you see. We have no evidence of anything. From forensics' examinations and what they've ascertained about matters, Marlene died of shock. So you're free to go but what I need to know and why I've summoned you here is to ask you what you know about recent deaths in your street; especially as you've got connections to a private detective business you see."

"What are you asking me exactly?"

"Ben, we need you to go undercover and to watch everything that goes on in the street. You've assisted us in the past and we're all very thankful for your help, but we need your services and skills now more than ever. If anyone move, breathes or even so much as leaves their house, we need you to follow them and to report to us whatever you are able to, even if it's the minutest of details. It may mean nothing at the time but everything means something, eventually. Now we can't force you to do this for us but we're short staffed and are already working all the hours God sends in order to trap whoever killed young Jan. Mel, I'm sure Ben's told you that he knew her, yes?"

Mel nodded.

"I have nothing to hide. Mel knows everything about my life," Ben replied, holding her hand under the table.

"We understand that you're a bit of a womaniser, Ben," the officer remarked, smirking and winking at him. Mel saw it and felt a combination of amusement and jealousy all wrapped into one as she felt his fingers brush hers. He squeezed her hand, just for a second, and then relaxed. She felt warm and safe. She also knew he loved her; not as just a mere lover, but their love was built on a strong foundation of friendship and that meant more than any quick roll in the hay. To her at least.

Ben coughed, clearing his throat. A slight redness flashed in his cheeks and he shuffled in his seat. "Who did you hear that from?"

"Oh people around here talk; you know? It's a small place but full of big mouths and even bigger imaginations."

"Mrs. Robinson, or Marlene was it?"

"No. Neither of them actually."

"What does my private life have to do with these recent murders? I don't see how it's relevant."

"It's very relevant though. We're trying to catch whoever is killing these innocent people and we follow up on everything and anything we can in order to do so. Your wife is staying with relatives until further notice and best that she does that too because if she's capable of taking anyone's life, we'll find out eventually and when she returns here we'll get her. But if you stay away from this area then you will be the prime suspect. Word gets about here in Porthcawl you know and we know that you didn't get along with your neighbour and now she's dead."

Ben shook his head. He had enough stress in his life without being carted off to court and then prison if he ended up being the only suspect. The officer continued:

"We called at your house last week, and after knocking on your door and getting no reply we went to Mel's here, and did the same. We then looked through the letterbox and saw you in well, a very passionate embrace. I wish my wife kissed me the way Mel kisses you. You're a very lucky man, Ben."

"Yes, I am. Thank you, I think." "When will Alice be back? Did she say?"

"No, she didn't. But she did tell us that as soon as she does intend on returning to the house she'll expect us to accompany her and to be positioned outside the house too, she's that scared, Ben. She keeps going on about seeing a ghost but I don't believe her myself. But she saw somebody that's for sure. And Marlene did too by the terrified expression on her face. The same expression that was on Mrs. Robinson's face too I might add."

"Such a shame she felt the need to move away. I'll miss her," Ben replied, not sure if he actually meant it or if he felt relieved. At least with Alice out of the way he could focus all of his attention upon his new love. He sure wasn't getting any meaningful company with Alice anymore and he certainly didn't want to be all by himself; especially with a killer on the loose. Or killers, possibly.

He gazed at Mel who was blushing beetroot red and looking around the room; her eyes darting all over the place but inside her heart melted into a million warm pieces. She squeezed his hand momentarily and played with his feet under the table with her feet. She gazed deeply into his eyes, getting lost in a beautiful world of familiarity and blossoming love. Their situation however, was about to change. And quite drastically too!

CHAPTER SEVENTEEN

Fishermen wiped cold droplets of salty seawater from their seawater-battered faces as they patiently waited for the next batch of fresh fish to swim near their tasty bait dangling from the end of their rods. Grey skies loomed overhead and ships' lights switched on as the sun began to sizzle into the horizon of the stormy sea. A stranger watched them intently from an old, cobweb-lined small window high up in the lighthouse.

A spider chased a fly around on a spiral iron staircase. Everything was quiet inside the lighthouse, except for the constant whirring of machinery powering the light and other equipment. Teenagers had attempted to smash it from outside on many an occasion but had failed. Protected very well, the light had been beaming for eons in time; a protector and welcome help to seafaring travellers for many years.

Freezing cold hands gripped a window ledge and ghostly eyes surveyed miles through a pane of partially dirty glass. The spirit then moved, momentarily merged with brickwork and white paint before emerging on the other side effortlessly. They floated at first and then, at warp speed, they were back in Mel's street quicker than the speed of thought.

Time, distance and physical restraints they were free from worrying about anymore and they relished their newfound freedom to go anywhere, at any time and to watch, observe and absorb, as much detailed information about other peoples' lives as they wanted to.

Other than Mel detecting them, and also the occasional cat, dog or small child now and again, they were unseen and unknown by the majority of human beings who lived in or who visited the coastal town. For now, anyway.

Sitting directly behind Mel and watching her as she slipped on headphones to listen to her new EVP's, they moved their face closer until hairs on the back of her neck stood bolt upright. She shuddered, feeling a wave of goose bumps popping up all over her body. She turned her face to where her fireplace was and she frowned. Logs crackled and she felt heat on her skin. Finding it odd that there should ever be a sudden cold spot next to her with that roaring away, she shrugged and continued with what she was doing.

The ghost backed away slowly and moved to her left side. As Mel strained to listen to what sounded like a very faint voice coming through on playback of a recent recording, she noticed something very unusual in her peripheral vision. A black pen she'd been using to jot down notes about her new novel had vanished.

Pushing her swivel chair away from her desk, she searched by her feet to find nothing. Opening a small drawer, she took out another pen and placed it on the top of the desk where the other had once been. Moving forward again, she placed both elbows on top of the desk and she closed her eyes as she rewound the file and pressed 'play' again. Turning the volume up slightly, the voice became a little clearer and she struggled to work out what was being said.

"Who are you?" she'd asked.
"You know who I am," was the reply.
"Are you male or female?" Mel had asked too.
"You'll find out," the disembodied voice said.

As Mel adjusted sliders on her computer monitor screen in a sound editing program, what sounded neither male nor female suddenly took on a totally different sound. It was definitely female and as she slowed down the speed of the playback, despite the voice being extremely faint, she was almost certain she'd heard it before.

Growing up miles away from where she resided now, she longed to return to her carefree and once stress-free life. When a child, she often saw spirits, but over the years, after her strict mother had lectured her out of this special ability, she'd closed down. Once, when sitting in a church, she'd distinctly sensed the presence of an unseen positive spirit person. Putting it down to her six-year-old imagination, her mother had waited until she got her home to advise her to stop glancing at nothing.

Congregation members talked about her behind her back and Mother needed to have their approval, not their whispering, mocking gossip echoing in her ears. Father had left them long ago; preferring the company of pubs and male banter to the warmth of family life. Absent from most of her young life at the time, Mel did occasionally remember some good times. He always brought her a little gift from his travels abroad with work and she loved to sit by his side as he helped her unwrap them. Although money was tight, he always found a way to show that he cherished his daughter.

Mel sat and pondered as wave after wave of memories washed over her out of nowhere. The spirit sympathised and placed their hand on top of hers. Mel flinched as if an electric shock had claimed her skin and she instantly pulled her hand away, shaking it. She felt her tears being wiped away by invisible fingers and she got up out of the chair and ran across the room to sit by the fire. The spectral visitor stayed put and simply observed her. Mel stared into the fiery flames of the fire and thought about her foster mother.

Red and orange danced into molten white and blue, dotted with bright sparks intermingling with smoke and she felt herself being carried away back into the past, into another life almost as remembered conversations burst back into life inside her head and ears. She recalled happier times, times when Mother had been nice to her. She travelled back to the age of two and saw herself being carried in a woollen shawl, safe in her father's arms as they both stood on top of a mountain as he rocked her to sleep. Then, after waking later, and after Father had gone to the pub to play dominos with his friends, Mother had a nice warm bath waiting in front of the fire for her.

A pink plastic bath, Mel fondly remembered how it felt to have soothing warm water on her skin as she watched the fire crackling from several feet away. They had a coal fire then and Mel could see in her memory, a coal bunker outside the house, filled to the brim with black jagged pieces of coal. Father had fixed a spare back wooden door on top of the brick bunker and, with the pull of a rope, and balancing on a metal spring, the door closed at the first sign of rain.

After years of bickering with Mother, mainly over money worries, he left in the pouring rain, and never came back. Mother began taking things out on her as time went by until Mel had had enough and moved out and away from the area. Clawing her way out of depression and other messes she'd gotten herself into, she'd learned to rebuild her self-respect and slowly but surely had reclaimed her power.

Marlene reminded her of Mother a lot and Mel often wondered if that was why she felt so uncomfortable around her, dreading to even go into her garden to peg her washing on the line for five minutes let alone the mountain of weeding she had to do. Meeting Ben and finding a friend in the street, well, he'd been her saviour at the time, she'd felt initially. Now he was her best friend, lover too, and a new life was beginning to unfold before her very eyes. As she sat there by the fire, she began to feel better as volumes of tomes of memories; mostly good, some not so engulfed her weary mind.

The spectral friend gazed into the flames along with her and also remembered times gone by; times when they too had someone to love them, someone to greet them when they came into the house. Someone who took the time to get to know them and to never let them go. But, at the cost of their physical life, they'd turned on a dime into a vindictive, nasty, vengeful being, out to get back at everyone and anyone who'd ever pissed them off. But not Mel. They could never hurt dear lovely Mel.

CHAPTER EIGHTEEN

Marlene's funeral went swimmingly. Swimmingly good in fact, because only four people bothered to turn up as everyone else went off to have a much nicer time – elsewhere. A hated woman, the majority of people had tolerated her for a quiet life; rather than confronting her about the obnoxious and rotten manner in which she treated most people in life, including her loved ones. She thought she'd owned the entire town and everyone in it. But she was wrong. In her own little narcissistic and psychological bullying selfish world, she had been her own worst enemy.

Even the undertaker couldn't be arsed to give her a proper service, rushing through proceedings and wanting to get away as far as possible from her nasty bones and putrid soul. Mel couldn't bring herself to go to the funeral, despite everyone in the street having an invite. Normally a very pleasant person with a forgiving heart and limitless compassion, she felt glad to see the back of the wretched witch; although she'd never be free from the dramatic impact she'd engraved upon her mind and very being. But she did send flowers. At least for the initial nice times when the cow had bothered to be civil to her when she'd first moved into the street.

As for Ben, he'd grown up farther away, had been to a grammar school and was extensively educated then and thereafter, had set up his own private investigation business with others and wasn't into paranormal things at all. They couldn't be more different yet they complemented each other perfectly.

Alice hadn't really been his type, not from day one, but he'd married her out of obligation due to an unexpected pregnancy but he'd loved her too. After the baby died, they remained together more out of keeping each other company rather than unbridled passion and an undying sizzling love and romantic reason. But with Mel, oh with her things were shown to him to be just how they were meant to be – white-hot passion mixed with a timeless friendship and a love he'd always craved yet had been out of his grasp.

He felt that things happen for a reason and at the right time. She fulfilled in him so much more than Alice ever could, even if she'd tried and had made more effort in their slowly dwindling relationship. Joanne had satisfied his baser urges, and had been a friend, but not having the same depth and quality of one that he has with dear Mel.

Being Mrs. Robinson's granddaughter, and not knowing yet, Mel always felt alone but was about to discover that she was far from it. Marlene had been the old woman's daughter. Mel was about to find out that who she assumed all her life had been her biological mother, was in fact her adoptive mother.

Marlene had given Mel up when months old, not being able to cope with it all. Never bothering to search for her when she'd reach the age of eighteen, and Mel not realising any of it all her life, she was in a for a very rude awakening and much more too. Marlene had left millions in her Will and the entire lot was about to go to Mel. Solicitors were on their way to her house after finalising paperwork and Mel's life was on the verge of being changed for eternity.

Would Ben be by her side when the overwhelming shock sets in? Will he be man enough to tend to her emotional wounds if she fell apart? Was he capable of real and lasting love when faced with a woman possibly going into psychological meltdown? Solicitors picked up a telephone and thought carefully how to word things. Time, and earth-shattering news simply cannot be taken back or erased. Were they doing the immoral thing in even contacting her in the first place or were they having her best interests at heart and a sense of justice?

One of the ghosts in Mel's house moved from the fireplace and soared back to the lighthouse to rest and to contemplate their next move.

CHAPTER NINETEEN

Police officers telephoned both Ben and Mel. Informing them that they had to go to the station as some new evidence had come to light, they set off immediately the following morning to find out what it entailed.

"Whatever it is they're going to tell us, don't worry about it, Mel. It'll be OK. We can get through anything together," Ben said, to a visibly nervous Mel who was biting her fingernails down to numbs as she watched fields morph into blurriness as the car sped down a motorway.

"I know. I'm just concerned that's all. You know what Marlene was like. The problems she caused me for years. Who knows what she's really been up before she died. Skeletons in the cupboard and all that. Figuratively speaking of course. She wouldn't really have any real ones in the cupboard. She was much too sneaky and clever for that."

"Oh you never know! I've read about many people over the years and have dealt with a few too in person who have done far worse and nobody ever suspected that they'd ever be capable of murder, let alone hiding bodies in places you'd never think they would."

"Like what places exactly?" Mel asked, looking at him now, curious.

"Well, I can't divulge too much information as you know. Ethics and all that. My line of work you know? But, just between us two, there was one man who had this horrible wife who thought nothing of disposing of her best friend in a bathtub of acid. And the weirdest thing was that all the woman had done was to flirt with her man. She just flipped and snapped one day. Some people are capable of anything. It was a shocking case."

"Sounds terrible. Tell me more."

"Don't breathe a word of this to anybody then, right? I'm trusting you."

"I won't."

"I was assigned by a member of the woman's family to track the couple and it was a chance meeting with the dead woman's sister in a pub that I became suspicious. She told me her sister was being stalked by a deranged-looking female who fitted the description of the killer. Naturally, I had to check it out and it came to my attention over time that the woman was not only being stalked by the killer, there was another suspect lurking in the shadows. The husband. But his wife got to her first. He initially propositioned the deceased for an affair but she turned him down. He didn't take lightly to being rejected so he was somewhat happy that his wife got to her first before he eventually did. His wife mysteriously disappeared. Nobody knows where she went to."

"Wow! And most visitors to this coastal town assume that Porthcawl is a relatively peaceful place don't they? It's shocking to think what goes on behind closed doors. What happened to the killer in the end?"

"Well," Ben replied, choosing his words carefully, "He finally left his wife and went into meltdown. He's currently in a psychiatric unit a few miles from here. He won't be released. They've kept him in indefinitely; mainly due to the dead woman's family insisting that if we and the medical authorities release him, they'll sort him out."

"But if anything did happen to him you'd just go and arrest them surely? Isn't that how it works?"

"No, not really. There's a little thing called evidence. We can't just go by threats. They'd be our first suspects of course, but without actual evidence the police can't go by just our word and snippets of information we may disclose to them."

"I see. You must have a lot of pressure on your shoulders most days. I didn't realise how difficult your work is."

"Oh it's that alright, Mel," he replied, turning a corner as they approached the station.

Mel's heart leapt in her chest as she sat in the car watching him remove the keys from the ignition and then he placed them in his jacket pocket. He looked at her.

"You OK? Look, you have nothing to worry about. You haven't done anything wrong. Well, apart from getting closer to me, and if that's a crime then they'd better lock half of the residents in this town up. From surveillance and other details my company has accumulated over the years I know a lot about a lot of people around here."

"Oh I bet you do. I bet you have such juicy secrets that you keep locked away in that sexy head of yours."

"Sexy head? I've never had my head complimented quite like that before. You're a funny one," he replied, grinning and rubbing her face with the heel of his hand. She'd managed to smear lipstick over a cheek when leaning on her hand, practically falling asleep on the journey after not much sleep. She smiled at him and, for a moment, time seemed to stop.

"Come on, let's get in there, see what they want. It can't be anything terrible."

They got out of the car and strolled toward the station door, hand in hand. Sunlight glittered on roof tops and Mel blinked when looking up. With lack of sleep and still in shock after hearing about Marlene's death, she felt as if she were in a dream state half the time. The woman had caused her so much grief over time and despite her physical absence, Mel still felt her presence around her; invading her mind, her very dreams too lately.

She thought of the EVP files and wondered if Marlene would come through some if she activated her recording device. Could she cope with hearing her and knowing she was still alive, just in another dimension of time and space? She shuddered and dismissed the thoughts from her frazzled brain.

CHAPTER TWENTY

Entering the police station, they squeezed each other's hand and resigned themselves to the fact that they'd be there for a while. Interviews were never quick and the last certainly hadn't been.

They recognised the officer from before who had spoken to them. He was in the process of chatting with fellow officers about a matter they couldn't quite hear details about. In hushed tones they continued discussing things as Mel and Ben sat down and made themselves comfortable. She looked at the officer and noticed that he had mud on his shoes. The rest of his uniform looked immaculate, but the dirt on his shoes caught her eye straight away. Where had he been to get them so filthy, she wondered? Ben whiled away the time by flicking through a car magazine he'd picked up from off a nearby table. Out of date and dog eared at the edges of several pages, he leafed through it, licking a finger now and again.

Mel sighed. She glanced at her fingernails and the jagged cuticles around them. Hiding her hands in her coat pockets, she hummed a quiet tune to herself and then yawned. A wall of black uniform came towards her and she stopped in mid-yawn and looked up. The man in front of her removed his smart jacket and threw it over his arm. His crisp, white shirt was so clean.

Sunlight flooding through windows soon showed up one or two drying drops of coffee on one of his sleeves. Mel wondered if she'd make a good detective. If she could spot that then she thought of what else she could detect too. She knew becoming an officer involved extensive training and a lifelong dedication to the job and she also knew that it wasn't her vocation in life but as a very observant person she'd noticed a lot in the street she lived in; sometimes much more than Ben did. She always noticed how people dressed and she often worked out what their body language portrayed about them as individuals. She disturbed a friend years ago who commented that Mel had some kind of unnatural ability of working out how a person was feeling within a mere five minutes; all based on their mannerisms, silent ways and little quirks and gestures that most people wouldn't even notice usually.

"Come with me. Good to see you again. Thank you for attending. You didn't have to but we do appreciate your cooperation with us regarding recent events," the officer said, pointing to a nearby interview room.

Mel and Ben rose from their seats and followed the man. He waved to a woman who walked into the station. She carried a large black plastic bag in one hand and a mop head in the other. She smiled and disappeared down a long corridor. Middle aged and wearing comfortable shoes, she took a pair of keys out of her coat pocket and unlocked a cupboard door. Mel kept on observing her until door frames blocked her view.

In the interview room, she removed her coat and licked her dry lips. Her stomach growled and she held both arms across her body. Blushing, she glanced at both men and then down at her misbehaving stomach.

"Would you like a sandwich? My wife has made too many and you're more than welcome to have one if you want one. You are both free to leave at any time and we're going to be here for a few hours so it's best you have something to eat now to be honest. What about you, Ben? Do you want one too? There's plenty to go around. Tea? Coffee?"

"I'll have a coffee please. One sugar, milk. Thanks. I'm fine about food, I had breakfast," Ben replied, as the officer then looked at Mel.

"Thank you. If it's not too much trouble I'll have one of your sandwiches please, and coffee for me, thanks. Two sugars, plenty of milk."

"Here you go. Help yourself. Two coffees coming up. I won't be long," he said, handing her a foil-wrapped parcel. She opened it to find thick slices of beef and mustard between wholemeal buttered bread. Her mouth salivated and she heard the loudest growl from her stomach she'd ever heard. Ben laughed like a hyena.

It seemed like an eternity later as the officer returned and handed them both their drinks. They remembered from the last time they were there how vile the coffee tasted but this one seemed rather nice! Ben nodded in approval and sipped the delicious and much-needed beverage. Mel felt satisfied and her stomach growled no more. She thanked the officer again and smiled. He returned her smile and sat down opposite the both of them. He had several more droplets of coffee on his white shirt. It resembled a jigsaw puzzle almost, different shapes scattered across a background of varying tones of brown, complete with what appeared to be tiny breadcrumbs. He noticed her staring and he cleared his throat. She looked up into his face, startled.

"Sorry. I've had a chest infection and am just getting over the worst of it. It's almost gone."

"All those endless hours hanging around outside when on duty I expect. You must get freezing cold most days. It's not exactly warm at this time of the year and if you're walking near the sea it can get bloody icy cold, especially on a windy day."

"Ben, tell me about it. My wife bought me a thermal vest but I still shiver most nights. Thank God for comfortable shoes though. I used to suffer with corns and bunions, and blisters were horrendous on the back of my heels until I began wearing better shoes. I do walk miles, you're right. It keeps me fit though I suppose."

"Mel has a spare pedometer at home if you want it. You'll be able to find out how many miles you cover every day then. It's a great motivator for keeping fit. I've got one too."

"Yes, you can have it if you want," Mel replied, nodding and sipping her hot drink. "I bought it as it was a buy one and get one free offer so if one breaks I'll always have a spare. I'll drop it into the station the next time I'm in the area, or you can have this one," she said, unzipping her handbag and feeling around for it. Her fingers rested upon a small, round hard object and she pulled it out. "Oh, I doubt you'd want this," she said, laughing as she lifted up a lipstick. Putting it back into her bag, she took the pedometer out by its strong string. It swayed to and fro and she placed it on the large wooden table in front of her.

"You sure?"

"Of course. I don't need two. You have that one. It'll be perfect for you. I should imagine you get quite bored when patrolling the area do you?"

"Well, we do normally walk around a lot with no action to pursue so it'll entertain me for a while that will. Thank you. We often chase after burglars and car thieves and the like, but it's quiet most of the time around here, well, it was before Porthcawl started having innocent folk strangled and killed in other ways too."

Ben winced as flashbacks of memories of seeing Jan swept throughout his mind. Despite seeing dead bodies in the past, to see one belonging to someone he not only had had an intimate relationship with but who he was very fond of was one murder scenario he'd never forget. He watched the officer play with his new pedometer as Mel explained to him how to change the different settings and functions and he felt a million miles away as the both of them chatted; their voices seeming to trail off and become quieter. He was brought back to the present as a door behind him opened, making him jump a little in his hard wooden seat. His gums ached after recent dental surgery and he wasn't a happy bunny at all.

"I'm just dropping this in, Sir. Speak to you later. Gotta go," a tall and thin officer announced, nodding to Ben and placing a stack of large papers on the desk. It had lots of data written on it in small but tidy writing. Before Mel and Ben could read a word, the officer slid it across the surface of the desk and put it in a drawer, closing it and locking it. He placed a tiny key in his breast pocket and looked back up at the couple again as the other officer walked out and closed the door.

"Another case?"

"I'm afraid so, yes. We get statements and all sorts every day. Never a dull moment around here. Hence my sandwiches going uneaten for hours. I manage to stuff one before situations get too hectic around here though but I'm still losing weight."

"That's the walking. You look quite fit if you don't mind me saying," Mel said, a glint in her eye. He held her gaze for longer than necessary as Ben felt a pang of jealousy well up in his chest.

"Right. Let's discuss matters shall we? I don't want to keep you here all day. I'm sure you've got work to do, the two of you," he said, coughing and holding his chest with one hand, making a scrunched-up facial expression.

Mel wondered if she'd embarrassed the man and felt silly for even opening her mouth in the first place. Ben held her hand again and she smiled at him.

"It's come to our attention that there is something you need to know, Mel. Something of grave importance. Now you can decline staying here and letting me tell you of what has been discovered but it's in your best interests if you do stay and do listen. We all have free will and it's entirely your choice."

Mel felt panic rising. She felt a wave of nausea creep across her stomach and goose bumps made her skin prickle and shiver. An icy cold spot suddenly made itself known to the right side of her body. Ben was on her left. She put her coat back on and huddled close to him. A ghost stood by her and listened intently at the officer's revelation.

"Do you wish Ben here to be in another room while I tell you something, Mel? You don't have to have anybody present if you don't want them present."

Mel had a moment to decide and didn't know what to do for the best. She suddenly felt as weak as a kitten and began having palpitations. "No," she replied loudly, "Sorry, I mean yes, I prefer him to be present. We're very good friends and anything you have to tell me I'll tell him anyway later so he may as well stay where he is, if that's OK?"

"Be it as you wish then. That's more than alright by me. How about you Ben? Are you comfortable with this?"

Without hesitation, Ben nodded in agreement. "If Mel wants me to be by her side then by her side I'll be." "Always," he continued, turning to look deeply into her eyes. She felt her body relax and her palpitations calm down. His warm hand in hers helped a great deal too and she felt that she could cope with anything. Losing him would be far worse, she felt, than any shocking news a police officer would tell her.

They both looked back at the man opposite them who opened a drawer and took a stack of papers out contained in a light brown folder. He put them on the desk and slid them toward Mel with the tip of one finger. He sat back in his chair and rested his chin on the back of his hands as he studied her responses.

Mel opened the folder and braced herself for whatever was next. On page one were detailed doctor's notes regarding her history of physical and mental health problems she'd had in the past. Her eyes scanned each sentence and with each minute that passed by she felt herself becoming increasingly ashamed and uncomfortable. She read everything and it felt as if she were reading about someone else's life, not her own. Sectioned under the Mental Health Act for extreme paranoia and once arrested for almost killing a neighbour with a thrown rock in a garden, and carrying a knife around whenever the neighbour came near her, she was later admitted to a psychiatric ward for evaluation for six months and was released after a year as her condition improved, she struggled to remember all and any of it.

"You had amnesia for quite a while then. No wonder you can't remember much after what you've been through, young lady," the officer quipped as a million unanswered questions flooded Ben's eyes.

Mel continued leafing through the folder and soaking up every single word. She'd left the psychiatric unit and had moved away several times; constantly searching for a street where only decent and non-argumentative people lived, where she could feel at peace inside and as stress-free as possible. After her husband, Mark, had ran off with Alice's sister, Anna, Mel was perfectly well aware of the situation but she'd changed as a person, resorting to locking herself away in her own little world, away from people and away from problems. She turned into a hermit. Getting to know Ben had practically saved her life on many a level and her sanity, once dangling from a thread, was now growing into something intact once more and stronger.

As she got halfway through the folder, she blocked out everything in that interview room and felt as if she were the only person there. A flashback in time, she pored over each page of details about her past and distant memories once hidden from her mind deep in her subconscious began resurfacing.

Ben felt her hand tighten in his, almost to the point that it began hurting. He felt her fingers like a vice around his. He looked down to see that his skin had changed from a healthy pink and fleshy tone to one of whiteness as the blood supply was prevented from reaching the surface. As pins and needles set in, he tapped her on the arm as he gently pulled his hand out of her grip but she completely ignored him. Tapping her again, she broke out of her self-induced trance and looked through him rather than at him, a dazed look clouding her vision. She wasn't now the Mel that he'd known for years, it was as if she were now someone totally different. He pulled away again and spoke to her but to her it was if he was a million miles away, not just a mere few inches.

A loud shrill of a telephone snapped her out of her own little world in an instant. The police officer stood up and took out his phone from his trouser pocket and answered the call. In hushed tones he chatted away with whomever was on the other end of the line as Ben tried to coax Mel back into the here and now. Her vision cleared and she blinked.

"Hey, it's fine. Whatever is in there you can deal with it. We can deal with it, together. Do you want me to read it with you? Do you want me to help you?"

"I'm OK. It's just a lot to deal with you know, returning to the past, to times I've tried to bury and forget about."

"Look, you don't have to read any more as it's obviously some sort of trigger for you. You were really out of things just then, not yourself at all. It frightened me to be honest."

She smiled. Relaxing her hand, Ben felt circulation returning to normal and colour coming back into his hand. Pins and needles and numbness started to go away and he moved his hand out of hers and shook it.

"Sorry. I didn't realise..."

"It's OK. But wow, you've got a grip there! Have you ever thought about going in for arm wrestling or brick laying or something?"

She laughed.

"Do excuse me please. I have to take this into a more private room. You're free to go but I prefer it if you waited. I've questions to ask you. I won't be long now."

They watched him leave the room, the phone still in his hand as he whispered something to the caller.

"I wonder if he's got a secret lover," Ben said, grinning at Mel.

"What, like us you mean?"

"Well, yes. Are you my lover now then?"

"I can be if you want me to be, yes. You're not a bad catch, even if you are older than me," she replied, smirking.

"Hey!" Ben replied, pretending to be insulted. "C'mon, admit it. Most women find the prospect of being with an older man quite enticing and exciting don't they?"

"I can't speak for all women but I do, yes. Look at you, you're a handsome man. Why wouldn't any woman fall at your feet and declare their undying love for you?"

"Love? Or lust maybe."

"You loved Jan though didn't you. Such a pity she was killed."

"I loved her, yes, but not in the same way that I love you. Sex is empty without love."

"Oh? You sound like a woman now. So strange to hear such profound words coming from a man's mouth. You're quite perceptive and deep feeling aren't you, for a private investigator anyway?"

"I have to be in my line of work, but I also have to be level headed and analytical too. Besides, don't be so cheeky. I've always been a deep feeling person. Not all men are horrible brutes you know. I'm certainly not that's for sure. You know that."

"I do. Shame you're married though."

"I loved her many years ago in a different way. Alice was difficult to live with. She blamed me for wanting too much sex when she was going through an early menopause and went off it but I'm a red-blooded male, I can't help it. And after she grew closer to Marlene and began acting and speaking like her and taking her bad moods out on me, my love for her kind of died a little. It was inevitable. I can't live with a woman who behaves like that. I much prefer your temperament; gentle and respectful. I've never even once seen you lose your temper with anyone up until recently, with Marlene. So, what's in the folder? You don't have to tell me if you don't want to. It's your private life after all and even if we were married you're not at liberty to disclose everything to me. I've had lots of secrets I've kept from my wife. And I'm sure many men in the world do from theirs too."

"Nobody truly knows anybody."

"No, Mel, they don't. We all have our little skeletons in our little cupboards. Fancy another drink? I'll go and get you one. I could do with stretching my legs. These chairs are so bloody uncomfortable. I think they make them hard like this so that you don't fall asleep when hanging around forever here."

"Yes, I'll have another, please. Thanks. You'd make a good husband if you were married to me," she replied, slapping him on the bottom as he leapt out of the way and laughed. He left the room and Mel waited until she heard the door click shut before she returned her attention to reading more in the folder.

Twenty minutes later, Mel was shaking. Ben walked back into the room along with the officer, both chattering away about manly things like: sport, cars and what not. Ben rushed to Mel's side as soon as he noticed the state she was in.

"May I?"

He picked the folder up. Holding her tightly, he waved the folder in front of her face, trying to get her to focus. She seemed totally out of it but had heard every word he'd been saying.

"Yes. But be prepared because I've lived shall we say, a colourful life. I forgot a lot of it. The medication at the ward saw to that."

"Ward?"

Ben began reading at page one. He put one hand on the desk as he stood and the officer spoke to Mel about it all. Silent and deep in thought for the next few minutes, Ben's eyes frantically sped read each page. He devoured every word and desperately needed, wanted, to find out as much as possible. If he could have taken the folder and its contents with him to read them alone outside, he would have but he didn't want to leave her in that room with just the officer. A jealous man, - especially over her – he wanted her all to himself. He'd noticed the exchange of mutual admiration between she and the policeman earlier and wasn't taking any chances. After his marriage had crumbled into dust over time and now with Jan dead too, Mel was all he had left.

Further into the folder he delved and completely understood why she'd been shaking so violently. He didn't want to believe what he was reading but they were the facts about her life, and was the truth. As reality set in, he began to see what a mess she'd been a long time ago and why she'd moved into the street where she was now and why she hated, detested even, Marlene's presence and Alice's too later on. Given up as a baby and unwanted by her birth mother, he nearly fainted on the spot when he read that her mother had been Marlene herself.

He felt his heart heavy as stone in his chest when he read that she'd been shuffled into foster homes on a regular basis, with virtually no friends and no understanding or sympathy from anybody. No wonder she keeps herself to herself, he thought, as he started to see the real her: a kind, forgotten creature, so beautiful in nature yet the ugly world and its so-called protectors had let her down so badly.

Abusive medical staff had been tormenting patients in their care, fucking them up psychologically and pumping them full of useless and mind-numbing drugs so that staff could spend time with their workmates, loitering around rather than looking after those they should have been keeping an eye on.

Escaping from the ward was futile as Mel had discovered on numerous occasions; each time spoiled by guards mocking her after allowing her to reach the outer doors, inches from freedom. After a while her mind shattered into a thousand miniscule pieces in order to protect herself from losing it altogether.

Her inner reserves of strength of character saw to it that they never could fully destroy her though. She simply retreated into herself and shut herself off from all interaction with people. So they put her in a ward alone, in her own little quiet world. It was only when senior officials intervened after complaints from her family and a spell in court that she was finally helped to get better by proper medical staff and later released and helped to adjust to the outside world again.

But the entire experience had changed something inside her soul. It had turned her into a potential killer. Unable to retaliate when in the psychiatric unit, now she was better and out of it and not drugged up to the eyeballs, she was capable of anything. But could she actually take another person's life? Would she have the guts and insanity to do so? The officer knew she could do it and so very easily snap after traumatic events in her past and his hands were tied, he couldn't keep her in the station indefinitely. He wondered if Ben as a PI could help him, but speaking to him about it would have to take place away from not only the station but from Mel herself too. He didn't want Ben's potential death on his conscience.

Ben reached the end of the folder contents. The woman he loved, her life displayed open to him like a lid prised off a box of shocking secrets. Abuse from medical staff? Abandoned as a baby? Numerous breakdowns? How was she still of sane and rational mind, he wondered? He put the folder on the desk and sat down. Reaching out to her, she responded and they held each other tightly.

The officer studied both of them and closely observed Mel's facial expressions. At no time did she look at him; either because she knew what he was doing or because she was still in shock. With all his years of experience, he couldn't work her out. On the outside a nice person who appeared to look like she couldn't hurt a fly, but what deep urges did she hide, he questioned himself? What killer instincts hid beneath the sunny disposition and niceness, he pondered?

"She's been through a hell of a lot hasn't she? No wonder she's in a state," Ben commented.

"She has, yes. More than most of us ever will endure in a lifetime," the officer replied.

"I'm still in the room you know," Mel interrupted, staring at both of them. She pulled away from Ben and stood up, pulling her coat tightly around her.

"I'm sorry, I didn't mean to upset you."

She flashed a fake smile at the man and looked at Ben. "Time to go home now, let's go."

"If that's okay with you?"

The officer nodded and got up out of his chair, seeing both of them to the entrance to the building.

"Thank you for everything. You've been very helpful. I need to speak to you about something, Ben, so please telephone me ASAP, please."

Ben nodded, letting him know loud and clear that he also needed to speak about matters. He too wanted to find out more about Mel's past and as much as he loved and trusted her, these new revelations about her past worried him immensely. He didn't believe that she'd ever hurt him but he'd never believed that his own wife was capable of treating him like shit either not long after their marriage after he'd moved miles away from his family home to be with her, to set up a life with her, to basically give up everything for her.

Could she have blamed him for wandering and finding other women to provide him with warm companionship he so desperately craved, needed and felt he deserved? He felt terrible about his philandering ways but a part of him also felt elated that he was having the best of both worlds and doing his own thing. But now his life had altered a lot. Not as much as poor Mel's had but he understood why she'd wanted to run away and to disappear when under a mountain of pressure. It was all becoming crystal clear to him now, like wiping a condensation-covered window pane with a cotton absorbent cloth until clarity and view replaced murky confusion.

"I'll be in touch soon," he replied, nodding to the officer as he turned and walked away, arm in arm with Mel. Mel noticed a dark-haired man standing by the doorway. He wore a suit and tie and flashed a smile at her, gesturing with his hand for her to pass by him.

"After you," he said.

"Thank you, very kind of you."

"No problem."

Puffing on a cigarette, he flicked it across the street. Coughing, he covered his mouth with his hand as several members of the public hurried past him. He watched them go up the street and then caught Mel's inquisitive eyes again. He smiled at her once more. She briefly smiled back and prepared to head back home in the car with Ben. She wondered who the man was.

"What did he say to you?", Ben asked, glancing at her.

"Oh nothing. He let me pass him when I was coming out of the station that's all."

"He seemed quite taken with you. Saying that, who wouldn't be? You're a stunner, you really are," he replied, a pang of jealousy jabbing him like a knife blade.

"And you young man, you could have any woman you wanted and you know it too don't you?", Mel teased, tickling his ribs.

"Well thank you, young lady. No. There's only one woman for me and she's not Alice."

Mel felt a mixture of pride, and also guilt. She watched traffic zoom past them and thought of the dark-haired stranger who captivated her. At least he'd taken her mind off more disturbing matters, something of which she was quite grateful for.

CHAPTER TWENTY-ONE

Upon arriving back home, Ben closed Mel's front door behind him and he slumped into an armchair, burying his head in his hands as he ruffled his hair with his fingers. Mel paced across the carpet deep in thought. She removed her coat and hung it upon a hook in the corner of the room.

Envelopes piled up near the front door on a small mat and she went to see what was in them. Among unwanted junk mail and pizza leaflets and supermarket coupons and vouchers, there was a bright, white large envelope with no writing on the front of it. Puzzled, she tore it open and peered inside. There was a single sheet of paper, neatly folded in the middle with precision; almost as if the sender had pressed a ruler along the edge. She shrugged and lifted the paper out, opening it. She screamed. Ben jumped up out of the armchair he was sitting on and ran to her side within seconds.

"What the hell? What's wrong? You nearly gave me a heart attack!"

In silence, and with tears running down her face, she handed him the piece of paper, nearly dropping it on the mat. He glared at it and clenched his jaw. The note didn't say much but the following handwritten words weren't written in ink. They were written in what appeared to be blood. Human blood possibly.

You two are next.

Police were in the house within five minutes after Ben ran outside and finding no officers patrolling like they usually did, he telephoned them, shouting down the line. Accusing them of not protecting residents in the street enough, he vented his anger loud and clear at them.

"We patrol this street every single night, and the neighbouring ones as well, what more can we do, Ben? We're short staffed. Our officers are in the other street at the moment but are going to be in yours, don't worry. You try and do our job and maybe you'll see what we're up against!"

"I do do your job though don't I?"

"Well, being a private investigator is similar to being a police officer I'll give you that but it's not exactly the same now is it?"

"No, but you know what I fucking mean."

"We won't accept that kind of language so stop right there. We're here to help you so calm down!"

Ben ground his teeth, nerves in his gums sending shooting pains up alongside his cheeks. "My apologies. I- I mean we've been through a lot today and now this?" He pointed to the letter that an officer was examining with a magnifying glass, careful not to smudge the paper. Every fingerprint was crucial evidence; if there were any on there that is. He couldn't see any. Tapping powder onto the letter and blowing it off into a small plastic bag in his hand, he couldn't see not one even partial print.

Shaking his head from side to side and cursing under his breath, he folded the sheet of paper and put that into a separate bag, a clear plastic one. Writing on a label on the top of it he folded the edge over, securing it, and placed the bag of powder, a rolled up pair of disposable latex gloves and the other bag into his jacket pocket as carefully as he could. The other officer scowled at him.

"Nothing? Not a bloody thing?"

The officer shrugged.

"Are you telling me that you can't get a scrap of evidence off that? It looks like its been written in blood for Christ's sake. Surely forensics can extract DNA from that and ID the sender?"

"It's not blood though. It's red ink."

"How do you know without taking it to the lab?"

"Because see this liquid here in this vial? It tells us if this is blood or not, and it's not human blood, or animal blood for that matter. It's red ink."

"Oh for fuck's sake!" Ben replied, standing with hands on hips, fury creating deep ridges on his forehead and saliva to spit from his mouth.

"Look, all we can do is post two officers outside this house; one at the back and one at the front, every night and morning until we ascertain who the person is that's doing this. Or persons. What would you do?"

"Well, for starters, I'd do that but I'd also try to interview everyone in the fucking town under the influence of a truth drug, and then I'd even resort to getting a hypnotist in, the best one in town to put them under and to extract the truth from them!"

"We can't do that, Sir. Not without the person's consent. You know that. Human Rights and the Data Protection Act and all that. If we just drag people off the street or out of their homes and inject them with all sorts and get them in trances, and reveal their identity to the public, chaos would ensue. We don't live in this kind of town, do we, so we have to do what we can and within the law?"

Both Mel and Ben sighed and glanced at each other and then back at the officer.

"Look, I well understand your frustration but imagine how it is for us for one moment. We're trying to catch this killer, or killers, because there could be more than one bastard doing this, but our hands are tied. There is only so much we can do and we don't have any leads really. All we've got is a big mess left, synthetic hair from a wig but no DNA evidence. Lots of people have contacted us and we've even had some who have insisted it's their ex-lover, ex-spouse and even their own parents bumping victims off, but without concrete proof then we can't arrest anybody. I have to go but I'll keep you informed every step of the way what's happening. You've got my contact details. I'll ensure at least two officers are patrolling this street and keeping an eye on things every single day and night and two others will be working night shift. OK?"

"Thank you, officer. That puts our mind at rest," Mel replied, affectionately rubbing Ben's tense shoulders. She saw him to the door and closed it.

"How do you think I feel that I can't catch whoever's doing this myself?"

"I know. But we're dealing with very clever people and you're not a magician!"

Ben frowned. "People?"

"Huh?" Mel replied, walking toward the kitchen to make a coffee.

"You said people. Plural. What makes you so sure it's more than one criminal doing this?"

"Just a hunch, nothing more than that. Several people have been murdered recently, do you honestly believe just one person could have carried that out all by themselves? Besides, each method was executed differently. Murderers usually have a pattern."

"Unless they want you to think that and are very clever. I do think one person can be capable of these deaths around here, yes. Some of the most hardened and most evil of people in the past have murdered hundreds of people, some expert serial killers have even managed to outsmart police officers, forensics' officers and even private investigators like me. I normally work with cheating spouses and that sort of thing but I have been contacted on occasion to deal with shall we say...juicier situations."

"Yes, we know, Ben. You've helped us on cases. When are you going back to work?"

"Tomorrow. I pop in and out of the office and as sole owner of the place and after the paperwork has been finalised for me to expand on the building for more staff to work there then I'll be there a lot more."

"So I'll be here by myself a lot more then. Should I get a guard dog do you think?" Mel asked, biting her nails.

Ben gently tapped her hand and she pulled it away from her mouth. "You really should stop doing that. Do you realise how much you do it?"

"Not really, no."

"Find a different and better coping mechanism. Ruining these pretty hands of yours, look at them!" He held her hand up to the light and they both saw how much her cuticles and nails were beginning to look as if she'd put them through a mincer. They weren't quite bleeding yet but they looked in a sorry state. The panic in her beautiful eyes though was worse and it broke his heart. He held her close and she sobbed into his chest until she sobbed no more.

"I'm scared. The letter said that we're next."

"No, we're not. Nobody is going to harm you, trust me on that."

"How can you be so sure? You can't outsmart an expert."

"Oh but I can. I'm an expert myself, remember? Nobody is going to ever hurt you so don't fret over it."

"It's hard not to."

"I know, but you have to trust me. I'm going to employ some people, contacts that were given to me years ago. I'll start using them if I have to."

"If you have to? Dangerous men?"

"You could say that, yes. Hitmen. Trackers and surveillance experts and hitmen. People who make this killer, or killers, resemble amateurs of the most pathetic and incompetent level."

Mel felt herself relax and slump into his warm and strong arms.

CHAPTER TWENTY-TWO

The following morning after a fitful night's sleep, Mel woke to the sound of birdsong. And herself screaming in her bed. Although not fully remembering her dream, she knew it was a bad one. Not prone to many nightmares in her life, this one left her with a feeling of dread and deep fear. She rubbed her eyes and looked over to find a folded piece of paper left on the other pillow. She reached over and unfolded it, her eyes adjusting to the morning's stark light, blinding her almost, golden rays lighting up everything in the bedroom.

I've gone to work and I'll be back at seven tonight. Any problems please call me.
Love you,

B

x

She re-read the last words over and over again. He really does love me doesn't he? She noticed the kiss at the end and felt calmer and protected. A muscular man, and a man filled with decades of wisdom and experience in his job, why was she beginning to feel sick in the pit of her stomach? she wondered. Something just wasn't right. Whether she was picking up on something she'd missed or whether it was her family and friends in the spirit world, she just couldn't shake off the feeling that there was an insincerity coming from him.

She believed very strongly that women were very intuitive and she'd learned over the years after making so many mistakes in her life to always trust her gut instinct. But she hated questioning things where he was concerned. Why can't I be like normal people? she asked herself. People who have nice things and nice people in their lives and who never have the amount of problems that she's had in the past; usually caused by other people, not happy with their own lives and who enjoy nothing more than trying to fuck up others' lives. Was trusting him and making herself vulnerable to him the right thing to do? she also asked herself that.

After a shower, she towel dried her hair and looked at her face in her bedroom's dressing table's mirror. A beautiful woman, lines of worry and age were creeping across her eyes as time swept by like a deceiving cloak across magician's secrets. She felt old today, very old indeed.

She just wanted to move away and to feel safer, but even then, would she feel safe ever, no matter where in the world she disappeared to? She couldn't get Marlene out of her head and the recent murders too. And now with Ben in her life more and more it was all getting far too much to handle.

She got dressed and decided to spruce up her appearance to make herself feel better. A lot of women do this and she was no exception. A quick spray of her favourite expensive perfume she normally only wore on special occasions like birthdays, Christmas and Valentine's Day, she thought 'fuck it' and practically covered her entire body in its sumptuous fragrance.

She slipped into an expensive satin pair of purple trousers over her best lacy panties and completed the look with matching bra and a gorgeous chiffon black long-sleeved blouse. She brushed her hair and styled it with curling tongs. Applying more make-up than usual, she looked a million dollars.

Stepping downstairs in her bare feet she only usually wore bright red nail polish on her toenails whenever she needed a boost, and she felt absolutely great. The thought of wading through thousands of words of writing her novel and once she got going she enjoyed it. She couldn't stop thinking about the EVP voices she'd heard lately and wondered if the person would come back.

Maybe I am really going nuts, she pondered as she got out her frying pan in the kitchen to make a full English breakfast. I'm not watching my bloody weight this week, she thought, as she got out salted butter from its little square plastic container and sliced a good inch off it, throwing it into the pan. She cracked open two fresh eggs and watched as it immediately began changing from transparent to opaque on the heat.

"Three rashers of bacon today methinks," she said, switching a radio on and dancing around to its lively beat.

A ghostly figure sat and watched her from the far corner of the room. They closed their eyes and smelled the delicious aromas wafting its way. With a smile on its face, it observed how much strength of character Mel possessed within her. And it felt so proud of her. It knew how strong she was and that when difficult situations arose how she detached herself from them and pushed them to the back of her mind. She was a survivor and always had been. The ghost knew this and knew that she'd be fine. Nobody was going to ever harm Mel, even if Mel herself worried that it'd become a reality, soon.

Eating her cooked breakfast, savouring every delicious flavour; from the smokiness and saltiness of the bacon to the delicate flavour of the egg, she munched on wholemeal buttered toast and licked her lips. Smearing her lipstick, a little with the back of her hand, she wiped her greasy mouth and didn't really care. She had a fantastic figure anyway and thought that one calorific-laden meal wouldn't really do much damage.

She read the morning's newspaper and closed its pages after a few seconds.

"No bad news today! I've had enough," she said, tossing it across the room where it landed on the floor, its pages strewn and blowing in a breeze coming from beneath the kitchen door that led to the back door and garden.

She opened a side cupboard door and pulled out a long and large stuffed cat, a draught excluder who she affectionately named 'Franklin'. Sliding it near the gap at the bottom of the door she slid it into place with her foot. It made a difference but she needed to draught-proof her house more. Heating bills weren't too high but she knew if she made slight adjustments in the house she could bring them down even lower.

"Let's go shopping for curtains!"

Her credit card had a lot of money on it, thousands in fact but as much as she paid it off, it always seemed to creep back up, taunting and luring her in almost with its monetary promises of a better and more lavish lifestyle, even though she didn't need one.

Solicitors knocked on her door. They told her how much money was due to her. After picking herself up from the carpet, they said that they'd speak to her in more detail when she came to their office. She made an appointment for a few weeks' time.

Mel booked a taxi and ventured into town. It was eleven in the morning and although it had been raining it had since stopped. It was April now and showers dominated most days; broken up with a little sunshine in between.

She took her umbrella nevertheless and stood by her front door for some fresh air before the taxi arrived. Looking up and down the street, it seemed as though she were the only person who lived there this week. It looked so deserted and not even one dog was in sight barking at cats or just wandering around searching for lamp posts to pee on.

For Sale signs were popping up further down the street she noticed and couldn't really blame residents for wanting to up and out either. Everyone around here seemed so terrified but were keeping a lid on things; doing their best not to fully acknowledge really how bad things were lately.

Despite the warning on the note, she'd managed to survive the night and was still alive. She pinched the skin on the back of her arm to make sure. It hurt. She cursed and checked her watch. The taxi was late as usual. She didn't use the service much but they always seemed to be at least five to ten minutes' late, never on time.

She pulled her light blue coat tighter across her neck and tidied her black wool scarf, making sure her cold neck was covered better. She had matching black woollen gloves and black leather shiny knee-high boots. She felt so sexy today and her mood was totally different to how it had been last night.

As the taxi pulled up outside her front garden's gate, the driver mouthed an apology through the window. A man in his mid-fifties, he had flecks of grey hair that always seemed to morph into the shape of wings on the side of his head and a large wart on the left side of his chin. With striking light blue eyes and a devilish grin, flashing white teeth and one gold incisor on the right-hand side, she often wondered how he could afford it on his wages. Maybe he's into other things, she wondered. Although a chatty and pleasant man, there was something quite sinister in his eyes at times; something that made her feel very uneasy. He looked like the kind of person who, if provoked enough, could very easily murder someone. She berated herself for her overactive imagination.

Opening a door and sliding into the passenger's seat, she made sure she had her umbrella and held it in her hand. She'd managed to leave one in there several months prior and despite telling the man about it he hadn't seen it.

"Late again I see, Trevor? How have you been lately? I haven't seen you for ages!"

"Sorry, young Mel, the wife had a problem with a leaking tap. I had to fix it. Coming home to a flooded house is not something I relish thinking about, you know?" "I'm fine, thanks. And you? You're looking glamorous today. Going somewhere nice? A birthday party perhaps, or someone's wedding?"

"I see. No, I wouldn't want to return home to a flooded house either. I'm fine, thanks. No, not a birthday party or wedding, I just fancied going into town and dressing up for a change. Nice of you to say though. You charmer!" Mel replied, grinning at him as he winked at her and looked her up and down. They always got along well, and he was a right chatterbox on all journeys, telling her all about his life, his marriage and anything else he could. Naturally she listened and nodded in all the right places, but sometimes wanted peace and quiet on a journey. She never got it though.

"It's awful about all these murders taking place around here lately. You must be worried sick, young Mel," he quipped, taking a shortcut and veering around a sharp bend much too fast, Mel sliding in her chair and banging her elbow on her door.

"Can you please slow down, Trevor? I'd like to get there in one piece if that's alright with you!"

"Sorry. I'm used to nipping about, you know that. I do keep within the speed limit but out in these quiet lanes I don't always." "I've never had an accident, so you're safe with me, don't worry."

"I know that. I'm just on edge lately that's all."

"Ah, the murders. Yes, I'd be too; especially as a taxi driver. I pick up all sorts. Weekends are the worst. Drunks, argumentative couples and friends, you know? I much prefer nice quieter ones like you."

"I suppose you're after a tip then are you?" she teased, looking into his flashing blue eyes as his gold tooth shimmered in the light. He reminded her of a film star; a suave and distinguished one at that. He always wore black smart shirts whatever the weather, and always wore his favourite cufflinks, given to him by his wife for his fiftieth birthday.

"No, don't be silly. I expect a tip from others but come on now, how long have we known each other? No need to tip me at all. You have a good time in town and just ring me when you need me to take you back."

"I'm thinking of getting the bus back for a change. I hardly ever take the bus. It's good to get out and about, Trevor. I need to do that more instead of being stuck in the house every day all day. I tell you what, if you're not busy after this fare, join me. We can walk around and I'll feel safer."

"With police patrolling the street I'm sure you'll be fine, young Mel. I wish I could join you but my wife will be onto you. You know what she's like."

"Ah, yes. Gwenda's quite possessive of you isn't she. I can see why though. With that gold tooth of yours, the cufflinks and your sexy shirt, I'm sure she's always worried you'll run away with a young lady one day."

"I'd run away with you, my dear. I'm sure you don't nag and tell me what to do like she does," he replied, joking.

"You never know. I might call you one day to whisk me away from Porthcawl, to somewhere abroad where it's sunnier and where I won't get strangled in my sleep."

"You're not going to get knifed in your sleep. And if you ever are I'll go after the bastard who did it and I'll murder them, young Mel," Trevor snapped back, looking angry now. His face softened within moments as she handed him a tip and the fare cost and climbed out of the taxi, her gorgeous black satin skirt slightly lifting to reveal a shapely stocking-covered thigh.

Mel turned around and smiled at him through the window as she shut the door. He smiled back, his gold tooth seeming to be the only thing noticeable in the vehicle. She waved at him and he waved back before speeding away around a corner in a cloud of dust and extravagance.

CHAPTER TWENTY-THREE

Three hours later, she got off a bus at the end of the street and struggled to carry several heavy bags. Full of food items, alcohol and some new shoes, toiletries and other things she'd bought on the spur of the moment on her credit card, she stopped every few feet to catch her breath. It was three-thirty-one in the afternoon and she looked forward to opening a nice bottle of white wine and settling down to enjoy a riveting film. Before she could even pick her bags back up, she felt a cold breath on her neck. She put a gloved hand to her skin and warmed where the cold sensation had been.

What felt like a finger brushing her hair away from her eyes, Mel began to feel unnerved by what was happening. She couldn't just leave the bags there and run to her house. She picked them back up and slowly plodded along, each inch of the pavement seeming to stretch into miles ahead of her.

Finally getting into the house, and with no angry neighbours waiting for her either, she felt good for the first time in a long time as she closed her front door, put a deadbolt lock across it as well as a chain and other locks too that Ben and police had installed. Even windows now had locks on them too but Mel knew that if a killer really wanted to take her life it wouldn't take much for them to do so. Especially a clever killer like the one professional police officers and Ben himself couldn't capture so what chance did she have, she believed?

Ben sat at his desk in work and thought about her. He thought about a lot of things that day as he settled back into a regular routine. At least being there got him away from Alice, he appreciated, as he sipped the last of his hot drink and checked the time on a large white-framed clock on the wall. It had Roman numerals on it and the second hand seemed to drag past the seconds like a snail. Actually slower than a snail, to him it seemed. It was 6 pm and he looked forward to going home and seeing Mel. He hadn't heard from her all day so naturally assumed that she'd been OK and safe.

Ten minutes later he decided to knock off and leave early. His colleagues had already gone home to their partners and he hadn't found out anything worth mentioning to anyone let alone to police so he logged off on his computer and put his jacket on. Raindrops pattered on the window panes. He didn't bother with an umbrella. His car was only a mere few yards away from the large office block and if he ran a few feet there was ample covering ahead to keep him reasonably dry. He switched an alarm on and made sure that all windows were closed and locked. Leaving security lights on, he got ready to leave.

A rustling sound alerted him to a corridor nearby. Rats and mice hadn't been seen in the building since day one before he'd helped his friend set up the business in the first place so he doubted it were them. Assuming he'd left a window open, he strolled up the corridor and whistled a tune to himself.

Mel sat and waited back home for his arrival. Seven o'clock passed and there was no sign of him. She thought nothing of it and continued watching TV and finishing a bottle of wine. When eight approached, she began to get concerned. Calling his mobile phone and getting no reply, she put it down to him driving or discussing work matters with workmates. When ten-forty-seven arrived, she fretted to the point she felt she had to do something. Ringing him again, her call went to voicemail.

"Ben, you said seven. Please let me know you're alright. Where are you? Call me!"

Not wanting to go out of the house into the dark street this time of the night, she paced up and down her living room and bit her fingernails, or rather what was left of them.

Just as she was about to ring Trevor to come and pick her up in his taxi, Ben walked through the front door. She'd given him a spare key.

"Thank God. I've been worried sick!"

"I'm sorry. I got held up at work. I tried to get away long before now but well, I haven't been there for a while have I? There was a lot to sort out. What's for dinner? Do you want me to get a take away if you haven't eaten?"

"I've had a pizza. I've left you half, its in the fridge. There's wine there too, I bought a few bottles."

"Ah, been shopping have you my dear? While I'm slogging my guts out in work you've been shopping?" Ben teased, pretending to look offended.

"Hey, I work hard here in the house and gardens. I do the work of at least six people and I don't get paid for it so I don't know what you're going on about. Now go and get your pizza and wine before I finish them off!"

"Oh, get you! All bossy like. Even Alice wasn't like this! I might go next door now in a minute."

"Go then. More pizza and wine for me then isn't there?" Mel replied, running toward the kitchen. He ran after her and they giggled like kids. Next door it was an entirely different matter. Jenny, a neighbour from a few doors down the street had been found decapitated by unusually strong gale force winds causing a washing line to snap and lash against her neck. The fence panelling at the bottom of her garden had landed on her too, breaking several bones in her legs, leaving her unable to walk and to get help before the line careered toward her. The poor cow hadn't stood a chance.

Sick of seeing police crime scene tape stretched around residents' properties lately, Mel downed a bottle wine and promptly got drunk. Despite Ben's helpful insistence that she try to remain relatively sober, she was gone past caring now. So he joined her in the drink fest session and they both fell asleep on settees in the living room, he with his trousers down to his ankles and she with her blouse off, strewn across a cushion.

Officers Jones and Davies were discussing the recent unfortunate accident.

"It's a shame about Jenny. I knew her well, used to go out with her a long time ago. Such a nice woman, even if she was a bit of a gossip and poked her nose into everyone's business. I would have stayed with her but she wasn't the one for me. We had some great times though over the years. I'll miss her."

"Davies, you're not getting sentimental on me are you? I didn't know her myself but it's not like you to get misty eyed over a woman. Not with your womanising past anyway."

"Hey, don't be so fucking cheeky, Jones, mate. I'm a changed man and you know it."

"Sorry! God, you're so snappy today. I'm off to interview residents in that street. I feel like I should move in there myself, I'm there so bloody much."

"Can't help it, mate. I'm just under a lot of stress. See you at the pub on Saturday night? You own me a round."

"Aye, no problem, mate. See you then. You're off for a few days so if you're knocking off now, Saturday it is then."

"Yes, I've got to attend my daughter's wedding in Chester on Friday morning. It's not something I can get out of, being the best man and all that. But I should be back by Saturday afternoon."

"Wind her up bigtime. She can take it."

"Oh I intend to, don't worry. I'll get her back for that time she smothered you in custard pies for a charity event, remember?"

"How can I forget? It took four showers and a good scrub until I got all the gunk out of my bloody hair. It was good fun though and for a good cause I suppose. Tell her I said hi and sorry I can't make it. Congratulations from me for her big day."

"Okay mate. See you later. Now go and get that killer so we can all have a break. There are other crimes to focus on and we've got a backlog building up right under our noses. What a headache. We need more men on the jobs. I hate this short staffed nonsense."

"Me too, mate. Me too. See you later."

Officer Jones sped off down the street in a police car. Davies looked into the distance beyond to see storm clouds approaching. He shivered and felt hairs on his body stand bolt upright. He felt bad for not joining his colleague as normally two officers were always patrolling the streets but Jones was a very experienced sort and an expert in martial arts and other life-saving skills too. He'd be fine.

Jones turned a corner and parked outside Mel's house. He surveyed the houses and the road, all was as quiet as a mouse. For now. Forensics had already been there. Tape blew back and forth in the wind and in several houses all lights were out. It gave an eerie feel to the place.

Mel had since sobered up and spotted him through a window just before she closed the curtains. Dark clouds loomed above her house and rain was well on the way. She always wondered if Wales had the shittiest weather on the entire planet; judging by the amount of rain they always seemed to have. Even the sheep on the hills and in the Welsh valleys should have little umbrellas, she thought.

She'd travelled to England once, to meet up with a former classmate friend, and it rained there too. She also noticed that they seemed to have about as many sheep as Wales had as well. So that theory vanished instantly.

She went to the front door, opened it and called to officer Jones:

"Fancy a nice cuppa? You've got a long night ahead of you and it's nice and warm in here. No pressure!"

"No pressure at all, love. Hi, Mel, that would be great. I've been meaning to speak to you anyway. Is Ben around too? I've got a few questions for him as well."

"Come right in. He's here. Not in a good state though I'm afraid. We've had a bit of a drink."

"Ah, I see. Celebrating something then are you? His wife's birthday? Is Alice with you?"

Mel rolled her eyes and muttered obscenities under her breath. Stupid fucking idiot. Surely the gossipers around here have let you know by now, she thought.

He got out of the car, closed the door wearily and locked it. Shivering, he hunched his coat around his shoulders, put his keys in his trouser pocket and rubbed his hands together.

"It's so damn cold today. I'll be glad when summer comes, Mel."

"Me too," she replied, goose bumps covering her bare arms as she shivered on her doorstep.

Officer Jones opened the garden gate. It squeaked and sounded like one of those scenes in a creepy horror film. He closed it and walked briskly up the garden path and all the while scanning every object, every piece of body language, straining his ears to hear any suspicious sounds, the lot. Even Mel wasn't innocent. Everyone in the town was now a suspect and a potential killer.

He walked inside, Mel closing the door behind her. Instant heat warmed their bodies as they headed toward the living room. Ben was in the bathroom, shaving and singing along to a radio.

"Ben, officer Jones is here to see us."

There was no reply.

"Be right back. I'll go and see what he's doing. Won't be long now."

"Okay love."

"Sit yourself down by the fire. Keep warm."

She ran upstairs as the policeman sat by the wood burning fire. He took his jacket off and placed it to one side on the edge of an armchair. As he stared into the orange and yellow flames, he was sure he saw a shadow ever so quickly move across the glass. Turning around, there was nobody behind him. As he turned to face the fire again though, a pair of eyes met his. He screamed and jumped up out of his seat. Right in front of him an ashen-faced figure stood, smiling at him.

Both Ben and Mel raced downstairs.

"What the hell is the matter?" Ben asked.

Officer Jones shrieked as the ghost lunged toward him; its gnarly bent fingers reaching for his throat. Just as Ben and Mel got into the room, the spirit dissipated into thin air, leaving the poor man speechless and trembling violently where he stood, unable to move his feet. Like a block of ice, he was rigid and not quite himself at all.

Mel crept up behind him and moved slowly to face him. His mouth was open and his eyes were fixed at nothingness straight in front of him. She followed his stare and all she could see was a framed painting above the fireplace. He saw a face full of anguish and pure rage before it dispersed into the atmosphere into nothingness. His eyes adjusted and he too saw a framed painting above the fireplace.

She looked back at him and noticed that his mouth was moving but no words were coming out. She glanced at Ben, shrugged, and returned her gaze to the petrified officer next to her. Ben felt an icy chill sweeping around his body and wondered if a window had been left open. He began speaking gibberish and slumped on the settee nearby, holding his head in his hands as he talked to himself.

"What do we do, just leave him there for a while?"

"Mel, best we do that, yes. Let's sit here and keep an eye on him. Whatever he saw it spooked him that's for sure."

Mel looked around the room to see if her ghostly visitor was making itself known to her too but there was nothing. The temperature increased in the air and a healthy colour began returning to the shaking officer's face. As Mel sat down, she distinctly felt a cushion moving behind her back, sliding upward. Rather than startle the officer further, she ignored the incident. It was much harder however to ignore what came next...

"I'll always protect you, but not him. He didn't listen to my complaints years ago when burglars broke into my house. He laughed my situation off and walked away. Thieves took valuable possessions of mine and he's got them. His friends made sure he got them."

Mel's eyes widened and she spluttered and coughed. Banging her chest with her fist, she got up and headed toward the kitchen. "I'm just getting a glass of water, won't be long. I've got a dry throat."

"OK Hun. Put the kettle on while you're there please. Thanks!"

"No problem," she replied.

"Officer Jones, we'll make you a hot drink now, that'll help. Would you like something to eat, a sandwich maybe?" Ben asked, placing one hand on the man's shoulders in front of him.

For the first time since his fright, the man snapped out of his trance-like state and glared into Ben's eyes.

"What the hell just happened?"

"Well, by the way you were acting, I'd say you saw a ghost or something. I couldn't see anything myself. Have you been overworking?"

"I'm under a lot of stress lately, all officers are but that was no stress-induced hallucination. I know what I saw," he replied, his voice getting louder, his forehead lined.

"I'm not saying that you didn't see what you thought you saw. I'm just stating an observation that's all. Just trying to help, you know?"

"Thanks, Ben. I appreciate it. God knows what just happened but it seemed so real, so lifelike."

"What exactly did you see? I'm curious."

"It was the face of a person; well it looked like a human shape anyway. I couldn't tell if it was male or female and the voice seemed distorted. Hard to make out really what it was. It frightened the life out of me I know that. Nearly gave me a bloody heart attack right there and then!"

"How about that hot drink? Which would you prefer, tea or coffee? I'd give you something stronger but you're driving today, aren't you?"

"I'm not from now onward, not until tomorrow morning. I've got to patrol all the streets in the town, especially this one. All night and all morning."

"Right then, if you're not driving, how about joining me and having a few pints of beer? It's good to have male company. I think the world of Mel but it'd be good to chat with a man. I've got some questions for you if you don't mind answering them, about private investigation techniques and all that. I'm looking for more staff so if you fancy a part-time job or even switching from your current one to working for me, then don't hesitate to let me know will you?"

"I'm happy where I am, Ben, but thanks for thinking about me. I'd like a beer, yes, thanks. Just the one though. I've got to stay alert. It's the same in your line of work I should imagine."

"It is, yes. Right, be right back. One beer coming up."

He walked to the kitchen as officer Jones composed himself and occasionally looked up at the wall and back at the kitchen again. He then did something very unusual indeed. He scanned the room and mentally and silently priced items on sideboards, tables, walls and even the rug on the floor. It was an Oriental-type of rug and he wondered how much it'd be worth if sold to a potentially interested friend who collected them.

A ghostly wagging finger appeared right in front of his face; just one finger, and it wagged and wagged from side to side and moved closer to his face with every second that passed. Just before it touched his nose he scrambled from his seat and ran to the front door, screaming his head off.

Ben stood there with a pint of ice-cold beer in one hand and another in his other hand which was extended out to the officer to take it from him. The front door flew open and all Ben could now see were the soles of the terrified man's shoes as he ran up the garden path and jumped over the gate without even opening it. He just about missed the top of the gate with the end of his shoes and he landed in a heap on the concrete on the other side. Getting up, he sprinted down the street and didn't stop running until he reached the corner, and even then he kept going!

"What a strange man," Mel said, secretly glad that she and Ben were alone now for a night of privacy. She closed the front door and locked it in several places. Turning to face Ben, she smiled and took the spare pint of beer from his hand and began sipping it.

"Hey!"

"What's the matter? He obviously doesn't want it, does he?"

"I'm not on about that. I would have had it."

"But you've already got one. Don't be greedy. You greedy piggy," she teased, taking another sip and licking her lips.

Belching, Ben wrinkled his nose at her and playfully slapped her backside as she headed back into the living room.

CHAPTER TWENTY-FOUR

Several hours later, along with several beers later and much dancing to music, they curled up on the largest of settees and cosied up by the roaring fire. Nodding off to sleep, they both felt more content in each other's company than they'd ever been.

Rain began pattering on the window panes and the street was deathly quiet and not a resident in sight, a far cry from a year before when everyone seemed to frequent the local fish and chip shops or pubs in the area. They were half empty now most evenings and were on the verge of closing down altogether if customers didn't return in droves.

Seagulls hovered over scattered bits of chips and batter and swooped down when out of the way of waving arms and 'shoo'-type sounds. They gobbled up the morsels of warm and tasty food and it was if they went away to tell their birdie friends about the banquet as more hurried over several minutes later to join them.

After officer Jones had managed to get to the police station, others replaced him to patrol Porthcawl. Boats, dotted all across the sea looked so small in the distance as they bobbed up and down on the sea. Winds were picking up but they didn't put fishermen off at all. They puffed on hand-rolled cigarettes and sat on a wall on a break before hauling in more fish for the local restaurants and cafes that relied on them, day in and day out.

The men were paid very well for their efforts and oftentimes they caught so many that they ate fish suppers several times a week. The oldest was a man named Tim, who was well-built and had dark cropped hair. The oldest among his friends at the grand old' age of 65, he had decades of fishing skills under his belt and took great pleasure in teaching younger men all that he knew. The youngest was a short and skinny man in his late twenties who initially thought that he knew it all but soon learned the hard way after pulling a net in too soon to find it empty. Not only that, it had snagged on an old rusty nail embedded in the seaweed and slime-covered wall at the bottom of it and had ended up spending the rest of that day mending the net as the other fishermen laughed at his predicament.

Time was getting on and darkness fast approached over the horizon, spreading in toward them all. Black clouds matched the black mood of a white-faced spirit sitting at the top of the lighthouse. They peered through dusty windows out to sea and didn't at all seem bothered that any one of the men, if they looked up, could probably see them.

The ghost had the ability to make themselves visible to other people, or not, but on this occasion they didn't care either way what happened. They felt sad at heart and sat there pondering.

The fairground was to be re-opened fully soon, after a harsh winter's battering against paintwork on rides; leaving bits peeling off and puddles of water accumulating on seats and rooftops of doughnut stalls and fish and chip cafes. A very small stall where fresh cockles were sold, was completely covered over in tarpaulin and not a cockle was in sight! Rinsed thoroughly of sand particles and bits and pieces of grit and whatnot, they were the best cockles in Wales.

A little girl and her father walked past and she nagged him to buy her some but alas, he couldn't. He lifted her up onto a small metal pipe that stuck out of the ground, so that she could look through a large window at her favourite ride. Too little to go on it next month, all she could do was watch workmen trying it out as a long carriage whooshed past, splashing water onto the window pane, much to her delight. Her father held her close to stop her falling off the pipe as her little feet balanced carefully. He picked her up and put her back onto the ground again.

They walked, hand in hand, to a nearby fish and chip shop on a corner where he shared his meal with her before they headed back to a caravan he owned along with his wife. They had two other children, older, and a dog named Pebbles too who often slept under the caravan, regardless of whether it was a sunny day or a rainy day. The dog thought himself wise to sleep under there anyway, mostly for a bit of peace and quiet; what with the kids squabbling or feeling bored most of the time with not much to do other than to watch a small television or wander around outside making new friends.

When Mother was busy cooking or doing something else, Father took the little girl onto the beach where she sang to her tiny heart's content holding her Dad's hand as he guided her across rocks so they could see the rock pools and the many creatures that lived in them. Limpets clung to the sides of rocks, in between crevices and nooks and crannies and other sea creatures scuttled around in the murky water in search of food or to hide somewhere safe from other predators who were after them. Dark green seaweed displayed itself like curly and swirling glistening ribbons all over the place and worms made their presence known by popping their heads just above the surface of sandy mounds nearby before quickly popping back down again whenever a wave or human foot moved toward them.

But today, the beach was empty. Even in winter time and up until March, there would always be at least a group of teenagers or dog walkers exploring the area but recent murders had put a dampener on that. There was an air of increasing fear in Porthcawl lately and nobody felt safe; despite police officers trying their best to reassure them that they were.

It was almost dark now and six o'clock loomed upon the town and beach. A bleak Monday evening, due to stormy weather, the fishermen had finished early for the day and were now sitting in a nice warm cafe yards away from the lighthouse. The ghost had left and everywhere was silent and still, other than inside that cafe and the hotels dotted all along the promenade and in the inner areas of the town. Shops were closing and people were hurrying home to their loved ones. Even buses seemed emptier than normal, with visitors and residents preferring to use taxis or to accompany friends and relatives in their vehicles to feel safer.

Many wandering spirits surveyed the town and beach and walked, floated and moved around, seemingly with no place to go, but they knew where they were going. As if stuck in different time zones, some passed right through other beings, not even noticing each other. Other ghosts definitely noticed each other and either chatted amongst themselves or avoided each other altogether. Animal spirits trotted by their sides; ranging from cats to dogs, to rabbits to other creatures.

Children had played in the rock pools and some had even dipped their tiny toes in the sea, giggling and enjoying themselves for quite a while before going home with their parents. An air of menace began vanishing into the dark clouds overhead and some ghosts dimmed their energy to the point they couldn't be seen by each other, let alone by humans who weren't physically dead.

Blinding bright light from the lighthouse slowly spun around and boats moved away from rocks and powerful waves. Fishermen were paid for their hard work by restaurant managers and cafe owners and they finished their supper before going home to their wives and girlfriends or to the pubs in the town for a nightcap and a quick game of dominoes or darts.

CHAPTER TWENTY-FIVE

Ben went to his office to pick up some paperwork to study for a few hours and to pick up a new laptop computer he'd left behind there. Unlocking the main door and disabling an alarm, he closed the main door behind him, locked it and stepped upstairs to a large room. In semi darkness he felt unnerved and didn't waste any time in getting his computer and getting out of the building as fast as he could. Before he got to the main door and was about to enable the alarm, he felt the presence of someone standing behind him. Fearing the worst and to be smacked on the side of the head by a burglar, he gripped his laptop with both hands and quickly spun around, moving it in front of him. There was nobody there.

"What the hell?"

Turning back around, he pressed keys on a panel and unlocked the main door, closed it and locked it again as a very loud and shrill sound rung in his ears. He shuddered and walked toward his car. Hearing footsteps behind him, he felt himself growing angrier and angrier with each step on the ground.

Stopping dead in his tracks, he spun around fully prepared to punch whoever was following him, only again to find nobody there. Standing, rooted to the ground, his eyes darted around in every direction. Expecting to see a shadow or a person jumping out from behind bushes, nothing happened.

Exasperated now and rubbing his eyes with the back of one hand as he put his laptop under his arm, he blinked in quick succession and tried to make his vision crystal clear. Wind was picking up and he felt tiny grains of sand lash against his face, stinging his skin. He licked his lips and tasted salt. The eerie footsteps had stopped now but as he got closer to his car, he noticed the driver's door was wide open. Picking up speed now and running, he got to the door and peered inside the vehicle. There was nobody in the back. He pulled a chair forward, expecting to see someone crouched underneath but it was empty, other than one or two crumpled up pieces of paper and a few lost pens.

He got into his car, closed the door and locked it and all other doors instantly. Sitting there for several minutes, he slouched down in his seat and waited. Everything was still and silent. He finally settled his gaze upon the large building he owned and felt a surge of pride wash over his heart. He'd spent every penny he'd had years ago on the place, managing to secure a bank loan to add to his own financial savings to start the business off.

The death of his workmate and friend had shocked him to the core but he couldn't just pack in his job now; he had to work and as much as he loved Mel, he didn't want to take time off to carry out endless and boring DIY jobs around another house. Mel was creative and a hard worker and he vowed to help her but police were relying on him to help them out with surveillance and monitoring the street he lived in and possibly the entire town too if he could find the time. He was a busy man and longed to take a month off to relax in one of the many hotels in Porthcawl but he simply didn't have the time to do so.

After twenty minutes and seeing and hearing no signs of trespassers in his workplace or its grounds and car park, he started up the engine of his car, slid his seatbelt around his chest and stomach and drove back home. His laptop rested on the passengers seat along with paperwork inside the black fabric bag it nestled in.

He travelled along a motorway and several dual carriageways. He couldn't wait to have a hot bath and to wind down for the evening. It was approaching eight-forty-five and he heard and felt his stomach rumbling. It occurred to him that he hadn't eaten for many hours and his blood sugar level was slowly going down. He felt lightheaded but not enough for concern. He was a very safe driver with no points on his licence and was a responsible, level-headed man.

His steering wheel began turning all by itself and try as he might with all his strength, he couldn't turn it the right way again. Several seconds later, he found himself moving down a quiet street on the outskirts of town. He felt confused as to why he was going this way and thought about stopping the car if the steering wheel was malfunctioning. It hadn't happened before. So why now?

The car slowed to a stop and he sat there baffled. Seconds later two police officers walked around the corner. From the shadows he watched them. They not only pulled out a suspicious-looking transparent bag of white powder, they also had blood on their hands. They laughed and Ben couldn't work out what they were saying but he got the gist of it. Something about 'doing him good and proper'. He continued sitting there observing them to see what they'd do next. They were too engrossed in chat to even notice him.

A man crawled across the ground toward their feet. They kicked him in the face and he crawled no more. Ben watched in horror as they bent down and dragged the defenceless man back around the corner before they ran toward their car and sped off in a flurry of dust and lack of conscience.

Ben got out of his car and looked around. Nobody was about. The last thing he needed was to be hauled into court for being wrongly convicted of hurting a person rather than helping them. He pulled out a small torch from his jacket pocket and shone it on the ground. Bits of discarded crap and broken glass dotted the surface and his light finally rested upon a human foot. No shoes were on the feet and the soles had painful-looking lacerations on them. A small trail of blood contrasted with the blackness of night.

He slowly lifted the light's examination upward and into the face of a battered and bruised elderly man. He was still breathing, thankfully. Ben rang for an ambulance from a nearby telephone box. And then he left the scene.

Tearing up the motorway he was raging now and slamming one fist on the passenger seat. "The callous bastards. I trusted them too."

The two police officers were the very same ones who had spoken to he and Mel on several occasions. A look of niceness and innocence on their faces, he felt utterly ashamed that he'd even entertained their conversation and so-called concern for their welfare, let alone them attempting to befriend them both as a couple.

He found two empty unmarked police cars at least ten miles away. He jotted down their car registration numbers in a small pocket notebook. Parking in the shadows again, he waited.

Waking in the morning to the sounds of dogs barking and birds tweeting, he jumped in his seat and winced. Rubbing his back and neck, it took a minute before he realised where he was. He wondered if he were dreaming but that thought soon took flight when a dog walker tapped on his car window, startling him.

Ben rolled it down and squinted in the morning's harsh light.

"You okay? Heavy night?"

"No, I'm fine. I fell asleep. Nothing to worry about but thank you all the same. Good day to you."

"Ah, good. You looked dead to the world then for a moment. I'm glad you're alive."

"So am I," he replied. "So am I. For fuck's sake!"

He roared up the engine and drove back in the direction he'd came from, cursing himself for nodding off on the job. I must be getting old, he thought to himself as he searched around for a burger joint to quieten the animalistic rumblings in his stomach. A coffee would be welcome too, he thought, his lips dry as a desert and sticking together like glue.

After sating his hunger and thirst, and visiting the men's toilets to relieve himself, he was relieved to have gone. The thought of a bursting dam of yellow all over the inside of his car was something he wouldn't want to endure, or to clean up. Used to long journeys going after clients' womanising husbands and wives doing the dirty on their spouses or ex-partners, Ben was accustomed to spending long hours out of the officer. His car had clocked up so many miles over the years it was time to get a new one, he thought. Not just yet though. Now that he and Mel were getting closer, paying for a new home to be together properly was priority now.

He swallowed the last of a piece of lettuce and dug a fragment of onion out of his teeth. His growling stomach silenced now, and his energy levels sky-high, he felt fantastic. His back ached but not as much as his gums had in the past few weeks and months after dental surgery.

Seeing no sign of the two police officers, he drove back to see if the injured man was still where he was. If paramedics hadn't turned up he was sure by now he'd be stone cold dead.

As he approached the scene there was not only no victim there, all glass, crap and traces of blood had been cleared up. That'd odd, he thought, usually paramedics just take the person to hospital and hose down the blood so as not to frighten innocent passers by, but to completely clean up every particle and to leave the ground spotless was very unusual to say the least.

He got out of his car and walked around the corner. There were no tell tale signs of any suspicious activity whatsoever and not only that the ground had been covered in tarmac. It was as if he'd dreamed the entire incident. Looking at his wrists, he noticed several spots of blood on his skin. Rubbing his nose and seeing the back of his fingers clean, he frowned. He got back into his car and sat there contemplating his next move.

Deciding to call in at the nearest hospital, he thought about what words to choose in order to go undetected. An uncle. He decided he'd use the victim as an uncle. He got out of his car and slowly wandered up to the main entrance of a large, looming white building. Memories of his dying father flooded his mind. He instantly pushed them to the back of his subconscious again, not even entertaining them for a nanosecond. He spotted the main desk and searched his mind for the correct way to behave; praying his body language wouldn't give anything away.

"Good morning, Sir. Can I help you?" a polite woman asked, donned all in pristine white clothing and having a smile that'd catch any red-blooded male off guard, regardless of their marital status.

"Oh hi. Yes. I'm checking up on my uncle, he was brought in last night."

"Name?"

Ben felt his heart thud in his chest and then skip a beat. Christ, his name?

"I'm sorry, gotta go. I'll be back. My wife's expecting me, it's her birthday today and I've just remembered I haven't got her a card. I'll get one for my uncle too, a get well one."

He ran out, leaving the woman open mouthed, her black mascara-covered lashes fluttering like spiders' legs gone crazy.

What the hell to do now? Ben asked himself, pacing up and down the car park outside. He stared up at the enormous building and felt a million miles away from answers, not several yards. He noticed an ambulance pull up nearby. After paramedics had wheeled a patient out of the back and in through the doors of the hospital, he grabbed the opportunity immediately. Climbing into the back of the vehicle, he almost laughed out loud when he noticed clothing hanging on hooks.

Dressed as a paramedic, Ben stepped out of the back of the ambulance and held his head down as he walked into the hospital and briskly walked past the receptionist. Busy chatting to a female member of staff, she hadn't even noticed him.

Ben scanned walls for directions and found himself facing a large notice board and a map. 'YOU ARE HERE!' informed him of exactly where he was at that given moment and where he needed to be.

Getting into a lift, he pressed the highest button up to the uppermost floor of the building. Starting with the ICU first, he thought it best to work his way downward from floor to floor and ward to ward. It was good that he had a few hours to kill. He'd telephone Mel later. Getting told off for chatting on a mobile phone in such a place was the last thing he wanted.

He found the ICU and peered around a doorframe. Lined with about ten beds, containing patients ranging from teenagers to the elderly, he examined each one visually for the merest flicker of recognition. Nothing. As far as he could ascertain, there was only on ICU in the vicinity. It would be highly unlikely that the man would have been taken anywhere else; especially with four empty beds in front of him.

A senior nurse tapped him on the shoulder. Swinging around, Ben was greeted with the sight of a curious older woman with a chest so ample buttons on her uniform were at bursting point. He dragged his eyes upward. A scowl on her face now, she tapped her watch with one finger.

"If you're looking for Mr. Ollsworth, he was expected at least ten minutes ago. I've had his family on the phone asking about him and where he is. Do you know?"

"I'm sorry. I've no idea. I'll go and find out for you. I've just been looking for him, he's not in here," Ben replied, lying. Flashing a momentary smile at her, he nudged past her and worried he'd get trapped between her huge, contained breasts and a Fire Exit door.

"So sorry. Be right back!"

The woman glared at him and flounced off in a hurry. He walked into the ICU and made his way around the corner. There were more patients and more beds but the victim was nowhere to be seen. Maybe he's died, Ben wondered. As he got to the farthest part of the sprawling room, he saw a family huddled around the man he'd seen the night before. He had tubes coming out of his nostrils and the beep of a heart monitor machine was one of the greatest sounds Ben had ever heard in his life. It would have been so very different indeed if the man had died. The shit would hit the fan bigtime if that had happened, what with Ben knowing quite a lot of officers back at the station.

Feeling himself relax, he smiled and turned around to leave. Getting back into the lift, two men got in with him just as the last moment. He didn't think twice about looking at their faces until he found himself staring into the end of a gun.

"Oh we noticed you last night, you prick. Don't even think of reporting us. Don't be a stupid little PI now will you?"

"You? I trusted you. And I don't trust many people."

"In your line of work I'm surprised you trust anybody to be honest!"

"Police officers though, come on, Davies and Jones!"

The lift doors opened on the ground floor and Ben felt his fight or flight instincts kicking in. Just as he considered doing some martial arts on the two men, several paramedics were rushing toward the three of them. Ben slipped behind them and ran out of the hospital. The officers barged past the medical staff and seethed with rage. Hiding the gun, they slowed down to avoid panicking visitors in the waiting area a few feet away. As soon as they got to the revolving door, they ran like the wind only to find Ben had long gone.

Just over an hour later, Ben decided rather than return to Mel's house, he needed to know what the officers were up to. He lurked outside the police station to see if they'd return. Sitting in his car scribbling a note, he thought about what to include in it and what not to:

Two officers were seen behaving suspiciously in town. A man was injured and they participated in his painful condition. Rushed to hospital after an anonymous telephone call, he...

Ben stopped writing and crumpled up the piece of paper. They knew where he lived and they also knew where Mel lived too. He didn't want to sleep with one eye open so he changed his mind and drove back to her house. Both officers saw him and followed at a distance. Rather than go to Mel's, he sped up and took them on a wild goose chase all across town.

Laughing as he observed their confused antics; them driving around and around a roundabout initially, he slowed down and parked outside a restaurant. Best to be around lots of people, he thought. They couldn't possibly do anything to him there. He sat and waited to see how they'd react. They did exactly the same. Playing cat and mouse chasing games with each other was amusing for him but Mel repeatedly texting him and asking where he was and that she was worried now as time was getting on, he had no other choice than to reassure her that he'd be home within the next thirty minutes.

Back at her place, he noticed that the two officers were no longer following him. Feeling tension in his neck and shoulders subside, he looked forward to a late evening cuddling up to someone who would never inflict harm upon him.

Using a spare key, she'd given him to let himself in, he closed the door and instantly inhaled a most beautiful of fragrances.

"Mel, where are you?"

There was no reply.

"Ah, playing games with me too are you?"

Still no reply.

The sound of water being splashed around caused him to smile. She was in the bath. Feeling groggy and dirty, he decided to join her. Stepping upstairs, he took off his jacket, shirt and trousers and neatly folded them on a bed. He slipped out of his underpants and felt goose bumps creeping over his body. The heating was on in the house but farting about outsmarting policemen in town on a cold Spring evening reminded him to stay warmer. He wasn't getting younger and seemed to feel the cold more lately.

The curtains were closed. Not that he was ashamed of his body or embarrassed even, he checked himself in a large dressing table's mirror and felt confident that despite middle age creeping in upon him as months passed by, he looked pretty good. Other than the odd grey hair on his unshaven face, he admired his toned physique and felt particularly pleased at how well endowed he was. Semi-erect, he knew that the instant he set eyes on Mel's exquisite body in the bathroom, the sight of her curves would soon alter that. She was humming to herself and had quite a good voice, he thought. He'd never noticed just how many talents she had until now. And he was about to show her one of his big talents too.

"Good evening, my gorgeous! Sorry I'm late. I called into the office and lost track of time. I'm fine, nothing to worry about."

"Hi, sexy. Just let me know in future, please. Preferably after my first text, not many of them."

"Will do. Sorry."

"Get in here. You look cold."

They both glanced down at his shrinking cock and burst into laughter. He took his socks off and climbed into warm and welcoming water and warm and welcoming affection too. Turning around and lying on her stomach and chest, he felt as if nobody in the world could ever hurt him ever again. She wrapped her arms around his naked torso and kissed the side of his head.

"Ah, so nice. Sorry I worried you. I won't do it again."

"I'm fine. I locked the doors, windows, and the baseball bat and knives stopped me panicking eventually. We must get a big guard dog too. What do you think?"

"I'm your big guard dog. I'll bite any intruders and I'll shit all over them too, no worries there!"

She slapped his arm. "Stop being so crude. I'll have no talk of shit in my clean and beautiful bathroom if you don't mind!"

"So let me get this straight. I can't even talk dirty to you?"

"That's allowed. Please talk dirty to me."

He turned around in the swirling water and kissed her passionately. He felt her hard nipples pressing against his chest and his cock responded instantly to her passionate embrace. Wind howled outside and trees swayed but in her arms everything was calm and so wonderful. Fragrant bubbles clung to their skin as they continued kissing; enjoying each other after a long and stressful day. He broke away for a moment to gaze into her gorgeous eyes, her lids half closed, reassuring him of her attraction for him. Her lips were parted and as steam enveloped her, she looked ravishing to him. He moved upward and with skin on skin, he and Mel writhed under the water as he slipped inside her.

She moved her head and rested it on the edge of the bath. Gasping and panting like an animal on heat, she opened her legs wider for him to have better access. Gripping the sides of the bath, she lifted her bottom up and wrapped her legs around his waist, drawing him ever deeper into her body.

Ben closed his eyes and felt as though he were in another world, not a bathroom. The heady intensity of pleasure and tight warmth of her almost made him empty himself right there and then but he wanted to last longer. Selfish at other times in life, when it came to the pleasures of the flesh, he was far from it. It turned him on even more to prolong a woman's pleasure. And now that he was at last with Mel, he'd make a lot more effort and wanted to do anything to please her.

CHAPTER TWENTY-SIX

Two days later things turned up a notch when Mel noticed that the EVP's were increasing in not only intensity but frequency. One of Mel's visiting ghosts had already informed her that they knew who killed them and they seemed to know a lot more too about other matters.

Mel decided to investigate and find out who the killer or killers were. The spirit seemed to be insistent on letting her know important details and if she was lucky and didn't give up then Mel believed she could possibly find out a hell of a lot more than even the local police ever could. Their efforts although admirable and daily, were discovering nothing of significance other than the condition and time of death of each murder victim.

It was noisy in the street today and with Ben in work fully now and because she'd finished writing her book she felt a little bored. Used to being extremely active, she found herself at a loss just sitting there doing nothing but watch daytime TV. One place she hadn't ventured into in quite a while was her attic.

After the last house move she'd packed away valuable items and reams of paper containing information regarding her family tree. She'd never fully looked at it and examined its significance up to now due to her traumatic childhood. What with her mother giving her up when she was a baby and not meeting her grandparents even, if Ben hadn't waltzed into her life she'd feel completely alone? Not a nice thought at all.

She made herself a coffee. After finishing it she walked upstairs. Yanking a steel ladder down, she climbed it and entered the attic area. Microscopic dust particles assaulted her nostrils as if angry at being disturbed from their dusty slumber in the darkness above. She spluttered and sneezed, holding one hand to her face and the other gripping the side of the ladder to balance herself.

After the sneezing had ceased, she climbed higher and up into the loft itself. Pulling a cord on the side of the wall, light glared, making her squint. Everything looked so still and eerie, a layer of dust and cobwebs clinging to every single item in front of her, and there was so much of it up there too. Creeping across the carpeted floor, she stood there contemplating what box to open first. Learning to write on boxes before each house move helped enormously to save time. Once, when searching for her passport, it was in the last box she opened; wasting three hours of her life when she could have been doing something more important.

Wandering around the large room, she couldn't help noticing how many spiders of all sizes were crawling around; mostly in corners but overhead too, inches from the top of her head. Not particularly having a phobia of spiders, she just didn't want them creeping over her body because she planned on being in there for several hours. Excited but hesitant too, she wasn't sure what secrets she'd uncover from reading many documents and other paperwork she'd never brought herself to read before.

Finding a large wooden chest next to a pile of boxes, she checked its lock.

"Shit! Where did I put the key for this?"

Sitting on the carpet and biting her fingernails deep in thought, she racked her brains to remember. A disembodied voice whispered in her left ear:

"Its on the shelf in front of you inside that ceramic cat you made in school."

Mel jumped and her eyes darted around the room. Feeling hairs prickling all over her body she shivered. Frowning and feeling a mixture of fear and curiosity, she waited.

"Over there. Where I said it is, it is. Go and see!"

Mel still did nothing. She even managed a smile. The smile soon vanished however when an invisible finger poked her in the shoulder, causing her to scream at the top of her lungs.

"Stop that! Who are you? Show yourself to me right now!"

The ghost didn't do as asked. Instead, it sat in the corner, watching her. Curiosity burning as brightly as the light above her head, Mel knew she just had to go and look. She knew if she didn't look, the chance of sleeping tonight would be impossible. Writers are a curious lot by nature and she was no different either.

She slowly walked toward a cobweb-covered black cat she'd made when five-years-old in school. A teacher had put it in the kiln but Mel herself had shaped the creature all by herself. A much loved 'real' pet, it never left her side for a long time until she grew into her teenage years where it was stored away out of sight, only to be brought back out when she moved to the house when an adult. She couldn't bear to give it away, yet it reminded her of childhood; a time when she needed her mother to be there to show her cat to, not to show only her teacher and foster parents who were now long dead.

Mel took the key out of the toy cat and gingerly walked over to the wooden chest. It had black metal bindings on it and grooves in the wood itself. Almost like a pirate chest, it made her think of ships and action and adventure times of long ago in many films and documentaries she'd seen over the years on TV and in the cinema.

Sitting cross-legged on the floor, she looked around for signs of the ghost. Everything was still, all was calm now. Only the ragged sound of her breathing and the drumming of her heart could be heard in her ears and she shivered in the cold and dark attic. It was almost as if every spider in that room stopped creeping and crawling over their intricate webs and cocooned prey to see, along with her too, exactly what secrets lay hidden within the confines of that dusty old chest.

Turning the key in the lock, she prised the lid open. Creaking, it sounded much like an old creepy-sounding door. Her heart hammered and she felt hesitant. Once opened, and its contents read, there was no turning back, no reversal of time or obliteration of memory. Mel chewed her fingernails and felt sick to the pit of her stomach. Feeling the unmistakable presence of another being next to her, she felt the urge to be brave, to be bold and to dive headlong into the mysteries of her past.

The first thing she took out to look at was a few bits and pieces she'd made in school. Memories came flooding back as she examined each and every object: drawings she'd created in art class when a very young child, depicting a house with child-like-drawn windows. No curtains decorated them, they looked dark and soulless. A swirl of grey smoke billowed from a tall brown chimney, disappearing between branches of old, gnarled trees dotted all across a mountain top. The only colour and warmth of the entire house was a single red coat on a tiny little girl. She was holding the hand of a woman, a woman who had no facial features.

Next to the house was the shadow of a man, drawn as if walking away from the two people. A black cat sat on a wall and seemed to be licking its paws, taking no notice of the deserter. Mel took out a small magnifying glass from the box and put it to her eye. Moving the drawing closer to her face she noticed that the woman was holding a book. She couldn't see what was written on the cover but the woman appeared to be handing it to Mel herself.

As she scanned each inch of the drawing, new things jumped out at her. It was only when she got to one window that she dropped the magnifying glass and gasped. Putting it back to her eye and looking again, she saw an old woman peering out of one of the other windows and a younger woman standing behind her. The younger woman resembled Marlene, the older woman she didn't recognise. She wondered if it was the woman's mother.

Mel sat there for a long time examining that scene and recalled being around about the age of six when she'd drawn it. She'd signed her name on the bottom-right of the paper. It looked as if a spider had crawled over the text. In bright red letters, it stood out. The only two colours on the entire sheet of paper was the coat she wore and the signature.

From nowhere she began sobbing, her tears mixing with the charcoal on the paper, distorting it, blurring it as her tears soaked into the fibres. Her heart felt as heavy as lead as distant memories of feeling abandoned and unloved filled her soul. Tossing the drawing to one side, she wiped her eyes and decided what to remove from the chest next.

A small white box sat in a corner, just beneath a dark brown folder stuffed with what appeared to be at first glance many documents like the folder she'd looked through in the police station. Taking the box out, she felt the weight of it. It definitely had something in it.

Excited now and her tears long gone, she felt as though it were Christmas Day. She loved the magical and special feeling that that day always had and this moment was no different. What if it contains something nasty and horrible, she wondered? Trying her best to remain positive-minded, she banished all negativity from her mind and pulled the top of the box upward. A flash of gold greeted her vision. Smiling now, she pulled the lid open fully and saw the most beautiful object she'd ever seen in her entire life – a pocket watch. It had a chain and the face of the watch had no scratches on the glass, no damage and looked brand new as if it had been purchased that very second from a quality shop. It had Roman numeral numbers on its face and in the middle were all its intricate and wonderful workings, all interlocked and ready to move. The time said two-twenty-six. It had stopped in the afternoon and Mel wondered why.

Turning the winder on the side, she carefully twisted it until the watch began ticking once more as if time had restarted from where it had left off. Mel felt the invisible presence by her side again and she glanced over her shoulder. This time, she saw the most serene and beautiful face imaginable and couldn't take her eyes off it. The being smiled at her and, lifting a hand, it pointed to the drawing that Mel had done as a child. Mel picked it back up and put the magnifying glass to her eye once more.

"Look at the old lady again," it said.

Mel did just that. Around the neck of the figure was a tiny little scrawling of the very same pocket watch and the time on it was two-twenty-six.

Mel looked over her shoulder again to speak to the ghost but it had left. Mel returned her attentions to the chest once again and placed the pocket watch around her neck by its chain. Psychometry took over and it was as if she were transported back into childhood again. The attic's appearance altered and she found herself standing inside the drawing she'd created, long, long ago. She felt a woman's hand in hers and she looked at her. She instantly recognised her; it was her foster mother who had passed away many years ago. Doris - or Mam, as she'd called her - had been a lovely person who had given Mel a wonderful love-filled childhood. Her husband, Maurice, although out at work most days, always spent quality time with her.

They lived in a little terraced street before moving to the countryside to the large house depicted in the drawing. She pulled out several photographs of them from the chest that seemed to hover right in front of her face and the both of them were in it. The man in the drawing looked totally different; taller and with dark hair. Maurice had white hair and was shorter. The shadowy figure in her drawing was her father who had left the family.

Mel had flashbacks swirling all over the place in her mind and all the while the ticking of the pocket watch reminded her of the here and now. It was if she were in two different worlds at the same time and everything she saw seemed to synchronise and make sense as each second ticked by.

The next scene that appeared before her face was when she was age just two-years-old. She could barely remember much from that time period but images of pushchairs and carried up a mountain, she wrapped in a warm woollen blanket made her feel secure and warm. She heard a very old song sung to her as a man rocked her to sleep as she lay her little head on his chest.

Fresh air took her consciousness within moments and she remembered drifting off to sleep and dreaming wonderful dreams of white and red roses covering the mountain, Gladioli too and Gerberas arrayed in lots of stunning and vibrant shades of colour; some two-toned in their exquisite beauty. She remembered how they all smelled and how they swayed in a breeze as she watched them over the man's shoulder before her eyelids grew heavy and closed into dream land. She remembered feeling as if nothing could ever harm her when she was with the person. She wondered if her father had returned or if the man had been Maurice.

She saw a woman walk toward him and join him as they both watched a lovely sunset sink into the sea over the horizon. The woman was Doris. So the man was Maurice, not her biological father. Mel felt a little sad and wondered where her Dad had gone to.

Snapping back to the present moment, Mel shook her head and saw the attic in its entirely once more. She felt groggy but her mind soon cleared as she rummaged in the chest again. Pulling out the big folder, she removed an elastic band and it twanged and rebounded onto the side of her hand. Fully alert now and wincing, she cursed under her breath and rubbed her hand. Opening the folder, it was her entire Family Tree history. Feeling a combination of joy and dread all at the same time, she took the plunge and began reading.

There had been scholars, coal miners, teachers and even very wealthy family members in her past, ancestors who had lived all over the world; many of them mainly in Wales and some not that far away from where she now lived in Porthcawl. It always amazed her how people never seem to stray far from each other; sometimes without even knowing the others were a mere few miles away, to later go on to discover the others' whereabouts. She'd read about things like this and had seen documentaries on TV detailing such incidents and here, right in front of her eyes, the exact same situation had occurred in her past too with her family.

As she scoured every page and its detailed facts, she came across two names that almost caused her to faint where she sat:

Marlene, and also Mrs. Anita Robinson.

Mel was convinced it had either been a misprint or a coincident. She felt herself swaying and her head felt as if it were stuffed with cotton wool. She got up and went to her kitchen to make a strong cup of coffee. She then decided to go to the library to find out more about the two women.

CHAPTER TWENTY-SEVEN

Sifting through countless records she found nothing. She went back home and booted her computer up. Normally she'd enjoy a nice big glass of wine when reading internet articles but this time she thought it best to keep her mind crystal clear. She had to know what was what in all its minute meaning and description and alcohol would just numb her alert brain. She searched for the two names and endless pages came up about other women, not those two. So she dug a little deeper and typed in all sorts of phrases and terms.

After an hour and a half, she landed upon a very old article about Marlene and how she'd enjoyed a string of affairs with married men as well as single ones too. That didn't surprise Mel one bit; she'd seemed the type to behave like that. Several of them had mysteriously died but there was no substance or proof that Marlene herself had committed the crimes. She delved ever deeper into the abyss and found a message forum where Marlene had complained to others that she'd never known who her own mother had been, being shuffled back and forth to many foster homes before moving to Porthcawl and starting a new life.

Mel continued reading and, expecting to find out much more, came to a dead end. She decided to go back up into the attic again and to look in the chest to see if things could be clarified for her there.

Sitting once again on the dusty floor, surrounded by umpteen spiders who were happily building new webs and others munching on their cocooned flies and other insects for lunch, Mel ignored them. As long as they stayed away from her, she could relax. The last thing she needed was to be deep in thought to find herself later covered in sticky silk webbing and crawling creatures trying to find their way into her ear canal or up her nostrils. Ugh!

She pulled more family photographs out and found a single, large oblong-shaped one that was folded. Opening it and peeling sticky clear tape off the edges, she found herself gazing into the serene and lovely face of the old woman in the drawing she'd done in school. At the bottom of the image were the words: Mrs. Anita Robinson, mother of Marlene. Mel's jaw dropped and she now felt like sinking a whole bottle of wine, not just a glassful.

How can this be? Mel asked herself. They never found each other yet lived doors away in the same street?

Looking at another photograph beneath that one, it was a very old photograph of a baby. Mel was afraid to look at the bottom of it but had to. It had the words: birth name, Joy, otherwise known as Melanie, age six months, on it. She felt her head swim with a thousand unanswered questions, all raging and battling to get in front first, the most important ones needing, wanting to be heard and acknowledged. Mel looked underneath that photograph and found ones of a man with dark hair, his face crossed out with some kind of sharp instrument. At the bottom of that photograph were the words: Left. Gone and forgotten.

That must be Dad, Mel thought. She could make out his features underneath the scratch marks. He looked very handsome but unhappy. He was holding a black briefcase and had a long black coat on. Mel stared at the photo and felt angry and sad too that he'd abandoned her. Had Marlene been her mother, Mel wondered. Shudder the thought! Had she been living right next door to her all these years and both of them hadn't realised who was who? A sheet of paper underneath the photographs gave her the answer:

Marlene, biological mother of Joy, the little girl was given up for adoption when a baby, looked after by Doris and Maurice, foster parents, renaming Joy, Melanie.

A document stapled to it explained that if Marlene ever wanted to search for her baby when age eighteen, she could. But she never had. Mel felt so sad inside that all these years had whizzed by and her own mother had not only abandoned her, she'd never bothered to take the time to come and find her.

To end up living next door to each other and not realising who they both were and how their lives were connected, made Mel feel a sliver of sympathy for her nasty neighbour. At least Doris had been a kind and loving mother to her, despite not being blood related to her. At least Maurice hadn't abandoned her like Dad had. Mel felt the need to visit Marlene's grave.

CHAPTER TWENTY-EIGHT

In the cemetery, Mel strolled among the most spectacular and beautiful row upon row of floral arrangements in pots, carefully placed upon countless tomb stones; some made of black granite, others white stone. Others still, made of wood. Gold and silver lettering, etched into the surfaces of many glinted in the afternoon sunlight. Each grave was immaculately kept and free of weeds and litter. A large cemetery, Mel felt that she'd be there for a while. In one of the oldest parts of the grounds, about forty tomb stones were lined up in a row; some were upright, others bent over at an angle. One or two had completely fallen over, exposing holes and cracks in stone surroundings at the base of them.

Mel felt uneasy walking past them, as if a hand could shoot out and grab her ankles, terrifying her in the process. She dismissed the silly thought from her mind and carried on searching for answers.

It was on the very last headstone that she had at least one of her questions answered. Upon it was the name David Williams, father of Joy, estranged husband of Marlene. Mel began to cry. A small photograph of her father greeted her teary eyes and aching heart. The same man in her drawing and the same man in photographs in the attic. She felt ashamed that she hadn't come to his grave before now, even though it hadn't been her fault not to. She sat on the perfect grass and buried her head in her hands until the sun went down.

A graveyard worker tapped her on the shoulder. "Sorry, Miss, we're locking the gates in a bit." He wore muddy trousers and black boots and had a shovel in one hand and rubbed his bearded chin with the other after looking at his watch. In his late forties, well-built and looking tired, he looked how Mel felt: drained, had had enough today and needed to go home.

"Thank you for letting me know, I appreciate it. This is the last place I want to be locked in."

"It's not the dead who can hurt you, Miss. The living, they'll make damn sure they hurt you."

"Oh I believe that one hundred percent, let me tell you. Bye!"

She hurried to the main gates as the man watched her leave.

CHAPTER TWENTY-NINE

Back at her house, she emptied a bottle of wine and sat by the fire in her living room. It was five-forty-two and Ben would be home soon. She decided to have a relaxing and soothing bubble bath.

For twenty-five minutes Mel soaked all her troubles away. The wine had gone straight to her head on an empty stomach and she felt a little sick. Sitting up, she played with fragrant bubbles on the surface of the warm water. Steam covered mirrors on walls. All of a sudden, an invisible finger wrote on one of the mirrors:

Go to the attic again tomorrow. The answers are all there.

Ben let himself into the house and hung his coat up on a hook. Mel dried herself and got dressed. Stepping downstairs, she flung her arms around him and didn't let go.

"You okay? Been drinking?" he said, spotting the empty bottle on the kitchen worktop.

"I've had a rough day."

"Oh?" he replied, lifting her up and carrying her to a settee. He gently put her on it and she sank into softness.

"Yep. I've had a really shitty day actually. I found out a lot of interesting things."

"Doing my job now are you? Come and work for me, I'm looking for another PI."

He sat by her side and stroked her wet hair and then her face. She looked up at him.

"Your eyes are red; have you been crying? What's been going on?"

Mel wondered if she should tell him exactly what she'd found out. She began biting her fingernail on her index finger. He tapped her hand and she stopped. Sitting upright, she held his hand and gazed into his questioning, kind eyes.

"I need you go into the attic with me tomorrow. I've found a few things; family stuff you know? I've also been to the cemetery and found my Dad's grave."

"Oh my poor thing," Ben said, cradling her in his arms as Mel slumped into them like a comforting duvet. "Of course I'll go with you into the attic. If there's anything I can help you with just let me know."

Mel sat bolt upright, her eyes wide open and her mouth too. "Fuck! Why didn't I think of that before? You're a private investigator, you can certainly help me! Do you have access to everything on the internet? And also access to family documents, whereabouts, history of scandals, disappearances from years ago, you know, everything?"

"Well, not everything, but more or less, yes. I have ways of finding out what needs to be found out. I have to be careful though, Mel, if I dig too deeply into matters best left concealed, I can get into a lot of trouble. Police and other authorities have probably even greater access to things than I do and my IP address can be traced back to me. So I'm very careful but yes, I can find out more or less anything you need me to."

"Good. We'll start searching tomorrow. It's Saturday, we've got all day."

"Right then. How exciting! Fancy an Indian take-away tonight? You look famished and you've got to keep your strength up or you'll make yourself ill."

"I'll open another bottle; it'll go very well with a take-away. Thanks!"

Ben watched her go into the kitchen and he wanted to ask her many questions. But they could wait. He gazed at orange and red flames in the fire and felt warmth spreading across his face and hands. He put the TV on and searched up and down on the remote control for a good film they could both watch later. There were many available and he wasn't sure exactly which one to choose so he put the remote control back on a small table and left it to her to pick something when she was ready.

He got up and joined Mel in the kitchen. She looked gorgeous in her white blouse and blue denim jeans. He hugged her and enjoyed her perfume before planting soft kisses on her neck and cheek.

They both enjoyed biryani and nan bread, washed down with wine. Cuddling up together on the settee, they watched one of their favourite comedy films and it lifted Mel's previously sullen mood a lot. She felt as if the harrowing situations she'd encountered earlier were of long ago, not of the same day, and tomorrow would no doubt be even worse, but for now, she could totally forget about it all and just enjoy the evening with her lover, best friend and soul mate. Wind howled outside and old dying trees swayed in the quietness of an empty street, but in the cosiness of her house, it was calm, wonderful and full of life.

As they watched the film, Mel couldn't help but go over in her mind all that had happened in the attic and how the ghost had showed her what needed to be seen. She thought maybe she'd imagined it but it had felt so real. She hadn't dropped off to sleep at all today so it certainly hadn't been some kind of surreal dream. It had been very real. She held Ben's hand and smiled at him. He turned to smile at her and then back at the TV screen again.

She huddled up into his arms and lay her head on his chest, slowly drifting into a well-deserved nap. As she felt herself sink into unconsciousness, like plunging into a black and murky chasm, she felt safe and very much loved. Even if her own mother and father hadn't wanted her company, Ben did. But still, Mel feared he'd too leave her, just as they had once.

There are no guarantees in life and life can change in an instant. But, for now, Mel focused on this moment; held close by a man who genuinely loved her. She felt her head and body relax and sleep captured her.

Ben watched the rest of the comedy film, had some more wine and he too nodded off, joining his loved one as they both astral travelled to the spirit world. Mel often remembered fragments of these visits, but Ben never did. He snored loudly but didn't once wake her. She was in a deep sleep and for once it was dream free.

They both slept all night into the wee small hours of the morning and it was only when the postman dropped letters and leaflets through the letterbox did they wake from their slumbers at eight o'clock the following morning. With hangovers from Hell. Copious amounts of caffeine helped enormously and they both had a few cups before starting their day which would involve many hours in the attic, discovering new things and answering so many of Mel's questions which were eating away at her soul. Ben looked forward to finding out as much as he could about her past. There was a lot he didn't know, a lot he did know but one thing was for sure – he would help her as much as he could because he'd never loved any other woman in his life as much as he loved her.

"Right. Let's get this over with," Ben said to a nervous but excited Mel.

She nodded.

Up in the attic, he shuffled around, checking out everything a bit at a time. Mel resumed searching through the chest. She sat in silence until a shriek from her made Ben jump. He banged his head on a beam and rubbed his head.

"Let me know next time when you're going to do that!"

"Sorry, I didn't mean to startle you. Are you OK?"

"Yes, I'm fine."

"Want me to kiss it better?", Mel replied, a mischievous glint in her eyes.

"Oh, you can do much more than that later, young lady. What have you found?"

"Take a look at this. It's nothing bad don't worry." She handed him an off-white sheet of paper, many years old but text was readable. He took it from her hand and began reading:

A sum of one million pounds to be left to Joy, active in her bank account on her eighteenth birthday.

"Why didn't you look at all this stuff long before now? It's important," Ben said, exasperated.

"I know," Mel sighed, "I could be living in a much nicer and safer area by now couldn't I?"

"With me, hopefully," he said, fishing.

"Of course!"

"I can't believe you let this situation drag on, you should have checked things sooner."

"God, you sound like my mother!" she teased, smirking at him and making a funny face.

"Well I'm not dressing up and wielding a rolling pin and donning an apron. You can forget that. And as nice as my manly legs are, they're never going near your tights or stockings."

"Glad to hear it! Besides, if you start doing all of that, you'll be after my perfume and make up next."

"Never!"

"Nah, my stuff isn't your colour anyway. You have different skin tone to me."

"So why didn't you find out more about your past long before now?"

"I'm not sure. Maybe a part of me didn't want to. Ah well, my fault. Never mind, the future's looking fantastic now. If I'd known who she was I would have spent more than a few minutes now and again chatting to her by her garden gate."

"Did she know who you were?"

"She does now!" Mel replied, shrieking.

"What do you mean, she does now?"

Mel paused for thought and looked at him, a serious expression on her face that he'd never seen to that degree before. He wasn't sure if he wanted to hear what was coming next.

"I've been doing EVP experiments and I've had whispers telling me who killed her. It must have been her voice because the voice told me they knew who was responsible for her death. At first I thought I was imagining it, hearing things you know? The voice is so faint, even with headphones on, but I've seen a ghost often around here who likes to follow me around. I saw it yesterday when up here. It showed me things that I needed to see and things that I needed to discover more about and that's why I'm back up here."

"EV what?"

"EVP. It means 'electronic voice phenomena'. You know? Spirit voices picked up on recording devices and you can hear them when you play back the tape or sound recording file or whatever other device has been used to record it all."

"Ah I see. And you believe in all of that do you?"

"I'm starting to. It's very fascinating to be honest. You should try it sometime."

"Did you recognise the face of the ghost you reckon you saw?"

Mel smiled. "Yes. It's my grandmother, Mrs. Robinson. Mrs. Anita Robinson."

Ben's jaw dropped and he stared at her. His eyes were on stalks. He tried speaking but no words came out. She got up and began screaming with happiness and danced around the attic. He looked at the document again, making sure he'd read what he'd read correctly. Yep, one million pounds was hers alright and he wondered why she hadn't mentioned it before now."

"So you've seen this money in your account then and never thought to mention it to me or to anyone else before?"

"No. Here's the thing. I've an old bank account, a different one that I didn't have much in, just a few quid for a rainy day. The money is with solicitors. I've also got a lot more coming to me which will be put into my main bank account. When I moved home I changed my telephone number and my foster parents didn't know my name, only my birth name. I need you to find me the best solicitors that money can buy. I need you to help me to sort things out properly please because we're talking about millions here and I need to know its secure and safe."

"Of course. I just hope that the firm is still active, otherwise God knows where your money's gone."

Mel stopped dancing and a look of horror filled her face. "Oh no. Where would it have ended up then do you think?"

"I'm not sure yet, but I'll find out for you. Now let's see what other wonderful surprises are lurking in that chest."

Mel looked down into her cleavage and back up at him again.

"You know what I mean. Dirty girl!"

"Ha ha. It's you who has the dirty mind, not me, young man."

"Whatever," he replied, placing one hand on her shoulder, the other in her hand as he twirled her around the attic, singing loudly as he did so. They both felt elated for the first time in a long time and basked in the warmth of each other's company. Her grandmother stood in the corner and smiled at the both of them, her grandfather and foster parents also appeared and joined in the happy show in front of them. Both Mel and Ben were oblivious to their presence, too wrapped up in what they were doing. The ghostly visitors turned and walked through the walls into another realm of existence.

Mel stopped dancing and led Ben by the hand back over to the chest. They sat together looking through its contents of which there were many. Rumbling stomachs reminded them to have something to eat so they took a break and headed for the kitchen for a snack.

CHAPTER THIRTY

In another part of town, by the lighthouse and beach, a woman was screaming for her life at the hands of a violent stranger. Unable to get any sound out due to the sheer weight of him on top of her, he bound her with rope in a vice-like grip. Her heart gave out and she died without freedom. Before he could drag her out to see, he could hear voices in the distance. The killer scrambled across the sandy surfaces into the night.

After an anonymous telephone call to the coastguard, hungry seagulls were soon accompanied by crowds of curious onlookers; a lot of them taking photographs and video footage of the carnage before them. Morbid fascination grabbed others as they stood over the dead, decomposing corpse, partly eaten during the night by all sorts of ravenous creatures. The tide had come in but quite reaching as far as to engulf the body to drag it out to depths unknown.

Ben kissed Mel on the lips and made her breakfast. For a change. She went back up into the attic and he set off to go to work. Monday mornings always got to him after a weekend of fun and relaxation. Well, that weekend hadn't been entirely full of fun and relaxation this time; with the police following him and he potentially getting killed along with the injured man in the alleyway, he felt grateful to still be alive.

He couldn't work out why they hadn't paid Mel's house a visit after the altercation but he wasn't prepared to stay indoors all day hanging around for them. He had work to do and lots of it now that Mel needed him to find out as much as he could about her past and those who were now influencing her future.

As he travelled down a motorway, he wondered what she was reading or analysing up there in that dark and dusty room. He thought about what she'd told him regarding seeing a ghost and it all made sense to him now, the ghostly incidents he'd witnessed too. Fearing an overload of stress had been causing hallucinations and audible sound effects in his tired mind, he felt somewhat relieved that the afterlife really does exist.

As he pondered on bits and pieces, it dawned on him that if the afterlife were real and if she'd truly seen her grandmother, other, many spirits were also out there. Everything he looked at in front of him as he drove down that motorway made him wonder if spirits would suddenly jump out from behind cars in front, or from behind signposts and other objects. With his senses heightened, he felt uneasy and very, very afraid.

Approaching the office, he felt very relieved to see that some staff had got there before him. Being alone in that place gave him the creeps and he didn't need to feel more nervous than he already was. Getting over the dental surgery had been bad enough: months of agony and slow healing had taken it out of him. He could almost feel his immune system crying out for him to take a holiday somewhere; anywhere but Porthcawl. Ironic, a holiday seaside resort and full of happy anticipation to thousands of children and adults alike every Summer, he was beginning to hate the place.

Mel, discovering millions of pounds was exactly what she needed right now. Too much for even both of them to live on for the rest of their lives, a lot of it would certainly secure a lovely new house for them in an even lovelier new place; far, far away from the endless Hell that this town had become. He preferred Heaven to this; not literally, but to be somewhere with her where he'd actually look forward to getting up in the mornings, rather than dreading it and what each day could bring.

He made his way to his desk and caught up with employees and other staff. It was good to be around familiar faces but still, he couldn't help but glance out of the window every ten minutes or so. Surely the police wouldn't come here? Part of him wanted them to; to get it over with. What could they possibly do to him if he was surrounded by other people? He felt safer here than back in Mel's house. He believed that she'd be safe always. She had spectral company a lot more lately and if she really had seen her grandmother then her other relatives would also look out for her and protect her.

As he sat and sipped a fizzy drink, it dawned on him that Marlene and other enemies of Mel's would also eventually manifest in front of her; even if they couldn't harm her, they could sure make her life unbearable. These, and a million other thoughts flashed through his anxious mind. He wondered if any of his enemies made it a habit of popping in and watched him when he worked.

The office had its moments of cold draughts but that wasn't paranormal. The heating system frequently played up. But what about the times his keys seemed to go missing, only to reappear later on? Had he done that himself and had been too tired and careless? What about the odd occasion when he thought he'd seen out of the corner of his eye in his peripheral vision chairs and doors move? No draught could have moved them several inches.

"Hey, Ben, you're deep in thought there. What are you thinking about?"

He turned his head to speak to a colleague but found nobody there at all.

CHAPTER THIRTY-ONE

Mel piled objects and more photographs on top of each other on the carpet beside her. She felt as though the chest was a bottomless pit and was beginning to get bored. That soon changed however when she found what appeared to be a book and an old one at that. Pulling it out of the chest, she examined the jacket of it. It had lots of wear and tear but the spine was still intact, keeping at least five hundred pages bound together. There was no way she was having a coffee break now with this beauty in her hands. She bit her lip and gulped, her heartbeat raging in her ears.

Opening the hardback cover, she read the title and copyright section and noticed the date: 1936. The title: Anita's Diary.

Leafing through to the first page and skipping the table of contents, she began reading. Her grandmother mostly mentioned how she had fond memories of her childhood and how, when growing up in a pretty and secluded rural area in Cheshire had shielded her from too much noise and stress. Being a sensitive, very psychic and with many other paranormal gifts too, she couldn't tolerate being around boisterous people or anyone involved with devil worship or the destructive type of witchcraft. The kind she was taught by her grandmother was whiteness itself; sending spells and positive intentions to friends and family, healing them and carrying out many other good things. Good people, they'd never caused harm to a living soul. But they were very misunderstood; branded witches by gossipers and by people who never bothered to take the time to get to know and to understand these peoples' gifts.

But could Mel be responsible for committing murders and not tell anyone about it? Police suspected everyone now. She was no exception. What about Ben? Or anybody else who lives in Court Street in Porthcawl. What if they've all taken part in killing people?

CHAPTER THIRTY-TWO

Officers back at the station mulled over recent findings, which weren't much to go on anyway. But something caught one of their eyes and he stopped dead in his tracks, dropping a stack of books and discs on the floor. Upon examining Mel's medical and other records given to the station by her psychiatrist, he noticed the tiniest of details but possibly the most significant of them all. She'd not only retaliated and had attacked a woman a long time ago, she'd also stalked and harassed her too; threatening her that if she ever reported it to police, she'd kill her.

The recent – and crucial - information had only come to light when the woman had seen the same psychiatrist and when she was out of the room the woman rifled through her files in an open filing cabinet. Out of curiosity she had to know if Mel had gone to the same shrink; Ben confiding in Alice about it after he'd downed half a bottle of rum.

Naturally, Mel told him everything because she trusted him but when inebriated he didn't think and had blurted it out when he and Alice were discussing him seeking counselling for his drinking problem. He'd mentioned to her that their neighbour and his good friend had sought counselling for matters relating to the past; mainly being adopted and Mel moaning to him on a regular basis that she often wondered if there was something wrong with her that her own mother had never looked for her when past the age of eighteen.

Alice had loved to gossip with Marlene about everyone and everything going on not only in the street but in the whole of Porthcawl too. Elderly Mrs. Anita Robinson had overheard them one day and, although not saying anything at the time, had stored it up in her long memory to deal with at a later date. Ben of course had completely forgotten about even letting slip to Alice about Mel's counselling sessions, and that her mother had given her up when she was a baby.

Alice and Marlene knew a lot about Mel but Mrs. Robinson knew far more about not only her own granddaughter but of those two and just about everyone else too. Living in the area for most of her life, she was excellent at observing and perceiving even the subtlest of matters; piecing bits of information together like a jigsaw puzzle over the years until a fuller picture was obtained.

After her murder, and with little to no family to sort her belongings out, they went to auction for charity. Mel just happened to purchase a desk that had belonged to her and the spirit of Mrs. Robinson was embedded within it and all around it too. That desk is the very same one Mel writes on and sits by, day in, day out. An old Grandfather clock she bought as well; its pendulum swinging back and forth but the time always seeming to stick at the exact same time the pocket watch stopped at. But, unlike the watch which now works after being rewound, the Grandfather clock although functioning every day, loses a minute daily. Mel adjusts it, it initially getting on her nerves, but people become accustomed to things and this was no different. An evening habit lately, Mel simply moves the minute hand a fraction until the time coincides with the time on her computer monitor screen.

Back at the station, the officer picked up dropped items and gathered his thoughts. But before he could get to his telephone to alert others who hadn't come into the station yet, he felt his gun being removed from his trousers and pointing directly at his head. Before he had time to fight the perpetrator off a single bullet ripped through his skull, ending his life.

Crimson liquid ribbons spurted from the back of his head, along with brain sludge and bone fragments. Some lodged in the adjacent wall and most splattered against it before sliding downward like a thick, multi-coloured spewing torrent. He hit the floor like a ton of bricks, dislocating his shoulder. It jutted out at a weird angle. Teeth scattered across the floor, along with tissue and congealing blood.

Smoke danced out of the barrel of the gun. The weapon placed in the officer's hand, footsteps faded into echoes of guilt. Ten minutes later, other officers entered the building before mayhem ensued. Forensics were on the scene within the hour but yet again, they were at a loss for words or understanding as to why they couldn't find one shred of DNA evidence.

The occurrence was plastered all over the newspapers the following morning. The killer read with much interest over the shoulder of a stranger in a newsagent's shop. As they skulked away, they sought out their next hit on their list of people to silence.

Mel had had a relatively quiet morning and weirdly missed the horrendous noise that often came from Marlene's house. Despite the house now being empty, Mel sometimes thought she heard odd noises coming from there. She also still woke at the same time each morning; the exact same time when Marlene used to deliberately wake her up; just for the hell of it.

Mel went outside and sat on a wooden bench in her back garden. Now April, she felt sunshine on her skin and a not so cold temperature in the atmosphere. Still a little chilly though, it was cardigan or jacket weather. She had a fluffy cream blanket wrapped around her shoulders and she sat there checking out many emerging weeds among daffodils; their bright and cheery yellowness lifting her mood from slightly anxious to content.

With Ben back in work more or less full time, she missed their chats over the garden fence. Her book now finished, she braced herself for lengthy editing of it before it becomes published and for sale to the public.

A noise diverted her attention from the flowers and weeds to Marlene's back door. Craning her neck to see around large barrels of rainwater and many tall shrubs and plants, she got up from her bench and walked toward her fence. She thought maybe workmen were in the house, renovating or sorting fixtures and fittings out for selling or giving to what family members Marlene had left.

Mel walked down the full length of her garden and then turned around to get a much better look at her nasty neighbour's back door. Astonished to see that it was not only closed but had a large brass padlock on it, and windows boarded up, she wondered what on Earth had made the noise: a cross between a tap on a window to a shuffle.

Five minutes elapsed and she decided to explore further. With Ben in work and Alice nowhere to be seen anymore, nobody would see her. Getting a pair of new running shoes from out of her shed, she slipped them on and tied laces tightly.

She climbed over a wall and walked along it until she came to Marlene's fence panels. Climbing over one of them, she lowered herself to the ground. Her running shoes sank into mud and horse manure. Even in death, the nasty cow was still upsetting her. Manure for Marlene's roses, it had lain there rotting away for ages, and it stank.

"Oh bugger, my new trainers! I paid a lot for these and now they're ruined," Mel cursed, taking them off and tossing them over the wall. She carefully stepped around the pile of crap and felt crisp, wet grass underneath her feet. It always amazed her how beautiful dew drops looked on blades of grass; like tiny jewels of light and clarity. She felt as if she were walking on water and the tickling sensation on the soles of her feet made her smile. Being very careful not to get any water inside them, she washed most of the smelly crap off her new running shoes with water from a small pond by Marlene's shed, and then she put the trainers back on her feet.

Approaching Marlene's back door, Mel gasped to see that the padlock was open. With no key in it she began to feel concerned that she'd been caught. Workmen were there, she thought.

Mel glanced around. No other neighbours were outside. The coast was clear. She wiped her running shoes on grass nearby. Swallowing hard, she braced herself for whatever was about to happen. Taking out some leather gloves from a pocket, she slipped her hands into them. They were a snug fit and her cold skin warmed up in them, seeing off the cold that had gripped them so fiercely.

Rubbing the sharp end of one of a set of keys in the pocket, she tried the handle on the door. Before she could push the door it opened several inches all by itself. She felt cold all over and her stomach was in knots. What the hell am I thinking? What if the killer is waiting for me and I'm the next one to die in this God-forsaken town?

"You can do it. You're safe. Trust me," she suddenly heard in her ear. Feeling a surge of courage, she pushed the door open fully. There was nobody there.

She must have stood there for what seemed like an eternity, praying that hands wouldn't reach out to grab her, or a rope or knife wouldn't get her either. Her legs began shaking. She felt as if she were teetering on a mound of jelly as she tried to get them to move forward. A strong person by nature mentally, her body felt so weak, as if it could shatter into a million pieces. She was sure she'd have a heart attack from fright if someone did appear right in front of her.

A murder of crows squawked behind her; as if they were enjoying being entertained and were feeding off her fear. Visions of her bleeding in the garden flashed through her mind, and the crows, hundreds of them swaying back and forth on tree branches would feast upon her eyeballs. She blinked.

Stepping into the house, guilt consumed her. What if police officers crept up behind her and put their hands on her shoulders? That alone would make her scream, never mind coming face to face with a murderer. She inhaled deeply and made herself stand as upright as possible. The crows were silent now but wind whistled through keyholes and cracks and crevices in the house and door, sounding much like lots of screaming banshees and creepy ghouls all singing at once; announcing the beginning of another life about to be taken away.

Mel didn't close the door behind her. Walking slowly into the kitchen of a woman who had caused her so much upset; even in death Mel wondered if the ghost of Marlene would come for her. Especially as she was trespassing not only in her back garden but in her actual premises too. Christ, as if that wasn't enough, to be attacked by a malicious ghost and a serial killer on this side of life as well would be the shitty icing on the cake of her dismal life.

Always positive by nature, she consoled herself with the fact that at least on the other side in the spirit world she'd finally get some well-deserved peace and quiet. Well, hopefully anyway. She believed angels existed, and spirit guides too, and felt less worried in the knowledge that they'd keep all spectral bastards away from her. But, putting herself deliberately in a dangerous situation like she was right now, they wouldn't protect her surely?

The wind howled outside and all throughout Marlene's house, causing the back door to slam against a refrigerator and then to close. Mel had two choices: leave right now, or be a brave girl and go forward. Time seemed to stand still as she stood there agonising as to what to do and what course of action was best. She decided to go forward.

"That's my girl," a voice uttered in her ear.

Mel turned a corner into Marlene's living room. Other than a layer of dust covering everything, the place looked tidy and maintained. Power had been switched off and although not dark outside yet, she was certain she saw a shadow dart across the room by a white wall. A sinister feeling hung heavy in the air. Mel likened it to a sensation of holding two magnets, opposing and repelling each other; it was a strange feeling, as if at any moment someone, or something would jump on her and suffocate her.

Nobody knew she was in that house and not even Ben with his expert surveillance techniques and abilities would stop to think that she'd be there and it wouldn't be the first place he'd probably search for her in either.

She sat on a settee. Rubbing her clothing and clapping her hands together, minute dust particles shimmered as they floated upward, outside light illuminating them like many pretty little shards of jewels. She looked at the white wall again. Was she one hundred percent sure that she'd seen that shadow, she thought to herself? Was she hallucinating; a build-up of stress and delusions taking over her life after everything she'd been through? What if I am crazy, she pondered, as she sat there, all her senses heightened?

Feeling thirsty and quite hungry too, she got up and went to the kitchen. All foodstuffs had been removed from inside cupboards and even the fridge was devoid of anything edible or drinkable too.

"Dammit!"

Going back into the living room, she strolled around, admiring and also loathing Marlene's taste in decor and wallpaper pattern choices. Some she loved the look of, others she detested. The thought of tearing the wallpaper off that she liked flitted through her mind but she pushed that thought out immediately. She didn't want anything of the nasty bitch's in her own house. Memories accumulated over years were bad enough; and unlike wallpaper, they couldn't be ripped away and disposed of.

Standing at the foot of the stairs, Mel looked up. A small landing window, stripped bare of curtains loomed above her. Grey skies with countless seagulls searching for their next meal seemed to stretch on forever. Why can't it be nice and sunny today? Mel thought. At least it would lighten the heavy atmosphere. She marvelled at how light and colour could transform a person's mood, as if the weather controlled people; dictating to everyone how they should feel at any given moment.

Mel stepped upstairs. Beautiful floral carpeting covered the stairs; dark blue, covered in tiny little light pink roses. The banister looked as if it had recently been repainted, shining white and with no scratches or unsightly bumps on it. I knew she was a control freak; it's even evident in her house, Mel thought, smirking to herself. Having OCD for many years, she believed that Marlene had had it also. And she hated their similarities.

Approaching one of four bedrooms, she went toward the nearest one and peeked around the door. An old Oak wardrobe stood proudly in a corner. A layer of dust covered everything and insects were happily making various objects their new playground or eating areas; scurrying after others and munching away to their heart's content; much like seagulls, crows and crabs were as they feasted upon a seaweed-covered corpse lying on Porthcawl beach. Another one in a short space of time, police were now at their wits end with plenty of suspects to watch but no actual certified convictions under their belt.

CHAPTER THIRTY-THREE

Forensics were getting closer to catching whoever was disposing of the town's residents however, as the odd stray hair and broken nail were giving them many clues. Computer analysis and fingerprint matches weren't set in stone however; the only culprit they could drag in from the streets to interview were one or two tramps who'd just happened to rummage through the pockets of the deceased.

Two of them had been in trouble with the law years' prior for stealing wallets out of pockets of the living who were meandering around the fairground, but they'd never been convicted of murder. Police let them go; especially as the both of them were relatives. Embarrassed more than grateful that they'd actually caught someone for a crime, they didn't even take statements from them. Let off with a caution, both tramps went on their way; resolving to behave themselves but knowing they wouldn't.

Wind howled outside and salty seawater lashed against window panes as Mel continued wandering around Marlene's derelict home. Every creak of her foot on a floorboard and every voice heard outside of dogs and birds made her jump. Morning turned into afternoon as she took her sweet time exploring the place. She opened several sideboard and desk drawers but they were empty. She stood there and racked her brains for a clue, any clue as to where Marlene would hide something, if she ever did that is.

Stepping into another room, Mel thought she heard a whisper. Standing by a window and feeling a draught on the back of her neck, she put the sound down to the wind through cracks and crevices and the wind squeezing through them. When she heard it again and louder, she began to feel afraid. It wasn't like the other whispers she'd been having from her grandmother on EVP recordings and into her ears from non-recordings and in real time. These were much different; deeper and seeming sinister in their tone.

Straining her ears and closing her eyes, she even held her breath for several seconds and concentrated. It always amazed her how much human hearing heightened when that was all a person focused on, as if all other senses were diminished and lowered in their efficiency. Mel wondered just how many other senses people had that they weren't even aware of.

"I'm still here."

Mel opened her eyes and gasped. Looking around the room, she saw nothing, but so felt a strong presence behind her. With ragged breathing and a heart bashing against her sternum like stormy waves of Porthcawl sea against jagged rocks, she felt open and vulnerable; much like boats bobbing up and down on the water on a watery expanse.

"Did you think you'd heard the last of me, bitch?"

Mel put one hand to her mouth and couldn't move. It was if glue were attached to the soles of her feet, stuck rigid on the carpet. She thought of her Grandmother, and other relatives in the spirit world, angels too, and silently called out to them. Out of the corner of her eye she was sure she'd seen ghostly fingers reaching for her neck. There was nothing she could do but pray that help could come soon. As quickly as the presence arrived, it went away. The previous icy temperature lifted and Mel shuddered.

"Thank you," she whispered. Her loved ones had heard her; she was certain of it.

Turning around, she felt an urge to go into the room she'd just left. Coming face to face with the old Oak wardrobe she'd admired earlier, she felt increasingly drawn to it. Grasping a handle and pulling one of the doors open, although it was empty inside that wardrobe, something – or someone – told her it was far from empty. She pulled the other door open and stared at nothingness for what seemed like forever. She suddenly heard a ringing sound in her left ear. Although it didn't hurt her eardrum, it was high pitched and insistent.

She remembered reading about abilities that spirits have and one of them was that they operate on a much higher and faster vibration than a physical, human body does, and the ringing was evident of this ability. She'd also read that if anyone delves deeper into bringing out their psychic abilities, or mediumship ones, the abilities start becoming much stronger over time and better. She concentrated and imagined her psychic ears opening up more. The ringing changed to a clear and distinct voice. A host of spirit people began speaking to her all at the same time.

"One at a time please," she said.

Silence replaced the voices. Feeling sad, she wondered if she'd stopped it altogether. She was still new at this kind of thing and fine tuning things.

"Please come back. Who are you?" She could smell lemon.

As clear as day, as wind blew through gaps in the window frames nearby, creating a kind of white noise to assist the spirits to be heard more clearly, a very familiar voice softly spoke into Mel's ear:

"It's Doris. It's your real mother. It's Mam."

Mel burst into tears and slumped to the floor. The lemon fragrance had been a reminder of when a little girl and her foster mother had rubbed leaves on a lemon plant growing in her front garden and putting her fingers to Mel's nose. Feeling a mixture of sadness, relief and happiness too, she sobbed into the palms of her hands until she felt all out of tears; drained dry, like a well. Red-eyed and shivering, she wiped her face with the backs of her hands and blew her nose into a handkerchief she took out of her pocket.

"So good to hear you, Mam. So great to know you're there."

"I'm always here, Dad too. You'll see us again. I have to go, I just wanted to let you know that you're protected. Nothing can harm you. See you soon. I love you."

Mel smiled as she looked up. A shimmering, very solid orb floated in front of her before vanishing through the window. It reminded her a firefly she'd seen in Corfu many years ago; along with many other fireflies; like little, tiny glowing flames of light that turned themselves on and off in darkness, like they were showing her the way, much like stars in the sky. She closed her eyes and remembered what her mother's voice had sounded like. It felt like she'd been wrapped in a cosy blanket on a chilly evening, kept warm and safe from the dangers of coldness.

Several minutes later, she got up and went to the big old Oak wardrobe again. There was nothing in it but dust and space. She heard a faint knock on the bottom of it. Crouching down, she tapped on the wood, twice. Two taps came back and replied. Rapping more firmly with her knuckles now, she knocked quite loudly on the wood, ten times in quick succession. There were no replies that time as she waited at least five seconds, counting in her head. On the sixth second however, ten, very loud knocks came back, making her jump.

"Who are you? Mam, have you come back?"

There was no reply.

"Are you a different spirit? Marlene, is that you?"

Still no response to her questions.

"You have to give me a name. I'm new at this and need help, please."

She suddenly heard scratching sounds coming from what appeared to be the underside of the wooden panel at the base of the wardrobe. Maybe a mouse or woodlouse has burrowed its way in there and can't get out, she thought. She had an idea.

Going downstairs to the kitchen, she looked for a cellar or under the stairs area. Finding it behind a door, she searched for a chisel or claw hammer. In the back of the cwtch (Welsh, for under the stairs, where coal or other items used to be stored, and still are in some houses), she spotted a holdall bag with a screwdriver poking out of it. Grabbing the bag, she took it upstairs. Several spiders crawled across her hand. She gently flicked them off and hoped that no more were lurking in the shadows once she put her hand inside the bag itself.

Sitting near the Oak wardrobe, she unzipped the top of the holdall fully and peeled back the top. Scrunching up her face, she looked through half-closed eyes, her body tense. There were spiders in there but they soon crawled out and scurried across the floor in search of holes in skirting boards or wherever they felt safer.

She saw a claw hammer and chisel amongst the tools. Holding them in her hands, she saw Marlene's face in her mind and began to see visions. She was aware of the powers of Psychometry, but didn't realise until that very moment that she had that gift too; of feeling and seeing things of whomever used those very same objects. Like flashes of scenes on a TV screen when fast forwarding using a remote control, Mel saw Marlene in different situations. She tried to slow it down in order to make sense of exactly what she was seeing but couldn't seem to find a way to do that.

Putting the hammer and chisel down on the carpet, she stared at them. The visions went away. Picking them up again, the visions started back up; going right back to the beginning again. She closed her eyes and concentrated. In blackness against her eyelids, she began to see what looked like a movie. In the movie, she could clearly see a little girl, quickly growing up and then giving birth to her own little girl. Then, Mel saw the woman handing the baby over to strangers. She then saw something very strange indeed. The woman's face. It was Marlene. She had her hands wrapped around a man's neck and was squeezing tightly. She then saw two police officers bundling the body into the back of a van and speeding off as Marlene waved goodbye to them before she turned around and walked away.

Time appeared to be speeding up at that point and Mel saw the woman sitting in a confessional box in a church, pouring her heart out to a priest. She couldn't quite hear exactly what she was saying but she definitely heard her birth name, Joy. Tears were streaming down Marlene's face.

The next scene then appeared, that of Marlene working and going about her day. Then the following scene showed her coming home from work and driving and then parking outside a cemetery in Porthcawl. Mel watched in utter fascination as Marlene walked through iron gates and placed flowers upon two graves. Mel couldn't read the details on the gravestones themselves, but she felt the same level of sadness that Marlene had felt at that time.

The next scene in time grew brighter and Mel saw her own street. She saw as if from an aerial view of a bird, looking down upon the houses from that angle. Oh what a great angle it was too, she thought! She could see each rooftop, each garden, even each person that walked around in their house. It was if she had X-Ray vision; it was fantastic.

Her eyes settled on Marlene's house. She could see a man in there, in the bathroom. He was shaving. She couldn't work out who he was as he had a hat on and a dressing gown. Mel wondered if Marlene had had lovers and hadn't told anyone about it, but surely not? Mel's grandmother had known for many years all about everyone and everything going on in the street but whenever speaking to her in the past Mel had never heard of any rumours of Marlene getting involved in sexual scandals. She had seemed the type though at the time; the manner in which she and Alice had often flirted with the gasman or electricity meter reading man.

Mel continued observing the time-travelling visions. She then saw Marlene, who was creeping around outside Mel's own house, much like she had done earlier – yet another thing they had in common. She then saw her speaking with Alice over the garden fence. Marlene was pointing toward her shed at the bottom of her garden and then she put one finger to her lips as if telling Alice to keep quiet about something. She then handed Alice a bag of something, but Mel couldn't see what it was. She suddenly had the smell of what seemed to be sage in her nostrils. How odd, she thought, shrugging her shoulders and waiting to see what else the visions brought. As quickly as the odour came, it went.

The next series of visions depicted Ben in his office. Mel smiled and felt all fuzzy and warm inside. Her heart melted whenever she saw his face and anticipated seeing only good things in the flashbacks. But her smile soon vanished when she saw him hunched over a body, a knife in his hands. He was looking around and a colder than ice expression filled his face. His normally gorgeous and kind eyes now were devoid of any of those positive attributes; they were, at that moment, dead and lifeless. Zombie-like. He didn't seem like the Ben she knew and trusted at all. He had the body wrapped in thick plastic sheeting and was dragging it out of the building, late at night and bundling it into the back of his car. Mel caught a glimpse of the corpse. It looked like a woman, a young one but with blood covering her face it was hard to make out her facial features properly.

He kissed her on the lips before wrapping and covering her face. Eyes full of terror and with her mouth gaping open in mid scream, she'd died quickly by the looks of it, Mel thought.

She was afraid to watch anymore but had to know. She braced herself as the visions changed from one to another in quick succession; each scene in order and imprinted upon time itself. She wanted to know who the woman was but she could hardly go to police and ask them a set of questions. She was already a suspect, Ben too, and the last thing she wanted was to end up behind bars for something she hadn't done in the first place.

There followed another series of images, speeding up now. They showed the police station where she and Ben had been interviewed and the comings and goings of officers doing what they usually do in a typical day. She saw a room in the corner of the building. It had two heavy padlocks securing a large black metal door shut. There were no signs or any indication of what lay inside the room. An officer went back and forth to it throughout the day and slid a small panel open, put something on it and then slid the panel back into the room again. Mel strained her eyes to make out more detail but no more details presented themselves to her.

Views of the beach came next, and in a fabulous aerial view of it, Mel could see what seagulls see each day; waves lapping at the big stone walls by the pier and lighthouse, many species of fish swimming around under choppy water and she could even see people who were sailing on many different kinds of boats and ships. She also saw fishermen casting their nets and, although she couldn't make out what they were talking about with their garbled and faint conversations, the general mood was one of contentment and calm.

What followed then shook her to the core. Over by the base of the big wall by that lighthouse, she saw stone boulders and plastic buoys with lots of thick and heavy rope trailing off from them and attached to countless grey dead bodies. Just beneath the surface of the sea, lifeless faces and many creatures chewing on flesh greeted her observance. Her immediate instinct was to look away but she had to know, needed to know, what came next.

The view shifted over to the centre of Porthcawl's town area. Partygoers lined the streets, waiting to get into clubs full of song, dance, booze and laughter. She recognised some of them; old friends from years ago when she too once joined them in merriment on a good night out on most weekends. A pang of regret took her as she watched them in their excited mood, preparing to enjoy themselves all evening and into the wee small hours.

Time slowed down for a moment as scenes glided from one into the next, bringing her up to the present day. She wanted more, much more, but that was it. She sat there, taking it all in, processing what she'd just witnessed. It all seemed much like a dream state. Unsure anymore if she was really in the here and now or sleeping and having some kind of bizarre dream, she pinched herself, hard. Snapping out of everything, it took her a moment for her eyes and mind to adjust, to realise exactly where she was.

Picking up the hammer and chisel, she rammed the blade of the chisel into the base of the wardrobe. She ripped wood off. It cracked loudly and flew in different directions, missing her face. A transparent plastic bag was stuffed in the hollow. Carefully pulling it out, she put it on the carpet in front of her. Inside it lay an object wrapped in black cloth. It was oblong-shape and weighed quite a bit. It sounded much like pieces of metal, clanging together.

She tore open the bag and peeled back the material. A large pile of gold and silver jewellery, all stacked together and barely held together by sticky tape sat in a pile, glittering and sparkling. Mel felt as though she had stumbled upon Aladdin's cave.

After counting each piece of jewellery; rings, necklaces and watches, earrings too, she then began examining them for any indication of value and authentic markings. Each one was definitely gold, silver too, and some were embedded with many kinds of crystals. On one watch, on the back of it, the initial A.R. stood out. Her grandmother's initials. Mel's eyes widened and she cursed under her breath.

"So, the little bitch has been stealing from her has she? How come police never questioned her about this then?", Mel asked herself. She put everything back into the plastic bag but kept the watch. It was hers now, and she'd hide it in her own house. Police wouldn't find it, Mel thought. She put pieces of broken wood back over the base of the wardrobe and pushed it until it fitted back together. Large cracks showed evidence that someone had been tampering with it but with gloves on her hands Mel felt safe in the knowledge that they'd never suspect her.

She closed the wardrobe's doors and stood up. Sliding the watch inside her jacket pocket, she thought about what to do next. Time was getting on and dark clouds hovered over the street. Wind had settled down somewhat now and Mel felt hungry. She looked around each room in the house in order to hide any signs that she'd been there at all.

By the time she got onto the landing, a human figure wearing a balaclava over their face loomed in front of her. The only thing she remembered before everything went black was how bright green their eyes were, and a familiar scent of aftershave.

CHAPTER THIRTY-FOUR

Mel woke. It felt like hours later but had only been ten minutes in actuality. Through half-lidded eyes she tried to make out what she was looking at. A ceiling. Not the one in her bathroom, this one was totally different. She wondered if she were dreaming, or worse, if she'd been abducted by aliens, having watched so many sci-fi films and documentaries about it. A pain in her head soon reminded her that she was far from dreaming. She was bound and gagged in a bathtub, still in Marlene's house.

She was alone, shivering and gagged. She tried moving her hands to pull the gag off, but couldn't. Her gloves had been removed and she couldn't feel them any longer. Her fingers clawed at metal beneath her and her shoulders ached.

Straining to listen, she couldn't hear any sounds other than her own rapid breathing and pounding heart. An anguished cry escaped the corners of her mouth. Panic began to set in quickly. Every tiny creak of wood settling in the house and every little droplet of water landing on a window pane opposite, made her jump and feel sick to her stomach. Get a grip, she thought, trying to calm herself down. Her heart was racing. It reminded her of a hare she saw once, years ago when driving up a leafy country lane in the dark on the way home from a cinema. In the glare of her car's headlights, its eyes were wide open and the creature had sat as if frozen in time. She felt much like that hare lying there. An empathetic person by nature, she completely understood now exactly how helplessness truly felt. But she wasn't a hare. She was a very strong woman mentally and psychologically and had overcome terrible things in her life that most people would find too daunting to cope with.

Wriggling, she managed to slide one hand out of rope gripping her wrists together, and then she pulled her other hand out. Keeping still for a few moments, just in case, she lifted her body upward a little to see if the person was still there. She was sure she was alone.

Her stomach muscles ached. She slumped back down into the bath. Staring at the ceiling, she thought of her next move. Although only living yards away next door, she felt as though she was miles away and felt grateful that she wasn't. It could be worse, she thought. She wondered if she was actually dead. Often reading that lots of people after sudden physical death weren't aware that they'd died and wandered around, carrying out the exact same movements in a situation that was stuck on rewind, play and forward like in a movie's moment being watched over and over again in a loop, she prayed that her situation wasn't like that.

Mel waited for a little while longer and, satisfied that she was indeed still alive; especially after pinching the skin on her hand with her fingernails of the other, she breathed an enormous sigh of relief.

Removing the rope from beneath her, she tried pulling it in front of her body. Pins and needles were shooting up and down her arms and across her shoulders but there was enough feeling in her limbs as circulation started returning. She ached all over and felt years older than she was.

Coiling the rope around in her hands, she placed it in her pocket. If she had to defend herself with it if the attacker came back, she wouldn't hesitate – despite knowing them.

Pushing herself upward into a sitting position, she waited until the grogginess cleared from her mind. Concussion is a serious matter but Mel believed that all of her mental senses and clarity were still intact. A large black spider crawled over the ledge of the bathtub. She watched how it attempted to grip the slippery surface with its tiny feet, sliding downward a few centimetres before climbing back upward again. Feeling much like that spider, Mel knew she was a born survivor who could get over any obstacle; no matter how daunting it seemed to be at the time.

She continued observing the creature. Behind it, it dragged a single strand of silk, followed by lots of strands of silk that were expertly wrapped around a fly. The spider yanked its meal behind it and tried once again to travel down the slippery slope into the bathtub. It didn't seem bothered at all that a human being was watching it, fascinated.

Mel left the creepy crawly to it as she hoisted herself out of the bathtub. Her movements caused vibrations, making the spider plunge into the bathtub, swaying and floating on its silk rope, its cocooned dinner now in front of it. The spider landed on the soft casing before scurrying off down the plug hole into murky depths.

On wobbly legs, Mel steadied herself by putting one hand on a wall as she tiptoed across carpet and onto the landing. Placing both hands on a banister, she looked over and down the stairs. Turning her head to the left and then to the right, she could neither see or hear anything untoward. Her heart was calming now and circulation fully back in her limbs, even though her head felt as if it were stuffed with cotton wool.

Her stomach growled. She put one hand over it in an attempt to quieten it. Satisfied that nobody was in the house at all, she went back into the bedroom where the big old Oak wardrobe was. Slivers of wood showed evidence that she'd been looking in there, but the hammer and chisel had gone!

She sat on the carpet and tried to prise the wooden panel off the base but it wouldn't budge. Snapping a fingernail, she couldn't prevent a scream of pain from leaving her mouth. Blood oozed out of her nail bed. Some had smudged on the wood panel. She wiped it off with her other hand and then wiped that on her jacket. Cursing, she stood up and kicked the panel. It cracked open. The contents had been taken away.

Out of the corner of her eye, Mel was sure she'd seen a shadow passing along a wall. She turned her head but it had gone. Turning to look back down at the panel again, she came face to face with a male ghost. He looked deeply into her eyes and rather than scream, she felt strangely calm; calmer than she'd ever been in her life. He had skin and an outline that appeared to glow almost, and the kindest and most beautiful eyes and smile she'd ever had the privilege to see.

"Mel, I'm one of your spirit guides. You're safe. Go and look over there by the bookshelf. You'll discover what you need to know. I'm always by your side."

"What's your name?" Mel asked, unable to take her eyes from his face.

"Henry. I have to go for now but I'll return very soon. I'm speaking with Doris and her husband. They're very proud of you and are helping you more than you know. We all are and there are many of us watching over you."

"I've always felt that I wasn't alone. All my life I've seen, heard and known things but wondered if it had been my imagination."

"No, it's real, Mel."

She glanced at the bookshelf. "Which book do I look at?"

"You'll know," Henry replied.

Mel looked back to him but he'd gone. Staring at a window, her eyes adjusted in the light. The sun was going down and she didn't have much time.

"Thank you," she whispered.

She felt a touch on the top of her head, like invisible fingers stroking her hair. Walking over to a large bookshelf, she sighed. Before her hand so much as touched one of the books, a large, leather-bound one moved. Sliding it out and holding it in her hands, she admired gold-coloured lettering on the front of it.

PRIVATE INVESTIGATORS' SURVEILLANCE SKILLS.

Mel opened the jacket and leafed her way to the first page. It had handwritten notes jotted down in margins and as she scanned a page she came across the name 'Ben'. She threw the book across the room. It slammed against a wall and then lay on the carpet, one or two pages torn and the hard jacket bent at a corner.

"The little deceiving bastard!"

On that page were details of houses in the town to watch. Ben had also written down information relating to her house too. But what really hurt her was what he'd written about her herself:

Gullible, will be easy to fool. Worth a lot of money.

Rage consumed her. She pulled the bookshelf and it fell toward her. Jumping out of the way, she watched as it cracked and made a hell of a din as it landed on the carpet; books squashed, some flying in different directions, landing all around her. One book had slammed against the wall, damaging plaster. Mel was astonished to see that it hadn't just damaged the plaster, a noticeable hole was now actually in the wall itself.

She climbed over the bookshelf and pushed her hand into the hole. Feeling around, cobwebs and dust was all she could find at first. Just before she pulled her hand back out, her fingertips brushed past what felt like a hard square object. She felt it, trying to work out exactly what it was. Grabbing it, she pulled it toward her. It was a small camera. Examining it, she was surprised to see that it still worked as she pushed a small switch on top of it.

The camera whirred into life and she checked to see if there were any pictures on it. Oh, there were plenty! As she viewed each one, her rage grew into full-blown fury. She turned the camera off and put it in her jacket pocket before heading downstairs. The back door was locked, so she smashed a window and climbed out. Explaining the situation to the police if they caught her would be a tricky one but after what she'd just seen on the camera and read in the book she was now well past caring what anybody thought – especially Ben. Running down the garden and climbing over a fence back into her own again, she flew up her garden path, let herself into her house and thought about what to do next.

CHAPTER THIRTY-FIVE

After some food, a hot shower and change of clothing, Mel sat at her kitchen table going over her recent ordeal. Other than rope marks on her wrists and a sore head, she was fine. She came to the conclusion that despite having spirit protectors, they allowed her to have rope burns and other consequences because she'd put herself in a dangerous situation on purpose and they couldn't override her right to have free will, but they had minimised her suffering. Plus, any physical trauma could be evidence if she reported it to police.

Her phone showed several missed calls from Ben and one or two texts asking if she was OK and that he'd be home later after work. She ground her teeth while reading them, imagining him in rope bindings and he enduring what she'd just gone through. She felt sick to her stomach that someone she'd trusted for so long could even think of putting her through what she'd just gone through.

With no time to change the locks in the doors, Mel grabbed her handbag and laptop and left her house before driving for miles until tiredness set in. She checked into a hotel and slept for nine solid hours, not even her dreams waking her.

She checked her phone again. There were so many messages now and missed call alerts but she refused to turn the sound back on, on her phone. Fuck him, she thought, familiar anger rising in her heart.

After breakfast, she sat at a table watching people; wondering if they could trust each other too, if they had dark secrets as well. Shaking her head, she went back up to her room. Watching TV and drinking coffee, she took her laptop out of its bag. Booting up, she thought of what to search for to discover answers to so many questions running around in her mind. Normally a patient person by nature, now was not the time to sit waiting for a bloody computer to start.

"Come on, you useless pile of crap! Hurry up!"

She opened up an internet browser page and began typing in search phrases regarding how psychopaths' minds worked, how she could report a crime without getting found out by others, how to move away at a moment's notice and to change one's identity and a few more things she needed to know. She couldn't go back to her house just yet and certainly not to Marlene's, yet an increasing needing to know what else could possibly be hidden in that wall was all she could think about.

She remembered how wonderful she'd felt when her male spirit friend had reassured her that she would always be safe and she also remembered the little spider and how it found its way over a very large obstacle. And like that spider and the spirit too, Mel knew in her heart that she also had the capability to see all, know all and to conquer anything that life threw at her. She could feel herself becoming much more powerful than she'd ever been up to now. And she liked the feeling and decided there and then in that hotel that from that moment on she vowed to turn the tables on anyone who had been playing with her mind and trying to ruin her life.

Mel suspected who had been murdering people in Porthcawl and she thought it about time she had a go at catching them for herself before they tried to snuff out her life. And she was going to start with Ben. There were others, and she was certain he was connected to them all in some way and had probably been for some time.

CHAPTER THIRTY-SIX

Ben returned to the street after work. He went to Marlene's house. Finding that Mel wasn't there, he stared at the hole she'd made in the wall and his heart sank. She wasn't in the bathtub and a trail of dirt across the floor and down the stairs let him know loud and clear that she'd managed to free herself and get out.

He thought maybe she'd gone next door to her own house. He thought of things to say and hoped that her knock on her head would render her memory useless. He felt bad that he'd had to make her unconscious but with several million quid coming to her, he had ways to persuade her to part with it, and he was certain she'd listen.

He let himself into her house with a key she'd given him and listened carefully as he closed the door. With senses heightened, he listened for even the tiniest sound. There was nothing. Racing upstairs to their bedroom, he checked her wardrobe. Things had gone missing. Grinding his teeth, his gum still hurt from previous dental surgery work on it. Cursing, he ran around the entire house looking for her. He even searched the attic.

Racing back downstairs, he was in no mood to mess about. Maybe she'd gone to the police station, he wondered. He took out his phone and called the station.

"Hi, is Mel there please? She's not here at home. I'm just curious if she's there at all."

"Who is this? Ah, Ben, I recognise your voice. No, I'm afraid she's not. If she does call in though I'll ring you back."

"Okay. Thanks."

Ben placed his phone back in his pocket and went to his car. He sent her text messages after ringing her and his calls going straight to voicemail. He also left a message asking where she was and that he urgently needed to speak to her. He waited a while longer and, fed up, he thought of plan B.

Sitting there for several minutes, he scanned the street. Although she spoke to and got along well with almost everyone, he wasn't in the right frame of mind to knock on doors. Time was of the essence.

He drove to town to look for her. It was dark out and as he sped up a relatively quiet road to speed things up, he slammed on the brakes. A white gathering mist loomed in front of him. He'd seen mist before but this was something else. It seemed to be forming a shape all by itself. The thermometer reading on the dashboard of his car indicated that the temperature outside and inside was dropping. A lot.

After about two minutes, he was astonished to see that the mist was now in the form of a human shape. It was so luminescent; glowing almost. He also felt as though he wasn't alone inside the car either. This is ridiculous, get a grip, he told himself in thought. He glanced to his left and then to his right. No people were around. No physically living ones anyway.

The shape slowly moved toward the right side of the vehicle. He couldn't take his eyes off it for a moment. He'd never witnessed anything quite like it and felt that it was one of those freaks of nature; a chance in a lifetime kind of thing, never to be seen again. Taking out a small camera from his jacket pocket, he snapped several photographs of the apparition.

Looking at the photographs on the camera's LCD screen, there wasn't anything strange in the first one. The second one either. But on the third one, what he saw shook him to his very core. Gasping, and with eyes wide open, to his horror he realised that he was looking at a face. Blinking a few times, he shook his head. The face was still there; he wasn't imagining it. Before he could look at the fourth picture, there was a loud bang on his window.

Jumping, he looked up and into the very same face. It was Marlene. And she was far from happy, as usual.

He rolled down the window, his hand shaking like a leaf. Speechless, all he could do was mouth words. He felt sick to his stomach. Putting up with her in person had been bad enough but she confronting him in ghostly form was far, far worse.

And just as she'd appeared in that misty ectoplasm before solidifying, she dissipated into the night until there was no sign of her anymore. Ben just stared at where she'd stood. He rubbed his eyes and looked again. Feeling tired most days, he convinced himself he'd hallucinated.

Continuing on his journey to town, he kept looking in his mirror. Other than one or two cars trailing behind him, there was no spectral beings following him.

He took out a mint from its open wrapper and popped it into his mouth. Peppermints often calmed his stomach whenever stress got the better of him. Sucking it, he enjoyed its soothing minty freshness on his taste buds.

Getting into town, he breathed a huge sigh of relief. Hunger pangs stabbing his gut and growling like a monster, he headed for the nearest fish and chip shop. They also sold meat kebabs. He had one of those. And a hot coffee in a disposable plastic cup with a lid. Enjoying his supper in the cosiness of his car, the apparition he'd seen played on his mind.

"Don't be so stupid. You imagined it," he said to himself as he picked out bits of meat from his teeth with the tip of his tongue. His stomach satisfied now and no longer growling, he felt warm and content. It was a pleasant night and winds had died down. He could smell the sea air and he closed his eyes, memories of childhood and walking along the beach washed over him.

When he opened his eyes again, he almost had a heart attack. Marlene's ghost was sitting in the back seat of the car and she was just staring at him. She'd solidified fully now and there was an icy coldness all around Ben, clinging to him despite the fact that he was wearing a thick jacket.

"What do you want from me?" he spluttered, almost bringing his meal back up. His guts and chest felt heavy pressure and waves of nausea were churning away.

"What do I want from you?" Marlene replied. Her voice was exactly the same but her 'physical' appearance was strangely better than it had been when she was alive in physical form before keeling over, he life force ebbing away from her.

"Yes. What do you want from me?"

"Now, now. You know what I want from you. Don't be such a silly boy. Her spirit protectors won't let me kill her, but you can. By the way, I was bloody furious at first, my life snuffed out, but when I woke and learned how much better it is on the other side and that I can do so many more things, and am looking better too, I soon got used to the idea. And now I don't want to come back. They asked me you see. They asked if I wanted to return to my body and life and I said no. I'm in a place where people like me stay. It's a bit like a solitary confinement cell in prison. There are others like me there, but I'm promised that if I ever feel remorse for what I've done to people on Earth over the years, I can meet up with my relatives and friends in higher places. My guides pass on message to them from me."

Ben nodded and stared at his car's steering wheel. He looked back up at her and then turned around. To see her sitting there, it was almost as if she wasn't physically dead at all. She looked three-dimensional and very much alive.

"They keep wanting me to go to the light and to be a better person," Marlene continued, "but I am not going anywhere what I want done in this town is done properly and completely. Do you understand? Now get on with it, and do it. I'll be watching you. I have such an advantage over here, Ben. I can see you all and can be wherever I damn please at any time."

"I will do it, Marlene. I'll make sure it's done by tomorrow," he replied.

As she drifted away again, Ben turned back around and shuddered. Noticing in the mirror that the colour in his face had drained from healthy to a greyish white, he waited until he felt better. The coffee helped a lot. Thank God for coffee, he thought. He sipped every mouthful slowly, savouring its stimulating properties. He needed all the energy he could get. He had a very busy night and morning ahead of him and didn't want to delay matters any longer.

CHAPTER THIRTY-SEVEN

Mel had a shower in the hotel. She was enjoying herself and felt glad that she'd taken a little break, even if it was to avoid being murdered. She'd still put a heavy chair up against the locked door and had wedged the top of it underneath the door handle and the rest of the chair had been positioned at an angle.

She dried herself with a nice big fluffy white towel. Sitting on the edge of a bed she began drying her hair with a hair dryer before getting dressed and putting make up on. She felt refreshed and alert.

Half an hour later, she walked to a public telephone box. Calling a local police station, she waited for the dial tone to stop.

"Hello. Police, how can I help you?"

"Oh hi. My name is Jennifer," she lied.

"Hi. How can I help you, Miss?" a man asked.

"I don't know where to begin to be honest. I've been attacked and kidnapped but I've managed to escape."

"Where are you now?" the officer inquired.

Mel paused for thought.

"I've left my house and am miles away. I need to report a crime, well, several actually."

"Several?" came the reply.

"Yes, several," Mel said, her heart hammering in her chest.

"Then come along to the station. We're in Court Street."

"Yes, I know where you are. I'm afraid that I can't do that."

"But Miss, you must. Unless this is a prank call of course. You are still being recorded, even if you are calling from a public phone box."

"The problem is though you see officer, police officers where I live know the man who did this to me and I'm not sure if they are in on things too and I'm not sure if your officers know him as well. So, do you see my predicament?"

"I do. But you have to report this officially. You have to come in and give a statement. Whether we know this man or not, if you don't report your crime how would you feel if he then went on to do this to someone else?"

"I've already thought of that. My life is in danger though, officer."

"Well I've been an officer for decades and I can guarantee you that you are safe."

"This man is a private investigator. He has ways of finding people. He can find me too if I report this crime. He has connections to local officers in my area and I'm not sure if they're as corrupt as he is too."

"Look, bring someone you know with you and they can sit in the interview room with you when I take your statement if that reassures you. Everything will be fine."

"I'll come in tomorrow."

"Make sure you do, Miss. Or we'll be looking for you, never mind that man looking for you."

Mel ended the call. She stood opposite the hotel and thought of who to take with her. She had friends but they lived miles away and wouldn't be able to get to her in a matter of hours. It was approaching midnight and she felt as though she didn't have a friend in the world as she watched strangers through windows, laughing together, chatting and drinking. Some were dancing along to music from a live band. She remembered being like that herself years ago and missed it. She wasn't old but felt it right at that very moment.

Strolling back into the hotel, before she had a chance to get to her room, a man smiled at her. She recoiled instantly, her eyes searching his for questions or threats. He flashed another smile and removed his hand. He appeared to be well groomed and decent enough but Mel was taking no chances. Almost everyone she'd ever trusted in her life seemed to either let her down, lie to her, die or be in their own little world rather than wanting to be in hers when she needed them the most.

"I'm sorry. I didn't mean to startle you, Melanie."

"That's okay. I'm a little jumpy lately," she replied, her shoulders relaxing as she noticed lots of people behind him, chatting away happily with each other. She turned to walk further into the hotel, to the Bar to get a drink. Stopping halfway, she leaned in and whispered to the man: "How do you know my name?"

"Allow me to introduce myself. I'm Mr. Morgan. Roy Morgan. I've been watching police in Porthcawl for many years and when you and your gentleman friend were in the station recently, I later read your file and statement."

"You can't do that. That's breaking the law on so many levels, Mr. Morgan!"

"Not necessarily. Although I'm not a police officer, I used to be one. Allow me," he continued, pointing to the Bar, steering her there by her arm, gently.

Mel fought against her instincts as curiosity took over. She joined him in a seating area as they waited for their drinks to be prepared. She watched every move he made and never once let him touch her glass. Sipping, rather than downing her drink in the speed she normally would, she hung on his every word. He looked a very imposing man, but had kind brown eyes. They say the window to the soul are the eyes and unlike Ben, who often had shifty-looking ones, his were soulful, and honest-looking. There was something about him that drew her to him like a magnet. Although a very handsome specimen of a man, she didn't feel remotely sexually attracted to him. Rather than passion burning in her body and mind, it was increasing intrigue.

"I'm a private investigator. That man you know as Ben, well, I used to work for him. I had a different name, then. He thinks I'm dead now of course but I'm not. You're not seeing a ghost, Mel, so don't worry about that for a minute. I had to pretend you see. When I discovered too many corrupt things about him, and the way he threatened me if I ever disclosed to police what I'd found out about him, I thought it far easier to just fake my own death. Oh I didn't used to look like this. I've dyed my hair and grown a beard and moustache. Even my own mother wouldn't recognise me, if she were still here."

"What corrupt things exactly?" Mel spluttered, wiping her mouth.

"Oh, this handsome middle age man you've fallen for? He's killed one woman that I know of; a secret lover of his. He's rifled through all of your life's documents. Everything. He's well connected with corrupt police officers, and he's been behind many clients mysteriously disappearing or friends and relatives of theirs being murdered but situations were made out to be accidents. And there's much more too. You see, even before you and he were interviewed in the station, long before he read your files there...he's already seen it all before."

"How did you find this out? You weren't in that interview room."

"No, I wasn't. But the officer who spoke with you is my brother, and he's what you call, how can I put it...?"

"A mole. A spy?"

"Bingo! Yes, he is."

"And none of the others suspect?"

"Mel. You don't seem to understand. Every officer in that station is involved with every kind of crime you can imagine. But it's Ben I'm after. Revenge and all that. He didn't just do me out of a job, he stole my life. He didn't sack me, no, but he may as well have done. Fortunately for me though, I come from a wealthy family. I only took the job on to monitor him. He thinks he's such an expert. He's an amateur," Roy said, laughing as he anticipated her reaction.

"The bastard. The complete and utter callous, lying bastard!"

"Oh he's that alright, Mel. But there's worse. Are you sure you want to know more? I can stop right now if you decline."

"No. I want to know everything. Tell me, please."

Roy finished his drink and got another one. He enjoyed a Welsh pint of beer and thought it was the best beer he'd ever tasted. He used to make some at home, wine too, but preferred to drink with his lifelong friends in his favourite pub. Mel was still only halfway through her drink. She needed to be fully alert. Although having a good memory, alcohol erased some of it and this was way too important to lose.

Hours crawled by as he told her all that he knew about Ben; how he'd laundered money over the years, how he'd blackmailed his lover, Jan, to see him, and if she refused he'd post false allegations to her family's house about her. He even had a vasectomy a long time ago and didn't mention it to his own wife even. Now with Jan murdered in cold blood, and with him coming after Mel now, Mel felt so stupid for trusting him in the first place. All those hours of chatting over the garden fence, going into town with him, getting along well with each other and finally having him make love to her; she felt an anger she'd only ever felt once in her life.

To be close to another woman's husband was bad enough, but for him to lie to her, knock her out and leave her alone in a bathtub? The rose-tinted glasses she'd worn were now well and truly shattered. Beneath his good looks, money and charm, he was a down and out asshole and the lowest of the low.

The more that Roy told her about Ben, the less she felt she'd ever known him in the first place. Like a stranger to her now, it was if she were viewing him and scrutinising him through binoculars from many miles away. She felt like a used, cheap whore, and he nothing better than the crap on the soles of her shoes. She fought back welling tears in her eyes as Roy revealed awful things about a man she'd even considered marrying one day. With every revelation Roy came out with, Mel felt so shocked that she'd lived next door to someone like this for years and had never suspected a single thing. With so many people in the hotel, she decided to have another drink. And then another. She was going to be a very rich woman soon and for once she let her hair down and celebrated. Ben wouldn't get one single penny.

CHAPTER THIRTY-EIGHT

Mel woke in her hotel room. Sitting up in bed, still fully clothed, she rubbed her head and squinted as sunlight hurt her eyes. Memories flooded back as she recalled the previous evening and what Roy had told her about Ben. She couldn't remember all of it at first but as the morning sailed by, fragments popped into her mind.

Finding Roy's card in her bag, she decided to telephone him. They both arranged to meet in a nearby park. Although cold out, Spring sunshine momentarily warmed her freezing heart as she felt glad to be alive at least; even if it wasn't in the company of Ben himself but rather in the company of a stranger who was helping her piece together a very complicated puzzle. A puzzle of her own life. She felt glad to be away from being cooped up in her house, worrying about murders and locking her door. But at all times she made damn sure she was never totally alone with this man. No longer trusting a single soul anymore, she sat in the park and waited for his arrival.

Feeding ducks with torn off pieces of a bread roll she'd had in her room with breakfast, she gazed at them and how carefree and happy they seemed. How she wished she could be like one of them with not a care in the world. She longed to be looked after and to have a friend, a real friend who looked out for her welfare, just like those little ducks who would never go hungry. But she was hungry for returned trust, loyalty and genuine friendship. She wondered if she'd find it in this stranger, but soon dismissed that hopeful thought from her mind. No, she'd be perfectly fine on her own.

She was realising that, slowly, that she could depend on herself and didn't need anyone else in her life. She was strong. And she had her ghostly family to watch over her. At least they were there for her to confide in. They could be trusted implicitly, she believed.

Seconds later, she felt an invisible presence sitting by her side as if a person was leaning against her shoulder. Closing her eyes, she attempted to tune in and to get a feeling about what kind of energy they had. She'd read that if you ask spirits to leave a 'calling card', some sort of sign that it is them, she'd be able to work out who they were; that's if they didn't visibly show themselves first.

Mel sat there a while. An invisible hand rested on hers and she felt as if the sun had risen in her soul; illuminating the darkness inside of her, scaring off dangerous shadows and all that has motive to harm the deepest parts of her very being.

"Hi, Nan."

"I told you that you'd always be safe. Before he had a chance to finish you off I put a thought into his mind so that he'd leave that room. You got out of your rope bindings and now you're here. See!"

"Thank you. I can see that now. You all see so much more on the other side don't you?"

"Yes, we do. We can be anywhere at a moment's notice and we can even be in two places at once. We're pure energy. Oh, you've no idea how wonderful it is to be free of aching old bones too. And eyesight, wow! It's so much better over here."

"Don't you mean up there, Nan?"

"No, Mel. We're all around you. It's a thin veil that you cannot see, but we see it. And we can cross it anytime we like."

"I see. It sounds amazing. I sometimes wish I were there."

Mel felt the hand tapping hers. She looked over and, although not seeing a face, she sensed that the old woman who loved her dearly, wasn't happy. Just as she'd done in physical life when Mel was younger, her Nan tapped her hand back then whenever she'd done something wrong, she was doing it now.

"It's not your time. You have a life to live over here on this side. Time doesn't exist over here. What is one day to you in your twenty-four-hour clock time, it's a mere blip in time to us."

"Do you know when I'm going to die? People are dropping like flies in Porthcawl. How can I go back home?"

"Soon. You can return soon. Your family, friends, guides and I are working to make sure that those in Porthcawl committing these murders, will be sorted out. Karma never escapes ones like these you know. Oh no, it always catches up with them, Mel. Sooner or later. But I know one thing for sure; you are going to be okay. Always."

"Who is that man, really? The one who spoke to me last night. Is he to be trusted?"

Mel nearly fainted where she sat at her Grandmother's next words:

"He's one of your spirit guides. How do you think he got into the locked interview room and in other places?"

"Why is he my spirit guide though? He used to work for Ben," Mel replied, gripping her Grandmother's hand.

"You think just because he used to associate with that corrupt man that he is like that too? No. We each make our own choices in this life, Mel. Roy's a good man through and through. He used to know your father too. He's been telling you the truth. Me, and your mother, Doris, and your father, Maurice, we listened in and we know without a shadow of a doubt that he's a good person. You can trust him."

"But if he's dead, how did he manage to finish his drinks? How is he seen by people here on this side?"

"We can materialise whenever we choose to, Mel. Some are better at it than others. We blend in much more than people here on Earth realise. He's got a very strong energy inside of and around him and that's how he can appear to you and others in a three-dimensional form. As far as being dead, in his eyes he never views himself as being dead at all. He's quite a funny chap. He's never lost his sense of humour despite all he's been through. Maybe that's why he's drawn to you, because you remind him of himself and your inner strength is like his is too."

"I always felt I wasn't alone. I've wondered about spirit guides and protectors all my life. If its his energy I've felt throughout my life, its always felt warm and friendly. I've never felt scared during the many times he's been around me."

"And that's how it should be. I'm glad you feel this way."

"Does he need my help to solve these crimes?"

"Yes, he does. He can do a lot but together you can do anything, and far easier too."

"We're a crime-busting team then. Cool."

"You are. He's told me that your new novel will do very well too, if that means anything to you."

Mel's eyes lit up. Little tears collected and gathered in the corner of her eyes, ones of pride and joy. She felt choked up and couldn't speak for a moment but her smile shone brighter than all the suns in the Universe.

"By the way, Mel, you have a lot more than one or two guides. They pop in and out of your life to assist you with many different things. You can call on them at any time you know. Try the EVP thing with them, see what happens. It's very important too, if you want to hear their voices louder, to put a fan on and also your TV in the background, or do EVP's near running water. It's white noise and amplifies their voices. You'll hear us at a proper volume then you see."

"I will. I'm getting into that bigtime. It's very interesting. I thought I was imagining it the first time I heard one but then I realised I'm not. I've even begun to hear spirits with my actual, physical ears lately."

"You're developing your abilities nicely. Keep it up. Few people on Earth even know about it or are aware of it. If only they'd try. They'd get a lot of their questions answered and would have hope, not despair. They'll see their loved ones again. In fact, their loved ones, even pets too, are often around, visiting them. Some can see or sense them, some can even hear them via clairaudience, with their physical ears without the aid of electronic equipment and headphones. You've reached that stage and it'll get much louder one of these days."

"Will any of my other senses develop? Clairvoyance and the other 'Clairs'?"

"You have them all but they need bringing out more, fine-tuning. Wait and see. All in good time," the female replied, winking at her and smiling a knowing smile. "I've got to go. I'm needed back Home."

"Thank you for everything."

"No, thank you. Now go get 'em for us. We'll help you find a way to put the bad guys where they belong. And as for your birth mother, Marlene, I'll personally make sure that she doesn't get to you from where she is. Just because she didn't want you, we all did. I couldn't tell you any of this, it would have traumatised you too much and possibly altered your destiny, but I always kept an eye on you in the street and you were always so kind to me."

"It's what we do now that counts, Nan. I've always felt close to you and even closer lately. It's funny how death can make us realise how much people truly mean to us isn't it?"

"We never really die, my sweetheart. Just physically that's all. I'll show you when it's time exactly who took my life. You need time to think all of this over first. You've been through a lot."

"What happens after that? How long will it take?"

"You'll know. We'll show you. We have our ways on the other side. Just rest assured that bad people never get away with what they do."

"Ah, karma! Yes, I've always believed in that too."

"See you soon, my precious child."

"Bye, Nan. I love you."

"And I love you too. Always."

Mel watched her beloved Grandmother vanish. The loving energy present was unmistakable and so tangible. Their bond crossed all barriers; seen and unseen, time neither existed or didn't exist, two separate worlds merged into one in that very moment in eternity. Mel wondered why now? Why not years ago when she wondered for a long time if there was anything after physical death? Maybe the timing wasn't right, she thought. Now though, when her own life was threatened, it was as if help arrived at exactly the right time, when she needed it the most. She wondered, now, if she had a very good reason to be here on Earth; if she had a purpose, one that would not become clear until later on. She sat there and pondered on this and many other things until tiredness took over her.

CHAPTER THIRTY-NINE

Fishermen had a good catch of fish that weekend. One of them was sure he'd seen a face at the top of the lighthouse through a window, but he wasn't certain. Working long hours into the wee small hours of the morning some weeks, he came to the conclusion that he'd imagined it. He hadn't though...

The coastguard and his colleagues, along with the fishermen too were becoming increasingly nervous, working so close to the beach lately. They'd never had cause for concern up to now; other than teenagers having parties late at night until the sun came up. None of them had got into trouble at sea and none had drown, but with alcohol and loud music involved, they caused a lot of people a lot of bother.

At three in the morning, a guest staying in one of the hotels overlooking the beach had shouted from a window for them to keep the noise down as he had to get up to go to an important work meeting later that day and when the crowd didn't pipe down and behave, police were summoned to see them off. Of course, the crowd returned most weekends but had a lookout who kept watch and they all soon legged it when police patrolled the area more often as well.

Several ghosts often joined the crowd, but none were seen by the naked eye. With sea breeze blowing across the sand, no people ever stopped to consider that they had spectral company; all they were worried about was daring each other in drinking games, or trying to find a secluded spot to enjoy some physical action with the same sex and occasionally with the opposite sex too.

Good kids overall, they never caused any serious problems for local residents, hotel staff or for police either. There were far more important and more serious things to worry about lately – murders. But those responsible for killings around Porthcawl weren't interested in taking the lives of the crowd, they were deliberately picking off people one by one on a hit list and Mel was on that list. The killer was running out of time and patience. With so much protection around her, they couldn't seem to find a way to snuff her life out at all.

Ben also had a killer after him too and his health was beginning to suffer. With so much work to do in his office, deadlines not met and other matters neglected recently, and now with Mel keeping out of his way, debts catching up with him and Alice leaving him, his mind first started to fragment when he began to realise that he was in a terrible mess. His life was going nowhere and he'd denied it up to the past few weeks.

Seeing Marlene's ghost and other paranormal visions as time went by made him wonder if he was hallucinating and going through some stress-related madness; slowly creeping up on him and driving him insane. He thought about checking into a psychiatric ward but what psychiatrist in Wales would even consider having him sectioned if he mentioned seeing spirits on the side of the road and being told to kill people? He checked into a hotel overlooking the beach and considered his next course of action to take.

Mel sat alone in her hotel room and thought about Ben. He'd been so tender and loving to her in the bathroom recently but now he seemed like a total stranger. After he'd attacked her and left her for dead in Marlene's bathtub, she couldn't believe that trusting someone and falling in love with them would lead to her harm. She sipped a drink she'd opened from the mini bar in her room and gazed out of the window. Although many miles away from him, she felt his mind searching for her. She shuddered and closed the curtains.

Police went about their day carrying out more or less the same things that they usually did: taking statements from people, interviewing others, cautioning others still and generally getting sick to death of the public wasting their time. Jones and several of his colleagues wanted to get their teeth into much juicier cases but were ordered by their superiors to stay where they were and to do exactly as instructed.

Forensics officers were banging their heads against a brick wall and were at a loss as to what to do next. Finding little DNA evidence to trap a killer, they felt frustrated beyond belief. People who lived in Porthcawl were starting to move out of the area out of panic and fear and visitors who normally flooded the seaside town were dwindling in number as months passed. It was beginning to resemble a ghost town – literally.

Mel woke to the sounds of waves crashing against rocks and small shops' walls. It was an unusually blustery day. Seagulls were struggling to stay level as they hovered over the waters; their strong wings fighting against wind currents in the air.

The young woman drank hot coffee and watched them, understanding completely how they felt. But her wings were stronger and no howling winds in the Universe could defeat her now. After visits from her Grandmother and other beings looking out for her and watching her back, she felt invincible. Knowing that she had free will was a liberating feeling but she knew full well that it didn't entitle her to place herself in dangerous situations on purpose. She wondered if the other side would help her then.

She packed her bits and pieces in her bag and brushed her hair. Wearing smart black trousers and a dark purple jumper and black knee-high boots, she wouldn't feel the chilly weather biting at her skin like an angry, invisible animal.

Stepping outside the hotel, she looked up and down the street. It was mostly empty, apart from council workers picking up litter. She buttoned up her jacket and went to get a newspaper from a local newsagent's shop and prepared herself for more cat and mouse games if Ben or others connected with him catch even a glimpse of her in public.

CHAPTER FORTY

Alice decided she wanted to return home to speak to Ben. Despite all that he'd done, she needed to sort things out for a divorce and to stay at the marital home they both once shared. He had no right to make her feel driven away, she felt, and she vowed to live there again; at least until she could find somewhere else.

With so much DIY work gone into the property, it was immaculate and she felt it a pity the same effort hadn't been put into their marriage. Having time away from him, she realised now that the breakdown in their relationship hadn't been all down to him. She knew in her heart that she'd have to take some responsibility for it too.

Burning curiosity afflicting her every day after hearing from gossip that he was now living with Mel permanently, she had building rage inside of her that wouldn't settle down. She hadn't heard the latest however, that Mel was far, far away and was about to turn the tables on him. In Mel's mind it was justice for her. But it would also be a twist in events and circumstances – providing justice for Alice too, all in one go. How convenient and handy! Others were observing matters though, and they also had a plan...

A week later, all was deathly quiet in Porthcawl, for a change. No murders had taken place and police had a rest, giving them adequate time to catch up on other cases and a tomes of paperwork. They had had more than enough lately and with forensics' officers at a loss for words and with no much evidence to go on, they were all tearing their hair out in frustration.

Mel rented a hotel room in the town centre overlooking the sea. She needed to speak to solicitors and her bank manager about the money left to her so she arranged an appointment with both to settle matters once and for all. Filled with a mixture of excitement and trepidation, she set the wheels in motion for her life to go forward into a better place. She felt safe being surrounded by a lot of people where she was staying. Nobody would come for her there, surely?

Nipping out to the solicitor's office, it was a Monday morning and a chill etched out in the atmosphere like a chalk drawing upon hard cement-like acrylic paint. Murky clouds obscured a beautiful blue sky overhead but songs were singing in Mel's heart for the first time in a long time. She felt elated, and hopeful for her future. She had realised, after having time by herself, that she would do just fine all alone with no man in her life. Not needing anyone but herself, she felt powerful, self-assured, and certain that whatever happened in the future, she had unseen helpers who would never let her down.

After sitting and waiting for over fifteen minutes, a solicitor greeted her and escorted her into her office.

"I see from the documentation you're showing me that you have quite a substantial amount left for you by family members, and other vast wealth coming to you from other sources too. Congratulations. Tell me why you haven't claimed it long before now because," the woman paused to get the most tactful words out, "you're not getting any younger. It was left to you for you to begin using on your eighteenth birthday, so why haven't you done anything about it up to now?"

Mel glanced out of the window and then back at the woman with questioning eyes and a stern expression on her face. She looked about fifty-five-years old and as battered as debris out on the sandy beach opposite. Mel wondered if all solicitors were an unhappy lot and she had the urge to splash out and celebrate with a bottle of champagne, taking the woman with her. She thought long and hard about how to word things and felt that keeping it brief and to the point was best.

"I let life get in the way and had suffered with depression for years but I'm alright now," she said, hoping the woman would be satisfied with that explanation of circumstances.

"Well, that may be it, Mel but I don't understand after many years that you haven't done anything about this. It's quite a serious matter. I may have to arrange to have my associates with me for a second opinion, you understand that don't you?"

"I do, yes, but I don't see what the problem is, it's pretty straightforward to me. I was left money and now I'm here to claim it and to sort out my life. I've got bills to pay."

The woman rechecked documentation and made a quick telephone call. Mel sat, fidgeting. She bit her fingernails and felt agitated, like a rat in a cage with no way out to freedom. She never expected this problem to arise, and felt as if her life was standing still, as if hands on a clock had stopped, frozen in time. It was all she could do not to roll her eyes and sigh impatiently, but she controlled herself. The woman got out of her chair and walked toward the door.

"I shan't be a moment. Make yourself comfortable. There's coffee over there, tea, soft drinks. Help yourself."

The solicitor left the room and closed the door behind her. Mel made herself a coffee and sat back down in a chair. Sipping it, she relaxed and watched children running around on the beach with their parents. She thought of her father and the memorable happy times searching for little creatures hiding in rock pools and she smiled; memories, like the hot coffee, warming the cockles of her heart.

The solicitor came back into the room along with two others; a man and another woman. They seemed to have softer, more approachable vibes about them and kinder faces. Mel felt confident that everything would be okay; especially as she heard a faint whisper in her right ear, letting her know that things would work out for the best.

"We think we may be able to help you. If you can provide us with every bank card and proof of identification, along with a doctor's letter and anything else to back up your claims, you can have full access to the money. We're just ensuring that everything is above board and meets our rules and regulations. I'm sure you understand, Mel. We have to do everything properly and thoroughly. We can't just take your word for it, not with this amount of money."

"Of course. I'll sort things out my end then. I'm in no particular rush to be honest. I've got enough in my savings account to tide me over and to pay bills. So when would you like me to come back?"

"Two weeks from today, if that's convenient for you. Is it?"

"Fine. Not a problem at all. I'll make a note of it and will see you then. Thank you for all your help."

"That's what we're here for," the first solicitor said, shaking Mel's hand. The others did the same and Mel left the room, feeling livid beyond belief. She cursed under her breath as she walked up the street back to her room.

CHAPTER FORTY-ONE

Alice pulled up outside her house. The street looked clean and tidy, thanks to the council doing an excellent job but her garden was overgrown and the house looked dark and depressing. She opened her garden gate and closed it.

Walking down the path, she braced herself for Ben possibly being in the house. She thought of things to say, and things not to say to him. Her heart sank when it dawned on her that the moment she did step inside, whether he was in there or not, he was no longer in her life like he once was.

She unlocked the door and went inside. She flicked a switch and light made the depressive atmosphere lift a lot. She put her handbag and coat on a sideboard and entered the kitchen. Cobwebs covered everything in a fine gauze-like layer. She burst into tears. Once, a house clean and sparkling, it now resembled a place of desolation, dullness and lacking laughter and joy.

Emptying a kettle full of stagnant water, she ran a cold water tap for a few minutes and filled the kettle with fresh water. Pipes made clanging noises but it settled after a while. The cold weather hadn't frozen pipework, fortunately, and she felt thankful that she hadn't walked into a flooded building.

Searching for something to cook and eat, she was grateful to see rows of tins, packets and all sorts. At least he'd left contents alone in cupboards, she thought, desperate for a nice hot cup of tea. She'd resorted to drinking more alcohol due to the marriage breakdown and had a small bottle of vodka in her handbag for later, with a can of cola.

Looking in the fridge, she was surprised to see that it was full to the brim of tasty treats. Ben had filled it up and had even bought a large carton of eggs for her. He'd always been a thoughtful man, even if they no longer had passionate encounters anymore. At least he had a kind streak in him, she thought. He'd actually left it for himself though.

She went back outside to get bottles of milk left by the doorstep. He hadn't stopped the milkman calling, something she was grateful for. She couldn't get through it all but at least she'd have enough for her needs over the next week at least. The rest she'd take to town tomorrow to a charity shelter. The least she could do, she reasoned. She couldn't help the state of her marriage, but at least the milk wouldn't go stale and lifeless, like it had. Locking all doors of the house, she unpacked her things and set about cleaning up before having an early night's sleep.

Mel needed to go back home to get much needed documents but was afraid to. Not knowing exactly where Ben was made her nervous as hell. She had a week and decided to see if he had duplicate copies in his office. If he could assault her and tie her up, then she was certain that he'd stoop so low as to do almost anything to get his hands on her money.

Time was running out but solicitors hadn't mentioned that her account was empty. She had a chat with her bank manager in person. Telephoning them about such private matters wasn't best, she thought. Ben's private investigative skills could possibly mean he'd bugged her phone at home. She could call them from a public phone box but they might be wondering why she didn't call them from a landline. And calling them from her mobile wasn't wise either. With no anti virus software on her phone, she wasn't prepared to discuss her bank details, just in case.

She called into the bank. Fortunately for her, there were no customers creating a queue that day. She detested waiting. Seen straight away, she spoke at length about her predicament. After going through security checks and satisfied her driver's license, bank cards and birth certificate that she had in her purse were almost sufficient to satisfy them that she was who she claimed to be but they required more. She explained to them her recent visit at the solicitors and the money left to her. Life was never that easy, she thought. She couldn't just withdraw a million pounds and without solicitors' say so, she just had no other choice than to wait until she saw them again. But the bank could confirm that her million and other money was definitely in two different accounts and for her to call back in to see them in a week's time.

Mel left the bank with a huge smile on her face and relief in her heart. "Right! Now let's sort that bastard out," she muttered under her breath as she got in her car and headed straight for his office. It was getting dark by the time she got there and on the way she picked up a crowbar and hammer.

Reaching his office car park, she switched off her engine and sat in the shadows, waiting for the right opportunity and perfect timing. Security lights were on in the office but Ben's car wasn't there. Happy that the coast was clear, she snuck out of her car and ran up to the back of the building. She'd have at most about twenty minutes before police or he responded to an alarm sounding so she had to work fast.

Wedging the end of the crowbar between the door and wall, she pushed forward with all her strength. It took several attempts before the door's wood creaked and broke, but she couldn't get it open. Shielding her face with her arm, she used the hammer to smash through the glass of the door. Slivers of glass fell, strewn across the carpet inside, crossing beams and activating sensors. The alarm sounded and was almost deafening. Mel carefully moved into the building and ran up a flight of stairs. Panting, she swung the fire exit door at the top of the steps open and sprinted across a large room. Security lighting gave her adequate vision to avoid bumping into desks and computers.

Reaching the end of the room, she saw a door with the word 'Office' engraved on a brass strip across the top of it. The door was locked. She prised it open with the crowbar and kicked it. When it didn't open fully, she hurled a computer through it, followed by a fire extinguisher aimed right at the lock.

Entering Ben's office, she rummaged through filing cabinets for any details about her or her family that he had no right to have, or anything about him and his dealings with people that would incriminate him and send him to prison. Nothing. Standing there, covered in fragments of wood, dust and sweat, she tried to get into his mind. "Now where would a devious rat like you hide something of importance?"

With the alarm ringing in her ears and adrenalin pumping through her veins, Mel searched in as many places as she could before time ran out. She couldn't find anything. A screeching of cars sounded outside. Perspiring, she scurried into a corner and hid behind a stack of boxes.

Muffled voices echoed nearby. Footsteps and shouting were heard getting closer, and closer until people were a few yards away from where she cowered. She did her best to keep her breathing as quiet as possible and prayed that she didn't sneeze or cough.

The alarm stopped. She managed to work out how many people were in the building, judging by the conversation and movements they were making. Five. Hearing the words 'the police are downstairs, they'll get forensics in to get DNA', Mel hoped that wearing leather gloves had been enough to prevent that. She tried to remember if any droplets of her sweat had landed anywhere, or if she'd brushed her arm or face against anything when entering the building. Just one skin cell could be enough to trap her. She recalled that she hadn't brushed against any doorframes or walls.

Straining her ears, she managed to hear that Ben was now in the building, but she couldn't quiet hear exactly what he was saying. She needed to pee but held it in. As she heard the tones of his voice she felt simmering anger rising in her soul. With the same voice he'd previously said sweet nothings to her, words of desire and promising of love and a wonderful future, but her future with him was in tatters now; much like an old duster that rested on top of the stack of boxes in front of her, its edges well used and torn in places.

Police came upstairs. Ben's voice was louder now as he and the other men stood nearer the boxes in the corner of the room. Mel felt like a frightened little mouse, sitting in that corner, potentially nasty cats prowling around and could pounce at any moment upon her. She couldn't hold her pee in any longer and with nerves getting the better of her she simply let go. A wet warmth spread across her crotch and through the fabric of her trousers before collecting in a yellowish puddle on the carpet beneath her. It didn't smell at first and she hoped that none of the men put the air conditioning on.

They walked away and searched around the office and upper floors for an intruder. Finding nobody, they assumed they'd got out of the building. Mel heard Ben shout that he'd seen someone, a figure crouching in bushes outside and that they were in white. Mel frowned and wondered who on Earth it could be. She heard everyone running down steps and, as voices became quieter and quieter, she slumped, feeling tension easing in her body.

"Ew, you disgusting woman," she whispered to herself, sliding around and standing up. A current of air with her movement caused the odour to drift upward, making her turn her nose up in revulsion and shame.

Stepping over to the nearest window, she ever so slowly inched her face toward the window pane. Her eyes darted around, searching for whoever the men had spotted lurking outside by the bushes. All she could see were the men, shining torches and hurrying around in different directions. Police gestured with a finger or entire hand for the others to go over there, or to stay where they were. She could see Ben in the shadows, chatting with a police officer.

Although she couldn't hear precisely what was being said, by his body language and hearing brief laughter, she gathered that it wasn't the first time he'd met the officer. She saw him pat the man on his arm and continue to speak with him. He didn't seem to be avidly searching around like the others were and she found that odd. In fact, he seemed very relaxed about the whole incident.

She watched them all for several more minutes until they all drove away and came back a few minutes later. Taking a large, thick sheet of what looked like plywood out of the back of one of the cars, two of the men boarded up the broken door. Mel panicked.

"How the hell am I going to get back out now?" she said, crouching down and creeping across the entire length of the office. She reached a fire exit door and pulled it ajar. On the other side of it were a set of concrete steps with a black metal banister running alongside them. A lift was next to them but the last thing she needed was to be stuck in it, so she chose the steps instead.

Ever so slowly stepping down them, she managed to work out that she was now at the back of the building. Relieved to find another fire exit door there, she waited ten minutes until hammering and banging outside ceased before she contemplated pushing a large metal bar across the door into freedom. She was so glad that she'd hired a car, leaving hers outside the hotel she'd been staying in. If Ben had seen her car she'd be in for it bigtime and he'd no doubt come after her. He knew every inch of his own workplace and she didn't.

When it was silent, she pushed the bar on the door with both hands and went outside. Coldness hit her skin first and then complete and utter relief that no person had. Looking up, she saw a beautiful full moon shining silver light upon her and upon everything else, lighting her way around the perimeter of the building.

Tarmac instead of gravel covered the ground; something she was so grateful for as her training shoes made virtually little sound when walking across its surface. She shivered into the night and pulled her jacket closer around her and right up to her exposed neck.

Getting to the very end of the huge brick wall, she peered around the corner and saw the car park in the distance. With her heart pumping in her chest and sticky trousers clinging to her legs, she felt in a sorry state indeed. She couldn't hear any talking or hammering sounds now so assumed the men had gone.

Just before she walked around the corner she heard car engines running so she stayed where she was. Pinning herself against the brickwork, she kept as still as possible until they drove away. She counted three cars and recognised the familiar growl of Ben's flashy car. Mel came around the corner when it was safe to do so. She got into her hired car and headed back to the hotel. Ben hid by tall trees and followed her, keeping a distance away so as not to be seen.

CHAPTER FORTY-TWO

Mel got a few miles up a motorway before noticing that he was hot on her heels. At least with so many motorists around he wouldn't stand a chance of attacking her surely? She was wrong. He managed to drive up alongside her. Keeping her hands firmly on the steering wheel and her head calm and rational, she ignored him. Traffic overtook them. Mel sped up but kept a watchful eye on her speed, slowing down whenever she saw speed cameras on the lookout. Ben always caught up, matching her. She decided to look at him. He looked at her too. For a split second she saw no warmth in his eyes, only cold, dead contempt and anger; his jawline clenched and his brow furrowed. She kept her expression neutral, not giving him even one tiny bit of satisfaction at whatever anxiety he was trying to instil in her.

Several miles down the road, she made the decision to attempt to outsmart him. She didn't want him to know what hotel she was staying in so she zipped in and out of traffic and headed down a slip road off the hard shoulder. Unable to cut across lanes to follow her, he banged his fists on his steering wheel and carried on where he was.

Mel reprogrammed her satellite navigation system on her dashboard and got to her hotel. It was coming up to eleven at night and she was looking forward to a well-earned drink and a hot bath. Little did she know that he was still out looking for her and was only a mere mile away.

"You'll be fine. We're keeping him away," a ghostly voice assured her in her right ear. Mel sat by the bar and couldn't respond. With people sitting nearby the last thing she wanted was to make them feel uncomfortable if she began seemingly talking to herself. She said 'thank you' in her thoughts and was hopeful that they had heard her efforts of an appreciative response.

After enjoying a lovely glass of Merlot, she wandered up to her room and locked the door. Running a soothing hot bubble bath, she peeled her trousers off and underwear and kicked her trainers across the room. She stank and scrunched up her face the second a rancid ammonia-type of odour reached her nostrils.

She felt so tired of everything she hadn't even cared if anyone downstairs had smelled her. They seemed too busy and engrossed in conversation to notice anything, she thought, and most were merry; alcohol numbing their senses, just like hers were too.

Soaking in the glorious water, she closed her eyes and thought of positive things in life to try to erase the very uncomfortable situation she'd just been in. And then it hit her, like a lightbulb moment making everything so very clear. Crystal clear in fact. The hole in Marlene's wall was probably where he'd hidden what she was looking for but not only that, he had a garden shed. It was worth a shot, she thought. But how would she get to these two places without being seen by him, she wondered?

Changing into her nightdress and slipping her aching feet into cosy slippers, she sat on the edge of the hotel bed and racked her brains as to what to do next. A good night's sleep was in order and tomorrow is another day so she forgot about it all until later. Ben however was still driving around, looking for her. A persistent man, he wasn't prepared to give up until he found her. He knew she wasn't at home but which hotel she was in was another matter entirely, and Porthcawl had lots of them. He didn't want to return to her house, if he hadn't frightened her on the motorway she could retaliate if she was back at home.

With sharp knives in her kitchen he wasn't taking any chances. He called in at the police station and asked if he could stay there. Despite knowing many of the officers for years that was out of the question so he checked into a hotel and drown his sorrows in booze until the sun came up.

MULTIPLE KARMA By ROSEMARY RAVENBLACK

CHAPTER FORTY-THREE

Alice woke in her bed and rubbed her eyes. It was so quiet, so empty without Ben or Marlene being around so she had a shower and put the radio on. Background noise made her feel better. For now, anyway. She got dressed, had breakfast and imagined that he was having a fantastic sex-filled time with Mel. Rage built inside her and she threw a ceramic plate across the kitchen. It shattered against a cupboard. She left the broken pieces there and went out into the garden. It wasn't like her not to clean things up but Alice was a totally different woman to the one she used to be. Like being on autopilot, she felt like a robot lately; detached and indifferent, but still, the rage and fury grew deep in her heart and wouldn't lie down to sleep. Like an angry animal, it was beginning to overpower her and she didn't know how to stop it. She sat on a wooden chair and rested her elbows on a table and sighed.

Mel got into her own car and drove to the police station she'd telephoned. Upon arrival, she almost bumped into Chief inspector Don as she entered the building.

"I'm so sorry. Hope I didn't hurt you," she blurted, as the gruff man glared at her before his normally miserable face softened into a beaming smile. He always lit up around ladies and with Mel's good looks and apologetic expression he only felt sympathy for her.

"Not a problem at all, Miss. How can I be of assistance? Are you here to report a crime?"

"Well, sort of. I need to speak to someone in confidence please, it's rather urgent," she replied, looking around and keeping her voice down.

"I was just on my way out but I've always got time for a pretty lady. I'll take you into one of our interview rooms, you can confide in me there if you like."

"Are you a constable or higher up because ideally I'd like to speak to someone who runs this place?"

"Then you've bumped into the right person. I'm Chief inspector Don Hallows. Come with me. Can I get you a drink before we begin?"

"No thanks. I'm sick of drinking coffee lately. I'm fine, thank you."

"This way, Miss...? I must say, your voice sounds familiar. Have you been here before?"

"No. It's Mel, just call me Mel."

"Mel it is then. A pretty name for a pretty lady. You'll have to excuse my flirtatious personality. I'm used to dealing with scum most days and that's just my colleagues," he replied, laughing.

She felt flattered at his attention and followed him into the interview room. Sitting down and getting comfortable, Mel felt she'd be there for quite a while. Ageing and walking at a slow pace, although not overly old, he wasn't rushing to get anything resolved quickly either. She watched him as he looked at his watch and sat down opposite her after closing and locking the door first.

"How can I help?"

Mel drew in a deep breath and thought carefully about how to word what she was going to tell him. On edge and ready to jump out of a window if Ben and his officer friends came to the station, it took all that she had to calm down enough to speak.

"I've been staying in a nearby hotel because I'm too afraid to go back home."

"Yes, we've had several murders in Porthcawl, I don't blame you."

"It's not just because of that though. Someone's after me and they've attacked me. My ex-boyfriend," she said, hearing her own words and finding it so strange to refer to Ben as 'ex' now after all of the tender and loving moments they'd shared before things went wrong.

"Ah! It's you. You're the woman who I spoke to on the telephone. I knew it. I'm glad you've had the sense to come here in person. I'm observant and I detected a truth and sincerity in your voice. So, it's a domestic dispute. I get a lot of them here; angry spouses or girlfriends, battered and bruised, some in a far worse condition. I won't go into the gory details, Mel, but we see it all here, week in and week out."

"It's more than a domestic dispute, inspector Hallows. This man is a private investigator. He knows a lot about me and my past and is after money left to me by family a long time ago. He attacked me, look," she said, rolling up her sleeves to show him fading rope burns.

"Do excuse me for saying this, but how do I know that you didn't inflict them upon yourself? I have to ask. We get all sorts in here and in order for me to get to the root of any problem I have to know every little detail. You seem the truthful kind so go on," Don replied, urging her to continue.

"If I give you the man's name, will you please check him out? He's very friendly with officers in the station near the lighthouse."

"Being friendly with officers is not a crime, Mel. What do you think I'll find if I do check him out? Give me more, I need more than that."

"He tried to kill me. How can I prove that if you don't believe me?"

"As you know with most crimes, in order for police to take action and issue an arrest, we need evidence. I need to know more. Convince me. He sounds like Ben. I'm aware of him alright. A right callous, lying shitbag."

Mel shuffled in her seat. "I was interviewed in that station with this man. An officer got hold of my medical records from a psychiatrist and I found out that a million pounds had been left to me a long time ago. I'm only now in touch with solicitors and my bank in order to access my money and I believe that this man is after me to get his hands on it. I also believe he's trying to take my life. He followed me on the motorway last night but I managed to get away from him."

"Like I said, Mel, without concrete proof, my hands are tied. I need more, but I will check things out for you. I've got a score to settle with that little twerp myself. I can't prove that he stole my parents' expensive jewellery and other items but I've always suspected him. He used to hang around the area a lot and I never did find out why. I also heard on the grapevine that he had been spotted by members of the public coming out of a park at night. Two women, friends of his clients had been killed around about the same time. He'd been interviewed but our hands were tied and the case never went to court and the culprit was never found."

She stared into his questioning eyes and she gulped. The urge to begin biting her fingernails was strong but she resisted. Digging her thumb nail into the palm of her other hand, she felt as though the room was about to spin around. Trembling and wanting to cry, she knew she had to tell him things that would get herself into trouble, never mind Ben.

"I broke into a neighbour's house. She died of shock before that and I was looking for something. I found stuff that belongs to this man and he caught me and knocked me out. He tied me up and I woke in a bathtub. I managed to escape but he's still after me."

Inspector Don raised his eyebrows and drummed his fingers on the table as he watched the initially calm and confident woman he'd met minutes before now turning into a nervous wreck in front of him.

"What were you looking for exactly? You do know that breaking and entering is a criminal offence don't you?"

She nodded and stared at her hands.

"Answer my question please. What were you looking for in that house?"

"Something to trap this bastard. Someone ought to sort him out. I can't report him to my local station because he knows them and I doubt they'd arrest him would they?"

"Not if they're corrupt, no. Are they? Are you going to use slander now as well as lies?"

"They're not lies. I'm telling the truth," she sobbed, digging her thumb nail harder into her palm until it hurt. She gave him Ben's car registration number and many other details about him. She also told him that whenever a murder had been committed in Porthcawl, he always seemed to know a lot about them and people connected to him always seemed to be hanging around relatively close to murder scenes and as a private investigator, he knew a lot of things about a lot of people; especially her.

"Just because this man is a private investigator, Mel, it doesn't make him a killer. Assuming someone did knock you unconscious and tied you up in a bathtub, how can you be so sure that it was him?"

"Because I know the smell of his aftershave. I bought it for him, it's his favourite. I also know what his eyes look like, I used to gaze into them enough. Look, I know it was him."

"So he had his face covered then, but you recognised enough to be absolutely certain that your alleged attacker was him, is that what you're telling me?"

"Yes."

"I still need proof, Mel." "I'm just nipping out for a sec, I need to use the toilet."

She watched him unlock a door and hurry out of the room. Seizing the opportunity, she ran out of the room and the station too. When he returned to the room he saw a small piece of paper with Ben's car registration number scribbled on it, along with the name of Ben's workplace, and his former address he shared with Alice too.

Mel pulled up outside her house. She sat in her car and bit her fingernails, worrying about going back to the bank and to speak to solicitors regarding her money. She needed to get into her house to pick up documentation they needed and so she realised that she was faced with a difficult choice: risk him being there waiting for her, or do nothing and live in hotels until her savings ran out. Waiting, until she was certain that he wasn't there, she braved it, got out and thought of her next move. Her luck was in. She saw her local postman doing his afternoon rounds.

"Hi, Brian, can you do me a favour please? It won't take long; I know how busy you are."

"Oh hi, Mel, of course. What's that then? I've always got time for you."

"I need you to come indoors with me. I've a parcel there but I don't think its mine. There's been a mistake."

"Has there? Okay, I'm running ahead of time so I'll take a look at it."

He followed her to her front door and she unlocked it. He went inside her house along with her. But she still felt hesitant. All she needed today was Ben skulking around and trouble. She went into the living room and then upstairs. Making sure that nobody was in the house but them, she breathed a huge sigh of relief and then thought about what excuse to give to a waiting Brian.

"Ah, sorry to waste your time, I gave it to a neighbour yesterday. Sorry, Brian."

"That's okay, Mel. Anytime. Got to dash, speak to you another time."

"Have a good day, see you soon."

She escorted him to the door and waved as he walked up the garden path. Locking and bolting the door, Mel headed straight to her back garden and jumped over Marlene's fence and ran up to her back door. It was just as it had been before, so she went inside and picked up a heavy piece of wood that was leaning against the door frame. Hurrying upstairs to the room she'd found items in, in the hole in the wall, she was surprised to see that it was exactly as it had been. Ben hadn't even bothered to block it up, which she found strange.

Alice heard movement coming from next door. She went into her own back garden and looked around. Seeing Mel through a window upstairs, she blew a fuse. It was bad enough that her friend had died, and now her arch enemy was trespassing and walking around in her house. She got over the fence and went into the house, hot on Mel's trail.

Upstairs, Mel was busy. She'd managed to stick her arm as far into the hole in the wall as she could go, reaching around for any objects that Ben or Marlene had hidden there that she'd missed the last time she was there. There was nothing but cobwebs and plaster. Frustrated, she eased her arm out and dusted herself down.

Alice was coming up the stairs. Mel heard a creak of a floorboard. Panic in her eyes, she hid by the side of the old Oak wardrobe. Alice stepped into the bedroom and stopped moving; her senses heightened and her anger boiling.

"I know you're in here, Mel. I saw you. Stop bloody playing games. Come out right now!"

Mel heard the anger in her voice and she gripped the piece of wood tighter in her hand. It would be self defence, she reasoned. Moving away from the wardrobe, she came face to face with her neighbour, and once friend.

"Why are you in here and what are you doing with that? Planning on hitting me with it are you? Are you the killer whose been bumping off residents around here then? I didn't expect it to be you."

"No, it's not me, Alice. Did you know that your husband attacked me? Do you blame me for carrying this? I have to protect myself. For all I know you're both in on things. I don't trust anyone anymore. There was a time when I thought I could trust you though, even when you were bothering with that cow. Did you know she was my birth mother? Did you also know Anita Robinson was her mother and my Grandmother?"

"Now, now, it's not nice to speak ill of the dead. I knew a bit about it, yes. But I was warned not to tell you. I'm not risking my life for anybody. Marlene's dead now and wherever she is, let her rest."

Best place for her, Mel felt like saying, but she bit her tongue. With Alice in such a state she thought it wise not to provoke her further.

"Well I'm not saying sorry. Look, have you been in touch with Ben, or not?"

"He's all yours. I don't want anything to do with that deceitful bastard. And you? Thanks for treating me like shit, Mel. I've been away. Had to clear my head. He attacked you, you say? Why was that then?"

"It doesn't matter. I just need to know if you've been in touch with him that's all. And the reason I'm in here is because I found items relating to me and my past and I'm back to find more to give to the police."

"Well I'll be contacting them myself don't worry. I'm sure they'll not take kindly to trespassing neighbours will they?"

Mel didn't want things to turn ugly so she started to walk around Alice in order to leave the property.

"It's your word against mine. Anyway, I've already informed police that I came here on a previous occasion. Not the local station, the other one miles away."

"And why would you do a stupid thing like that? Landing yourself right in it aren't you by doing that?"

"Like I said, Ben attacked me. I had to tell the officer everything. He bombarded me with questions."

"And he let you go? Breaking and entering and trespassing, and he let you go?"

Mel looked at the floor sheepishly. "Not exactly, no. I left."

Alice rolled her eyes and ground her teeth. She took out a knife from one of her pockets and played with the sharp blade between her fingers and all the time she never took her eyes off Mel's. Mel backed away slowly as the blade glinted in the light and was getting closer and closer to her. Alice was no murderer, she thought. She ran past her, closed the door and bolted down the stairs and out of the house. Sprinting down to the shed at the bottom of the garden instead of going to her own house, she hid behind the shed and got her breath back.

Alice stood by the back door, still wielding the knife. "I need a word with you. Get back here!"

Mel didn't respond. She watched her until she went back indoors, put the knife down and closed the back door. Mel waited and still had hold of the piece of wood, just in case. Out of the corner of her eye, something fluttered in a breeze. She turned to see what it was. It was a white plastic bag, the handles on it moving back and forth just on the inside of an ornamental wishing well. She checked to see if Alice was watching. The woman must have gone to her own house, she assumed.

Mel walked over to the well and pulled out the bag. It felt heavy. She lifted it out with both hands after putting the big piece of wood down first and peered inside. A large square object wrapped in black plastic lay there at the bottom. Looking up again to make sure she was still alone, she carried the bag over to the back of the shed, went back and picked up the piece of wood and carried that over too. Sitting down, she pulled the black plastic off to see jewellery and a small video camera. Switching it on, she was horrified to see footage of her coming and going in her house, including bathing times and when she was sleeping too. Not only that, there was a small notepad taped to the underside of it, detailing every little thing she'd said or done when alone. The fucker had planted a bug in her house, even watching her when she slept. She had the perfect reason now to incriminate him. Chief inspector Don would now get his evidence.

Twenty minutes ticked by. Mel decided she had to pick up important documentation from her house. Climbing back over the garden fence, she left the piece of wood there. She had bigger knives in her own kitchen than Alice's, and would use them if she had to protect herself.

Getting what she needed, she packed clean clothes and other items and headed back to the hotel. Alice followed her.

Upon arrival, Mel sorted things out and telephoned her solicitor and bank. They agreed to see her earlier than previously arranged. Relieved she'd now have full access to her vast wealth, she thanked them and set off to the first police station she'd called to report Ben's crime against her. But first, she had to find sufficient evidence to get police to arrest him.

Sitting in her car, she prepared herself for one hell of a stressful time. Sick of feeling that police were incompetent and that she was doing a much better job herself, she sat there trying to figure out a way to end the situation once and for all. She looked up and saw Alice behind her, doing her best – and failing miserably – to hide the fact that she was stalking her. Mel wondered if she still had a knife on her but came to the conclusion that it'd take a very stupid person to sit outside a police station with a deadly weapon on them.

A few seconds later, Mel mustered up the courage to confront the bitter woman. Alice rolled down her window and said nothing at first; she just stared into Mel's eyes with a mixture of anger and also fear. And then she told Mel something that knocked her for six.

"Didn't tell you about the hidden cameras all around the house then did he?"

"Which house? What are you on about?" Mel replied, still unsure and standing a few feet away from the car window.

Alice looked off into the distance and chuckled under her breath before returning her stare, more intense now than before.

"When I returned to the house I only had to plug a HDMI lead in and saw what he did to you. I also saw what you did too. Every house in the street has the cameras, except in yours of course. I knew about his affair with the young woman and obviously I know about your relationship with him too. Gets around doesn't he?"

"Well, I'm not with him now so take that as my karma visiting me if that makes you feel better, Alice!"

"Not really, no. See, I, unlike Marlene, actually really liked you. But you ruined any chance of us ever having a strong friendship. Yes, we all make mistakes, Mel, but to steal another woman's husband and to have him living right next door, how would you feel if someone did that to you?" Alice spat, rage filling her face now.

Mel moved away a little farther and didn't quite know where to look nor what to say either. All she could do was to feel utterly, utterly sick to her stomach. She wasn't sure if remorse consumed her to a deeper level than fear as she saw something glinting in the light on Alice's lap. Her fingers were toying with something. Mel got ready to run, the very moment the car door opened. She glanced over her shoulder to see the police station door was open and she looked back at the furious woman again.

"I'm sorry, Alice. I truly am. If I'd known what he was like, what he was really like I mean, I never would have befriended him in the first place, let alone have an affair with him. I always liked you too but Marlene made sure that a friendship between you and I could never develop. You know what she was like. And the fact that you associated with her, knowing how disgustingly she treated me for years is far worse than any woman having an affair, in my opinion. Have you any idea what it's like to feel like a prisoner in your own home? To feel like a trapped rat in a cage and never comfortable in your own garden even, have you any idea how horrible that feels?

"Well she's dead now isn't she, so maybe her karma has visited her?" Alice replied, shifting in her seat.

Mel flinched as Alice began to open the door.

"I've got something for you."

"I bet you have!" Mel responded, staring at the woman's hands.

Alice looked down at her hands and then back up at Mel again.

"Oh, I see. You really think I'd stab you right outside here? I'm not that stupid!"

"I didn't think so, no. That would make you deranged, just as he is."

"Here. Give it to chief inspector Don, if he's here. I've dealt with him in the past over family matters years ago. He's a decent man. Don't let his grumpiness put you off."

"I've already met him. He didn't believe me that Ben had attacked me. No evidence you see!"

A sinister smile crept across Alice's face.

"Oh this will change his mind. Show him this."

Mel took a silver and black small cassette tape from her hands. Both women, for a moment in time felt a kind of shared respect for each other, both desperately needing justice and peace in their lives, to move on.

"Goodbye, Mel."

Mel watched as Alice closed the door, rolled up the window and raced off down the road, not even looking back. Mel examined the small tape in her hands. It felt warm and she wondered if its contents would end up securing Ben's future in the bowels of Hell. Prison would be too good for him.

"Can any of my family in the spirit world confirm if whatever is on this tape will be a good thing, or a bad thing?" she whispered, tuning in to the spirit world.

"It's a good thing. Give it to the inspector."

"Thank you. That's all I needed to know."

"We're always near you, Mel. Everything is going to be alright."

Mel walked into the station, her nerves in tatters, but positive hope shining a light in her heart. Born an eternal optimist, she'd suffered a series of setbacks lately but she was a survivor.

CHAPTER FORTY-FOUR

Alice pulled up outside her house. She opened the glovebox in her car and pulled a sharp knife out. Putting it in her handbag, she got out of the car, locked it, and went inside Marlene's house, using a spare key. Going upstairs, she went straight to the room with the hole in the wall. Using the knife, she dug away at the plaster a few feet away and six inches up from the original hole. Picking away, she eventually made an opening large enough to slide her hand into. Reaching in, she pulled out a small plastic black bag. It was covered in dust and cobwebs. Not bothered by spiders, she was more concerned that Ben would come back and that would make things very awkward indeed.

Going over to the window at the front of the house she checked that the coast was clear. Other than a few cats prowling around in neighbours' gardens, no residents were visible. She crouched down on the floor and tore the bag open, its contents scattering onto the carpet. Over the years she'd seen Ben skulking around the house and he always asked if Marlene wanted DIY work done upstairs. He seemed to take a bit too long up there, Alice thought, and she caught him one day, standing by the walls and tapping them. When she needed to use Marlene's toilet on a different day as hers was broken, when creeping across the landing as she'd taken her shoes off downstairs, she'd seen him sitting on the carpet and measuring the bottom of the wardrobe and had heard him speaking into his dictation machine about hiding something. When he'd gone to work, she'd acted fast and had found out all she needed to know.

When Mel handed Chief Inspector Don Hallows what Alice had given her, along with bits and pieces that Mel herself had discovered too, her spirit family and friends gave her additional information through her physical ears via whispers. It was more than enough to convince Don that not only Ben was one of the killers in Porthcawl, but most police officers in the other station were in on things as well. Not only that, Marlene had been in a huge conspiracy and had planned to eventually murder not only Mel, but as many people in Porthcawl as possible – regardless of whether they had pissed her off in the past or not. She really was unhinged and Mel had had a very lucky escape.

Don made a quick telephone call in front of Mel. Within five minutes her favourite taxi driver walked into the interview room and sat down.

"What are you doing here?", she gasped, as he flashed his gold tooth and grinned at her like a Cheshire cat.

"This man here is an old friend. We go back many years. I didn't tell you because along with him and others in Porthcawl, we've been making sure that they never killed you. Not you, my dear young Melanie. I pretended to be a lookout man for that corrupt lot in the other station, but in doing so it enabled me to gather as much crucial evidence and information as possible in order to finally get the bastards once and for all. They thought they'd slipped through the net but my fisherman mates also kept a lookout as well and relayed information back to Don here, myself too and although several lives were lost, with you and Alice helping us out, we can now put the lot of the buggers away for good. Life in prison will be facing not only Ben, but all the others he's connected with too. I always told you that you were safe, didn't I?"

"Yes, and you looked at me so strangely recently. Now I know why. You knew he was going to sort me out didn't you?"

"I did. But when you telephoned this station, despite giving a fake name to Don here, we managed to trace the call and with me as a taxi driver, I kept an eye on you. I know every road in Porthcawl like the back of my hand and as well as picking up passengers outside the hotel you've been staying in, it gave me the perfect opportunity to tell Don here if Ben was stalking that street or not. Fortunately, he never did. Being a private investigator I would have thought that he'd find you."

Mel smiled. "You wouldn't believe me if I told you but I will tell you. I have spirit friends who promised me they'd keep him away from me."

"I don't believe in ghosts myself, it's the living you want to worry about, but if you're telling the truth then that would explain why he never seemed to be able to track you down. He was tracking your movements, and lots of other peoples' movements too all over the town but he couldn't quite get too close to you could he?"

"I let him get close to me. I loved him. But I don't need a man in my life. I'm stronger than I used to be and I'm fine all by myself."

Don looked at her, his eyes softening and a smile like the sunshine flooded his face. "Would you go for a drink with me sometime? I'm not really married you know. I've just never met the right woman but as soon as I set eyes on you I couldn't stop thinking about you."

Mel was about to say no but she decided to say yes instead.

They got married six months later. The taxi driver was their best man. Alice sold her house while Ben was in prison and she went out with the taxi driver and eventually married him. Her menopausal symptoms cleared up and the couple ended up having the best passion they'd ever enjoyed in their lives! Alice and Mel rekindled their friendship and all was fine again.

Ben looked out of a small prison cell window and wondered if police had bothered to look underneath his garden shed. When new owners of he and Alice's house moved into the street, their two dogs wouldn't stop digging by the shed. It was only when a big mechanical digger got under there did police see what Ben had hidden.

"Will you look at all of this? What the hell?", one officer said, holding a spirit board, black candles and other occult items up in both hands.

"He was into all of this macabre stuff then was he? Did his wife know do you think?", another officer asked, moving away from the objects.

"Who knows? She doesn't seem the type to be delving into all of this. He does though. Well it can't help him now, not where he is and he'll be there for a very long time. None of them will get out of prison for at least twenty-five years; maybe fifteen for good behaviour but as the Judge slapped several life sentences on them all I can't see it myself. They'll rot in jail. Best place for them I say."

"Aye. Now let's see what the Chief Inspector wants done with this lot. Burn it most probably."

"What do you think he used it for?", the first officer asked.

"My cousin is into stuff like this. It has no power if the recipient doesn't believe in any of it but saying that, if Ben had advanced knowledge and skills and if you believe in the devil then that would explain how he knew things he couldn't possibly have found out through his private investigating abilities."

"I doubt very much the devil or anybody else can help him now. Nobody's managed to get out of that prison in the past and I can't see them doing it in the future either."

Both officers gathered everything and took it to Don. He burned it and, as he wiped smoke and dirt off his hands he was sure he saw a nasty-looking entity rising from the ashes. He held Mel in his arms and discussed the recent sale of her house. With millions of pounds in her bank accounts and with the protection of a respected and powerful Chief Inspector and of her spirit family and friends too, she felt more relaxed and content than she'd ever been in her life.

"Good riddance. Come on, let's go on holidays. I need a break."

"Mel, where would you like to go? Do you have anywhere in mind?", Don asked, holding her close.

"I've always wanted to go to Scotland; lets go there please."

"Sounds great to me. I've been to Edinburgh lots of time over the years, to watch the Welsh rugby matches."

"I've never been but I hear they have haunted castles for sale there. I wouldn't mind buying one to be honest. We can still have a nice place here in Wales too though."

Don gazed into her excited eyes and he saw such life in them, such zest and hopefulness that he found so endearing. She kept him young and blunted the edges of his former grumpiness and gruffness and he boosted her confidence in herself and put her mind at rest that she'd always be safe in his arms; but she already felt safe and had rebuilt her self-confidence all by herself. With her invisible spirit protectors, she knew that whether she stayed with Don or not, she didn't need anyone to look after her. She had more than enough power to keep everyone in Porthcawl safe and sound.

As they walked away hand in hand, her ghostly parents, Grandparents, Roy Morgan and many others watched them.

"Our Mel will be fine. She always was; she just didn't realise it for a long time. I'm so glad she heard me on the first EVP she did."

"We would have found a way to reach her, don't worry," her mother, Doris replied.

"There's always a way to reach the good at heart and she is good at heart too," Maurice said."

Porthcawl bustled with tourists and residents as Spring swept into Summer. With murderers under lock and key, the seaside town came alive once again and warmth and trust permeated everywhere. Fishermen still cast their nets and rods, bin men still emptied bins, and the postman still posted letters in Mel's former street.

She, however, had moved on. She was finally free. Unlike Ben and all the others who had let her down, hurt her, inflicted pain upon her heart and mind and had made a young woman's life an utter misery for so many years. But what they didn't know was that in doing so, they had simply made her a much stronger person. They say we are all here on Earth to learn lessons from other people in order to improve ourselves as souls. Mel sure learned a lot and with suave and handsome Chief Inspector Don Hallows by her side and in her heart now, she'd improved dramatically.

THE END

About the Author

Author Rosemary Ravenblack sincerely hopes that you've enjoyed 'Multiple Karma', her very first paranormal murder mystery novel, dear reader. It is available in e-book and paperback formats. As of March 2017, she's working on and is writing a paranormal science fiction novel and also a comedy novel too; both available for purchase and reading in the very near future. When not writing, she can be found exploring haunted castles and other cool buildings, tending to her two beloved cats and her handsome partner in beautiful Derbyshire, she enjoys painting abstract art and generally enjoying life and, as a psychic, spirit medium, Reiki master and having clairaudient, clairvoyant, clairsentience and all the other 'Clair' skills, she's made it her mission in life to give people in this world understanding, strength, hope, comfort and information about the spirit world, through her stories. And you don't have to be religious either; she's not, but if you are, then great, if it makes you happy and gives positive meaning to your life.

She's seen her parents and many others in spirit form for real and although she writes fiction novels, there is always truth among the pages. She hopes that you too discover that the afterlife is actually real, and you too have invisible protectors in your life as well. Never give up hope. You are never completely alone. Ever. Your spirit loved ones are only a thought away. Try EVP, it works. Do some research on it. Can you hear them when you play back your tape recordings? Rosemary hears hers often. Who knows? Maybe her loved ones in spirit inspire her written words. She believes that she's here to help people through her books in many ways and if she's helped you in any way then her job is done.

For news, updates and other information regarding what Rosemary is working on, and all the many stories she's written under different pen names in the past, or if you'd like to say hi, please see her website and Twitter page. She'd love to hear from you and if you enjoy her work too.

Take care, enjoy a fantastic day and thank you for reading!

www.rosemaryravenblack.com
@AuthorVividMind

Made in the USA
Middletown, DE
08 April 2017